A COUNTRY MANOR MURDER

BOOKS BY ALICE CASTLE

Sarah Vane Mysteries

Murder at an English Pub

A Seaside Murder

Murder at the Tea Shop

Murder in the Choir

A Beth Haldane Mystery

The Murder Mystery

The Murder Museum

The Murder Question

The Murder Plot

The Murder Walk

The Murder Club

The Murder Hour

The Murder Garden

The Murder Affair

A COUNTRY MANOR MURDER

ALICE CASTLE

bookouture

Published by Bookouture in 2026

An imprint of Storyfire Ltd.
Carmelite House
50 Victoria Embankment
London EC4Y 0DZ

www.bookouture.com

The authorised representative in the EEA is Hachette Ireland
8 Castlecourt Centre
Dublin 15 D15 XTP3
Ireland
(email: info@hbgi.ie)

ISBN: 978-1-80550-458-0
eBook ISBN: 978-1-80550-457-3

To Ella and Connie, with love

PROLOGUE

'Who's that?' Madeleine Brett-Coates said sharply, peering over her shoulder. From outside the judging tent came the usual sounds of the Vanstone Spring Fair – the joyful tune from the carousel, the shrieks of the children playing Splat the Rat, fathers trying their aim at the coconut shy – but inside all had been still and quiet, until that odd little noise behind her.

'Oh, it's you,' the old lady said, turning to smile at the newcomer. 'That's a relief. I thought it was... It's so dark in here, I can barely see this year's bake-off entries.'

She turned back to the trestle table groaning with plates of scones, cakes and biscuits. 'I'm glad you've come at last,' she said, a quaver in her voice now. 'That means I can go in a minute. I'm not feeling at all well. I'm rather queasy, and my stomach's aching terribly... Anyway, you can help me make my decision. Which do you think is worth first prize this year, the sponge or these chocolate chip cookies? Not scones again, though, surely.'

There was no reply, and Madeleine Brett-Coates turned round again. 'Didn't you hear me? Why aren't you answering?

And... what on earth do you think you're doing with that bunting in your hands?'

ONE

Sarah stood by the wonky wrought-iron gate outside her seaside cottage, still waving, even though the car containing her two daughters and two tiny granddaughters was already out of sight. It had been a wonderful week, full of peals of laughter from the toddlers, who were growing so fast and already adored the quaint little town of Merstairs. They had spent hours on the beach, making – or more strictly, destroying – the sandcastles patiently constructed by their doting granny, egged on by the excited woofs of Sarah's sturdy black Scottie, Hamish. The dog loved nothing better than proudly standing guard over the children, protecting his young charges from any marauding seagulls who thought they could get their beaks on the girls' mid-morning biscuits... though he wasn't averse to hoovering up the odd crumb himself.

Sarah sighed and patted him. 'Just you and me again, Hamish,' she said, turning back to the cottage. It had been perfect spring weather during the girls' stay, with china blue skies smiling above the wide Kent coast. But now, all of a sudden, there was a chill in the air. Opening the door, she surveyed the trail of devastation left behind by two very small children. Oh well, tidying would give her something practical to get on with, taking her mind off the sudden silence in the house. She was just lugging out her mop and bucket, ready to give the kitchen floor a spritz, when there was a rap at the door.

Two seconds later, a familiar whirlwind burst in, bracelets clacking, colours clashing and arms reaching forward for an all-enveloping hug. 'I knew you'd be lonely, once the girls had gone, so I thought I'd pop straight over,' said Daphne Roux, Sarah's oldest friend and next-door neighbour. 'Sorry I couldn't bring Mephisto, but he's busy at the shop at this time of day.'

Sarah, rather glad Daphne hadn't brought her enormous ginger cat to persecute Hamish, wondered what on earth the creature was up to in Daphne's beachfront Tarot emporium. 'Lovely to see you, Daph. Cup of tea?'

'Just the job,' said Daphne, settling down and hefting her purple bag onto the table, displacing a book on antiques. 'Listen, I've had a brilliant idea, the perfect thing to keep you busy.'

'Righto,' said Sarah, putting the kettle on and shaking some custard creams onto a plate. 'Tell me all about it.'

'Well, you know I love a biscuit as much as anyone,' Daphne added, looking askance at them. 'But I really miss a proper slice of cake. You know, like Hannah Betts used to make...'

Both women were thoughtful for a moment, remembering the café proprietor who had now gone to prison for a very long stretch after three sponge-related murders. Her red velvet cake had been a triumph – when it wasn't laced with arsenic.

'So this is my brainwave,' Daphne continued. 'I've signed us up for the Vanstone Fair bake-off. We should win it easily,' she said, absent-mindedly scooping up and munching one of the despised biscuits.

'Vanstone? Oh, that's nearby, isn't it? But Daphne, neither of us is great with cakes. That's why we appreciated Hannah's so much,' Sarah reminded her friend gently.

'That's true, but I was thinking we'd make scones. They're easy,' Daphne said confidently.

'Are they? I've made a few in my time. They're perfectly respectable, but I'm not sure they're prize-winning.'

'Respectable?' Daphne chuckled. 'I think we can do better than that. Come on, Sarah, let's do it. I can't wait to show off my rosette.'

Sarah thought for a moment. Then she smiled. 'All right,' she said gamely. 'Let's have a go. If we do nothing else for a few weeks, I'm sure we'll be fine. When is the contest?'

'This afternoon,' said Daphne, crunching another biscuit.

* * *

Three hours later, they were loading up the boot of Sarah's trusty Volvo. 'Careful, now,' said Daphne. 'That's precious cargo.'

'Hmm,' said Sarah. 'I think we should brace ourselves, Daph. I'm not entirely certain we're going to win.'

'Course we are. Those are tip-top scones, aren't they, Hamish?'

Hamish could normally be relied upon to rally round when support was needed, and he'd quite enjoyed the day in the kitchen, with pastry flying in every direction. But he wasn't sure he was a scone fan. His mistress's were fine, if a little small and dry. Daphne's, meanwhile, were as big as hub caps and had a tendency to rawness in the middle. So he maintained a diplomatic silence, merely jumping onto the back seat with a waggy tail, ready for pastures new.

'Right, off we go,' said Sarah, setting the satnav for Vanstone. Soon the car was pootling along the winding country lanes, past hedgerows decked in their spring finery. The fields were a brilliant billiard table green, and the trees were unfurling tender young leaves. Daphne's scarf was fluttering in the breeze, and all seemed right with the world.

Until they rounded a corner, and were confronted by a huge Land Rover veering over onto their side of the road and doing at least seventy miles an hour.

Sarah slammed on her brakes, and the little car came to a halt half in a ditch, before Daphne even had a chance to yell. The Land Rover went into reverse, then there was a screech of tyres and the white-faced, red-haired, thin-looking man at the wheel revved up again and zoomed past them.

'Not a word of apology! Well, I like that. We could have been killed,' said Daphne, looking pale.

'No harm done, I suppose,' Sarah said shakily, feeling they'd been very lucky to avoid a collision. She turned to give Hamish a reassuring pat. He was absolutely fine, and excited, if anything, at the unexpected turn of events. 'Oh well, not far now to Vanstone. And where do we go then?'

'To Coates House, of course,' said Daphne. 'Don't tell me I've never mentioned it?'

Sarah started the car and they set off far more sedately than the Land Rover. 'I don't think so. Is it special?'

'It's only one of the oldest houses in the area. It makes Francesca's place look like a Portakabin,' she said with a giggle. 'In fact, rumour has it she was quite keen to marry one of the Brett-Coates boys back in the day, just to get her hands on it.'

Francesca, who was the mayor of Merstairs and took herself extremely seriously, lived in a fabulous Georgian house that Sarah secretly envied. While Sarah loved her own cottage, it was a tiny bit cramped – especially now Francesca's ex-husband Charles was more or less a permanent resident as Sarah's official boyfriend. If Francesca had once manoeuvred to become mistress of Coates House, it had to be quite something.

'I must see this, then,' Sarah said drily.

'Oh look, here we are,' Daphne pointed out the sign up

ahead. They were entering Vanstone. The little place was picture perfect, with a village green in the centre, complete with a pond surrounded by weeping willows. There was a tiny post office and shop-cum-café, both with pretty Victorian gables, and over the way a village pub, the jolly-looking Coates Arms. Everywhere there were strings of gaily coloured bunting, the flags waving gently. A few late daffodils were peeping through white-painted fences. The spire of an ancient church pierced the blue sky, and the sound of children's laughter rang out as two little boys chased each other across the green.

Sarah looked around, drinking in the sight. 'Isn't this lovely?' she said, driving slowly past the duckpond.

'Coates House is here on the right,' said Daphne, pointing ahead to a wide driveway with ornate gates. There was a banner strung across the drive. *Vanstone Spring Fair Today*, it proclaimed. Up ahead, Sarah got her first sight of the house. It was a Jacobean masterpiece in creamy local stone, flanked by two huge cedar trees and a sweeping lawn. She could see why a young Francesca might have developed a sudden crush on anyone with the keys to such an impressive front door. 'We can park over there,' Daphne added, indicating a field to the left.

Sarah edged forward, joining a slow-moving queue of cars, and they were soon easing into one of the last spaces available. Once Sarah had got Hamish out, they only had to pick up their scones and drop them off for judging.

'What time did you say the competition starts?' Sarah asked Daphne as she hefted her friend's entries out of the boot.

'Oh, four o'clock, I think,' Daphne said idly.

'Daphne, you're joking, aren't you?' Sarah said urgently.

'What? No, why?' Daphne was looking around absently. 'Now, where did I put my bag?'

'It's four o'clock now, look up there,' Sarah hissed, pointing to the large clock tower on the top of an old stable block.

'Oh my goodness, why didn't you say?' Daphne snatched up her container of scones and sprinted across the car park.

Sarah, shaking her head, yanked out her own contribution, locked up the car, and followed her friend. 'Come along now, Hamish. We're going for a rather fast walkies. Do you know where you're heading, Daphne?' she called out, cursing the fact that she'd relied on her friend for the logistics of this endeavour – a mistake she really shouldn't have made after knowing her so long.

Sarah couldn't quite hear what Daphne was saying, but she followed doggedly in her footsteps, huffing and puffing to the large field where the fair was taking place. Daphne paused for a second to take stock, then she darted off again, weaving through the busy stalls.

'Daphne! Wait for me,' Sarah protested.

A few moments later, Daphne had drawn up at a gaily striped blue and white tent, its flaps tied shut with bows. She feverishly started to fight these open. 'We need to get in here and leave our stuff on the table before the judging starts. Look, there's the committee over there,' she hissed, pointing in the direction of a small group of people, making their way slowly but surely past the candy floss machine towards the white elephant stand. Luckily they seemed easily distracted, lingering over the crafting stall selling knitted mice and babies' hats and mittens. As Sarah watched, they all stopped to chat to the lady manning the tombola.

'Quick, now's our chance,' said Daphne, who'd got the last knot undone, and was holding the flap up for Sarah. 'I'll stay here with Hamish and keep them talking. You get inside, and put our scones out for judging,' she said, giving her friend a shove. 'Stick them right at the front, where they can't miss them,' she added with a wink.

Sarah almost fell inside the tent, her eyes adjusting gradually to the dimness. Ah, here was a long table laden with wares – lovely china plates in assorted patterns, each bearing a delicious array of cakes, biscuits and scones, all of which looked, frankly, much better than her and Daphne's best efforts. Oh well, she supposed she'd have to arrange theirs as temptingly as she could. She was just putting the last of Daphne's hub caps out, when she finally looked up.

That was odd. The rows of bunting, ringing the portion of the tent where Sarah was standing, and doing a sterling job of jollying up the interior with their bright innocent colours, had all been yanked down on the other side. Sarah could now see the flags were trailing messily along the ground. Everything else in the tent was beautifully neat; this looked all wrong. She began to feel acutely uneasy. Something was amiss. What was going on here?

She squinted into the gloom, following the line of fallen red, green, yellow and blue bunting as it snaked across the canvas floor. It was all bunched up in a huge, tangled pile in the middle of the tent. Then she saw something that made her gasp aloud. Was that – surely it couldn't be – a pair of feet?

'Good grief!' Sarah rushed forward. Now that she was much closer she could see that there were, indeed, two legs sticking out from the pile of flags. They belonged to a lady, lying flat out in the middle of the tent, almost covered in swathes of fallen bunting.

'Is everything OK?' she asked, her voice sounding croaky and fearful. She just couldn't believe she'd been fiddling with scones instead of helping this poor stricken woman. 'Are you all right?'

There was an ominous silence.

Sarah felt a prickle of dread run up her spine. This couldn't be happening, could it? But as she leant over the still figure, she saw the bunting wasn't just piled up harmlessly on top of the woman, bizarre though that would have been. Instead, horrifyingly, it was pulled cruelly tight around her neck, while her blue eyes stared vacantly up at the tent roof.

This poor lady was certainly not all right at all – and never would be, either. It looked very much as though she'd been strangled.

TWO

Sarah couldn't help giving a yelp of terror. Normally calmness personified at a crime scene, she had been taken completely by surprise this time. She had been in the tent for a full five minutes before she'd even noticed the calamity. Her hands were shaking at the thought that she'd been unaware of this poor woman's body, though judging by the cloudiness of those staring eyes, the killing must have taken place a while before Sarah arrived in the tent.

The lady was elderly, and despite the gloom, Sarah could see she was well-dressed in a smart fitted pink suit in boucle wool, which now rather unfortunately matched her face. Her white hair had been rigidly styled, and those eyes were wide in what looked like astonishment. And then there were all those flags, almost covering her body, and wrapped so horribly round her neck. What a cruel and awful thing to do. Sarah wasn't sure she would ever look at bunting in the same light again.

Wait a minute. There was a patch of jacket that was free of flags. She could see something caught between the shining gold buttons. It was a snippet of bright red cloth, frayed as though it had been torn from something larger. And underneath the lady's head, like a floral tribute on a bier, there was a bouquet of spring flowers.

Taking a shaky breath, Sarah stepped away. Just at that moment, Daphne stuck her head through the tent flap. 'Sarah! What on earth are you doing? You've been in there for ages. The judging committee is just arriving. You need to get a move on!' A yap from Hamish seconded her friend's urgency.

Sarah backed carefully out of the tent – only to run slap bang into a red-faced middle-aged man wearing a bristly tweed suit.

'A cheat! And we've caught her red-handed,' the man said, wrapping his arms hard around her and pressing her into his tweedy chest. Sarah fought to free herself, but to no avail. He was a lot stronger than a woman in her sixties, and she found herself subsiding crossly into this strange prickly embrace, while Hamish, who'd got loose from Daphne, leapt forward to defend her honour.

'Hey you, call the police,' the man said angrily to one of the other committee members, a wan-looking woman of about forty. 'And call off your dog,' he said even more crossly to Sarah.

'Hamish, it's fine, boy. This man is just being very silly,' Sarah said in her most reassuring voice, aware that the Scottie was quite capable of sinking his teeth into anyone who threatened her. 'But yes, please do call the police,' she said, twisting round as best she could to address her captor. 'There's a dead body in that tent. Someone's been murdered.'

* * *

Half an hour later, Sarah, Daphne and Hamish had taken refuge in the tea marquee, while the judging tent was cordoned off by Merstairs police constables Dumbarton and Deeside, often known as Tweedledum and Tweedledee. Sarah had cause to be grateful to Dumbarton, at least, for his timely intervention on a recent case and now felt she must address him by his real name. A stream of shocked visitors to the fair were making their way out past this duo, leaving their names, contact details and brief statements.

Though she'd been spared the sight of the corpse, Daphne was even more wobbly than Sarah. 'I just don't want this to be happening again,' she wailed. 'Why do people have to die? And why are you always finding their bodies?'

'Try not to worry, Daph,' said Sarah. 'With any luck we'll be home soon. Now drink up that tea. The cake is very good here, isn't it?'

'If you think talking about cake is going to distract me, then you've got another thing... oh goodness, this is moist, isn't it?' Daphne munched on a mouthful of sponge for a moment, an expression of rapture on her face.

Sarah was eating too, rather surprised she had the appetite, when there was a light tap on her shoulder. She swivelled round, to see Mariella, Daphne's daughter and a recent transfer to the Canterbury police force.

'Mariella, thank goodness you're here! Does this mean...?'

'Yes, the case has been taken off DI Brice and given to us.'

'Is it in your jurisdiction?' Sarah asked, as Mariella gave her mother a comforting hug.

'Not exactly... It's more a matter of who we're dealing with. The Brett-Coates are big cheeses round here.'

'Is that who's died?' Sarah asked.

'You didn't know? Yes, it's Madeleine Brett-Coates. I suppose you'd call her the matriarch of the family. Ah, look who's here,' said Mariella. A tall, slightly gangly figure was rushing towards them, an expression of acute concern on his handsome face.

'Charles! You didn't have to come,' said Sarah, getting up and melting into his embrace. 'But I'm very glad you did.'

'I got your text earlier about the bake-off. Thought I'd cheer you on. Now this ghastly thing has happened. You poor love, it must have been terrible.'

Sarah sniffed a bit into Charles's reassuring arms, then took her seat again. Charles sat next to her and patted Daphne's arm. 'How are you bearing up, old girl?'

'Less of the old,' said Daphne spiritedly. 'As well as can be expected. Given that I've been starved half to death,' she added, looking at her empty plate.

One of the advantages, if there were any, of having to stay when everyone else at the fair had been sent home was that there was now a tentful of baked goods going begging. Daphne accepted a fresh slice of sponge and seemed to rally.

'Well, as you're here, and you've somehow got involved again,' Mariella said drily, 'I suppose I should fill you in on some background. It might be useful in the days to come.'

Sarah sat up a little straighter, all ears. She was dying to know more about the Brett-Coates clan. As Mariella was about to speak, though, there was a commotion outside the marquee, and the bluff middle-aged man in the tweed suit who'd been so aggressive with Sarah pushed his way inside and made for their table. Sarah instinctively shrank away, though it was unlikely she would get manhandled again with Charles at her side.

'Ah, Diggory,' the man said, frowning down at Charles.

'Brett-Coates, dear chap,' Charles said, leaping up and grasping the man's hand. After a hearty shake, and a bit of back-slapping, the men seemed to remember their audience, and both sat down a little sheepishly. 'Old schoolfriend, you know,' Charles confided to Sarah.

Sarah nodded, by now aware that such ties meant a lot to Charles.

The man looked over at Sarah. 'Bernard Brett-Coates,' he said. 'Sorry about earlier. Thought you were meddling with the competition,' he said. 'Didn't realise you'd found Mumsy,' he said gruffly.

'I'm so sorry for your loss,' Sarah said. 'I can't imagine how awful today has been. But you said something about cheats – have you had problems with that?'

'Oh, just villagers,' said Bernard, in the way his ancestors might once have said 'peasants'. 'Some of them sneaked in last year and changed the prize cards around. It sounds like innocent fun, but people build up to the fair all year. They get upset. I saw you coming out and assumed the worst, I'm afraid,' he added.

'I see,' said Sarah. She normally had strong views about people who acted first and thought later – but in view of the poor man's bereavement, that didn't seem important now. 'Quite understandable.'

'It's appalling,' said Bernard, his face going an angry red. 'Poor Mumsy, who always had other people's welfare at heart. But I told her doing the fair wasn't safe.'

'Why was that?' asked Sarah.

'What? Oh, just a turn of phrase,' said Bernard quickly, though Sarah could have sworn he'd meant a lot more than that. 'Listen, it's getting late. Perhaps you'd like to adjourn to the house? It's getting chilly.'

It was true, while they'd been sitting there, the temperature had dropped and there was a strong breeze getting up. Besides, it would be fascinating to see inside the house that Francesca had once had her eye on, even under these grim circumstances. Sarah buttoned up her cardigan and looked towards her friend for confirmation.

Daphne looked torn. 'Well, I suppose we could pop in for five minutes. But really I should be going to check on Tarot and Tealeaves. I run my mystic business empire from there, you know,' she said to Bernard Brett-Coates.

Sarah wasn't sure he would have been interested in Daphne's concerns even on a good day. But, following the death of his mother, it was clear Brett-Coates had automatically assumed their acceptance. 'That's settled, then. See you in the drawing room. Better show these blighters what to do,' he said heavily, gesturing towards the constables, neither knowing nor caring that it was Mariella who was in charge of the entire operation.

As Bernard Brett-Coates stumped off across the field, Sarah carefully gathered up Daphne's scarf and bag and Hamish's lead. Charles offered both ladies an arm.

'Are you coming, Mari?' Daphne asked.

'I'll just make sure all this is going smoothly,' Mariella said. Sarah realised she must be waiting for the pathologist, and wondered if she should stay behind as well, but the policewoman gave her a tiny shake of the head. She wasn't likely to forget the sight of that bunting anyway.

From the outside, Sarah found the Brett-Coates mansion rather forbidding, but as soon as they were through the imposing oak front door, she realised the interior was very different. The air was full of the welcoming scents of beeswax and fresh flowers, and although the hall was magnificent, with a vast and very solid oak staircase rising up at least three storeys, it still managed to be warm and inviting.

There was a vase filled with purple and white tulips and blue agapanthus on a console table, with an oil painting behind it of the house, painted a century ago when the cedar trees were just saplings. Beside the bowl was a big, highly polished mahogany box and some silver-framed photos, including one of a smiling lady in a lilac dress. Sarah stepped forward. It was, surely, the woman in the tent, perhaps twenty or thirty years before this fateful spring day, her smile now poignant.

'Poor lady,' Sarah whispered.

'Hmm,' Charles said. 'The drawing room is through here. Been here before, you know,' he said, in answer to her unspoken question. 'Oh, ah, house rules. Everyone has to drop their phones into this box,' he said, pointing at the mahogany chest.

'You're kidding?' said Sarah.

'Afraid not. They're very strict about it.' Charles popped his mobile in, holding the lid open for the others. 'It was one of Madeleine Brett-Coates's big things. Said phones were wrecking family life.' Sarah and Daphne looked at each other and followed suit. There was already quite a pile of handsets inside. Sarah immediately wondered what Mrs Brett-Coates had hoped to achieve. Did she want to keep everyone here incommunicado? And if so, why?

Charles opened a sturdy oak door and ushered the ladies in. The drawing room was exquisitely pretty. It was dominated by a fireplace so large Sarah's cottage could have fitted into it.

At right angles to this were two squishy sofas upholstered in a cheerful chintz. Daphne sank onto one of these gratefully, as though she'd been made to trek across the desert for hours. Immediately, she picked up a copy of *Country Life* from the upholstered ottoman between the sofas and started flicking through it.

Sarah and Charles sat opposite her, sinking into the sumptuous cushions. 'What a lovely place. And a gorgeous room,' said Sarah, looking out onto the lawn. There was a magnolia tree close to the window, its large pink-white blooms bobbing as though they were trying to peep in.

'I can't believe all this has happened, though,' Charles said, rubbing a hand over his face.

'Of course. It must be so awful, knowing the family as you do. Did you see much of erm, Mrs Brett-Coates, when you were growing up?'

'She'd appear at the odd Founder's Day or whatever at school. It'll be tough for Bernard, that's for sure.'

'Was he close to his mother?'

'Oh,' said Charles. 'It's more that all the cares of running this place will fall on his shoulders now. Needs a lot of upkeep, a house like this.'

Sarah wasn't surprised to hear it. So far, Coates House seemed as plush as any luxury hotel. The heating bill alone must be eye-watering. 'They'll be sitting on a tidy fortune, I suppose,' she said idly.

'Hmm,' said Charles again.

Sarah was beginning to get the feeling that he wasn't telling her everything. If it hadn't already been quite an emotionally exhausting day, she would have pressed him for more details. But as it was, the sofa was very comfortable, the room was lovely and warm, and she felt quite cosy sitting with her head on Charles's shoulder. Perhaps she should just close her eyes for one minute...

It seemed like only a second later that she received a rude awakening. Someone had erupted into the room and was shouting right in her face. 'What did you do to her, you evil old woman?'

THREE

Sarah, jolted into wakefulness, gaped at the furious-looking dark-haired woman who was yelling at her. She looked to be in her early fifties – only ten years younger than Sarah herself. Old woman? Charming, she thought. At her side, Charles jumped to his feet.

'Now wait just one second, Helena,' he started, when someone else came through the doors and rushed over to the woman.

'Come on, Hells,' said the man, who had the same dark hair but was younger and slighter. 'No good flying into a rage about this. We're all inconsolable about Mumsy, but assaulting people doesn't help, does it? Take deep breaths. Think of all your mindfulness stuff.'

He pulled the woman away, and shoved her into a plush armchair near the sofas. 'That's better. You stay quiet and I'll get you a drink.'

He went over to a trolley stationed near the door and took the stopper from a cut-glass decanter. 'Oh,' he said as an afterthought, turning to the sofas. 'Would any of you...?'

Sarah shook her head, but Charles stood up. 'Actually,

Jonathan old man, that might be just the job. Tricky afternoon, you know,' he said with wonderful English understatement.

'Sorry, Charles. Didn't recognise you for a second. How did you get dragged into this mess?' Jonathan said.

Charles raised an eyebrow. 'You may well ask. It does, er, happen,' he said, glancing at Sarah. 'Daphne? A little something?'

Daphne shook her head and pressed a tissue to her eyes. 'I'm sorry. All the shouting is tangling up my chakras. I think it's about time we got going.'

'I think we're going to have to stay until Mariella gives us the nod,' Sarah told her. 'Our car is parked right by the crime scene, if you remember. They'll be really busy out there.'

Daphne groaned. 'Oh, honestly. How is my poor little Mephisto going to manage?'

'Shall I give Mrs Jones a ring and ask her to feed him?' Sarah asked. Mephisto wouldn't have the slightest trouble fending for himself, but she wanted to put Daphne's mind at rest. Mrs Jones lived in the last cottage in their terrace of three, and sometimes helped out with Hamish.

'Oh goodness, not her. She hates me, ever since I read her palm and said all her plants were going to die.'

'Have they?' asked Sarah.

'Not yet,' said Daphne darkly.

Sarah couldn't help smiling. 'Well, I'll just go and send her a text.' In the hall, she got her phone out of the box and quickly messaged Mrs Jones. 'That's settled,' she confirmed when she returned and sat down again. 'She's sent a thumbs-up.'

'I still don't understand what you two old— well, you *women* are doing here, twittering on about your domestic arrangements,' said Helena, scowling at them fiercely.

'This is the lady who... found Mumsy, Hells. The police want her here. This is her friend, and you know Charles, of course,' said the man with an apologetic smile. 'We should all introduce ourselves properly. I'm Jonathan Brett-Coates,' he said, leaving a small pause. 'And this is my sister, Helena,' he went on.

'Just a minute,' said Daphne, clutching her headscarf. 'Don't I know you from somewhere?' she said, staring at Jonathan. 'I'm sure I do. Don't tell me... Ah, got it! You came to fix my drains last year, didn't you?' she said with a triumphant smile.

The man's face fell and Helena let out a whoop of delight. 'That'll teach him! Jonathan thinks he's a huge star these days, don't you?'

'Shut up, Hells, of course I don't.'

Charles put his head on one side. 'Ah yes. Do a telly show, don't you?'

'Do you watch it?' Jonathan said quickly.

'Sorry, old boy. Bernard, ah, happened to mention it.'

'Oh yes,' said Jonathan crossly. 'I can just imagine what he said.'

'What sort of programme is it?' Sarah asked politely.

'Gardening makeovers. I help viewers who have issues making their outdoor spaces reflect their dreams,' he said earnestly. 'Sometimes I assist with community projects. Just last week we were revamping a school playground. They were about to put in a yew hedge,' he added, shaking his head.

'Oh? Wouldn't it have thrived?' Sarah was trying to sort out her own pocket handkerchief garden, despite the combined efforts of Hamish and Mephisto, and was always interested in tips.

'Yew's a deadly poison,' Jonathan said, with a downturn of his beautiful mobile mouth. Sarah could really see why he was on the small screen – he was a very attractive man. 'The berries could easily kill a child.'

'Thank goodness you were there to advise them,' Sarah said.

'Oh yes, thank heavens for Jonathan,' sneered Helena.

'Always on hand at just the right moment. Aren't you, Mumsy's boy?'

'I don't know what you mean by that,' said Jonathan, withdrawing into himself immediately.

There were a lot of undercurrents with this family, thought Sarah. Poor Mariella. It was her first big case since the transfer to Canterbury. And it looked as though it wasn't going to be straightforward at all. Sarah would just have to do everything in her power to help the girl prove herself. If that meant trying to get this murder solved, then so be it.

Just then, there was a knock at the door, and the policewoman poked her head round. 'Sarah, erm, Dr Vane, could I just have a quick word?'

Sarah got up from the sofa, struggling slightly to free herself from its soft embrace, and joined Mariella in the hall. 'Everything OK?'

'Well, it's a crime scene after a sudden death, so... But anyway, there's a bit of an anomaly. We're not working with Dr Strutton as Canterbury has its own team. To be honest, I... well, I just wondered if I could get an unofficial sounding from you.'

'Oh. I see,' said Sarah. It looked like she was being called upon to step up immediately, and in a way that could be a little tricky. No doctor liked being second-guessed by a colleague. Mind you, Sarah was now retired – maybe that would take the sting out of anything she suggested. 'Very happy to help in any way I can, of course.'

She squared her shoulders, and they were soon traipsing back out to the fateful tent. Its jaunty blue and white stripes looked rather sinister now to Sarah, knowing the sight that lurked within. Through the flap, instead of the previous murky darkness, she was greeted with blinding light from a rig spotlighting the crucial area. Standing with his back to the corpse was a short man in jeans and a hoodie, who turned and gave Sarah a huge smile as she advanced.

'Sarah Vane,' she said, holding out a hand while thinking that, like policemen, doctors were getting younger every day. She knew this chap must have completed a seven-year medical degree and then undergone at least five or six years of specialist pathology training, but his fresh round face, pleasant open expression and the way he was almost bouncing on the balls of his feet meant he didn't seem a day over twenty. No doubt he was thinking she was a total dinosaur, she thought ruefully.

The man did jazz hands with his latex gloves to show he wouldn't be shaking hers, inclining his head towards her in a friendly way instead. 'William Jarvis. Lovely to meet you. Bit of an odd one, this. I understand you have an interest?'

'I was the first on the scene, yes,' said Sarah, as they moved over towards the corpse. 'And I'm a doctor. Well, a retired GP.'

'Marvellous! I bet you've seen it all,' he said cheerfully.

'Mm, yes.' She'd definitely seen a lot since moving to Merstairs, anyway. Now, as they both approached the body, she braced herself for the sight of the garish bunting, pulled so cruelly tight, but it was gone, presumably having been cut away by one of the SOCOs. They were diligently working away, fingerprinting the long table, which was still laden with forlorn cakes and scones.

'What did you make of it?'

'I didn't get a very close look,' Sarah said hesitantly, reluctant to admit how much the sight of the body had spooked her. Now, with the forensic team's arc lamps in place, presumably powered by a generator somewhere, the tent was bright as day. But when she'd been in there alone, it had been quite gloomy, and the sudden unexpected discovery of the corpse had been horrible.

She inched forward, careful not to tread anywhere outside the delineated path as they got closer to the body. Now that the victim's throat was clear of its knot of flags, she could see something rather surprising.

'Curious. I'd assumed it was a strangulation, of course, though the colour of her skin was a bit off. But now I can see that the flags weren't actually tied tightly enough. I'd have expected deep striation marks, possibly even breaking the skin, as the bunting seems to be strung on a strong but thin cord. That would leave very nasty indentations if someone really had strangled her.'

'Exactly!' said Jarvis, as excited as a small boy on Christmas Day. 'And did you get close enough to examine the eyes?'

'No,' said Sarah, rather apologetically. 'And it was very dark.'

'Well, have a look now,' he said, moving from foot to foot as though he couldn't wait for her verdict.

Sarah approached, and peered down at the poor lady. Death was so unfair, robbing people of all dignity. This woman, possibly in her late seventies or eighties, with her rigid crown of white hair set in old-fashioned waves, her face thickly adorned with powder with brave patches of rouge, had got up this morning, determined to make the best of herself for the fair. No doubt it was quite an ordeal, at her age, but she had put on this attractive (and expensive) pink boucle suit and floral silk blouse, strung on a triple strand of pearls and found matching earrings, never guessing that people would be staring down at her only hours later, noticing the asymmetry of her make-up and the fact that there was a toothpaste mark on the collar of her frock. Her eyes, a faded blue, stared sightlessly at the roof of the tent.

'No petechiae,' Sarah said succinctly, referring to the characteristic pin-prick red dots that usually appeared in the whites of a strangulation victim's eyes, and occasionally ran across the face too.

'None at all! Wonderful, isn't it?'

Sarah wasn't so sure this was a win. The woman was, after all, quite dead. 'I suppose you mean it proves she wasn't strangled after all,' she said slowly, straightening up.

FOUR

Dr Jarvis almost clapped his hands with suppressed excitement. 'Yes! I do love it when the body helps us out, don't you?'

Sarah was a little bemused by the pathologist's extremely cheerful bedside (or should that be graveside?) manner. 'You'll be looking for another cause of death. Are you thinking stroke, heart attack?'

'Ah, that'd be telling,' Jarvis said, wagging a finger at her. 'In the meantime, have a look at this, just under her shoulder and behind her head. What do you make of that?'

Sarah leant forward and studied the squashed blooms underneath the body. 'Yes, I noticed that before. Very odd that she seems to have fallen on a bouquet of flowers.'

'Perhaps she was arranged on top of it?' Jarvis countered.

'Is there any sign of interruption of lividity?' Sarah asked, looking sideways at the woman's forearm. It was lying uselessly at her side, and so far the colour of the flesh was uniform.

'You're right, I'll be keeping an eye on that. As you know, later on it could show whether she was moved after death or not. And while I'm doing that, you'll be looking out for someone who didn't like this lady very much, I imagine.'

'Me?' said Sarah in surprise.

'Oh yes,' Jarvis twinkled. 'Pamela Strutton has told me all about you.'

'I see,' Sarah said, feeling quite daunted.

'Wonderful, isn't it? I love a puzzle.' Jarvis was almost rubbing his hands together with glee. Sarah was all for an enthusiastic attitude to work, but this was a little much.

'This poor woman has died. It isn't a game,' she said, then rather wished she'd bitten her tongue. Jarvis might be acting like a child, but he wasn't one, and it certainly wasn't her business to tell him off. Luckily, he seemed to take it in good part.

'Oh, of course not,' he said airily. 'But I do like to work stuff out,' he added with a grin.

'Well, perhaps I'd better get back to the house,' Sarah said. 'Unless I can help out here?'

'Got it all in hand, haha,' said Jarvis, waving his gloves at her again.

'Bye,' said Sarah, making for the tent flap and heading outside, where Mariella was waiting.

'Well? What did you think?' said the young detective.

'About the body? Or the pathologist?' Sarah said with a slight grimace.

'Oh, I know,' Mariella said with a shake of her head. Sarah immediately felt sorry for her. Her recent transfer to the Canterbury force had put some troublesome colleagues behind her, but it looked as though she was finding out that staffing issues were a universal problem.

'Well, it's great to have lots of enthusiasm,' said Sarah, taking Mariella's arm. 'Now, is there anything you can tell me about the family? You were just about to give me a run-down before we got interrupted.'

'I'll go over the basics. Well-to-do local bigwigs. Madeleine was the matriarch, the widow of Tobias Brett-Coates, who was a financier. Rolling in it, as you can probably tell from the house and grounds. There are three children, Bernard, Jonathan and Helena. I suppose the unusual thing is that they all still live at home. Well, Helena has only returned recently, she was living in Los Angeles, of all places, before. But the boys have never left Vanstone.'

'They must all get on well, then,' Sarah mused.

'I'm not so sure. There are rumours in the village, according to some of the people who were at the fair. Friction between the brothers, a rift with the mother – and they all find the sister really hard going.'

'Actually, I'm not surprised at that,' said Sarah, remembering the way the woman had flown at her. 'Why would they all stay together, then? They could have gone their separate ways. If the mother was loaded, and it looks as though no expense is spared on the house, then surely they could all afford to buy their own places?'

'I have a feeling she had a tight grip on the purse strings, and they only got their allowance if they stayed with her,' said Mariella. 'But hopefully you can make some enquiries about all that.'

'You wouldn't mind?' Sarah was surprised. Mariella had never encouraged her to get involved before – quite the reverse, in fact.

'Well, you're going to do it anyway, even if I tell you not to,' Mariella said with the ghost of a smile as they trudged up the gravel drive. 'Actually, I've got a good reason for asking. You see, there was only one entrance to that tent.'

'Oh yes. I remember. The flaps were tied up with bows. But that's not exactly barbed wire and padlocks, is it? Anyone could have got in.'

'But that's the thing, you see. Only the family had been in there.'

'How do you know?' Sarah asked, puzzled.

'Well, right opposite the entrance was the white elephant stall, run by two ladies from the village, Beatrice and Jessica Weatherspoon. And they are adamant that, from three p.m. onwards, the only people in that tent were the family – and you. They didn't take particular note of who went in at what time, more's the pity. Apart from the fact that you were the last in.'

Sarah felt a shiver go up her spine. 'Mrs Brett-Coates was dead when I got into the tent at roughly four o'clock, her eyes were already starting to look cloudy, which happens within two hours of death. So if these ladies are right, it's only family members who are under suspicion. How reliable are they?'

'The Weatherspoon sisters? They're leading lights of the local Neighbourhood Watch. The beadiest eyes in Vanstone. Put it this way, I wouldn't want to try and get anything past them.'

'But what about the sides of the tent they couldn't see?' Sarah couldn't help asking.

'Ah,' said Mariella. 'It's an unusual tent, very expensive, and specially made for Madeleine Brett-Coates. The ground sheet is zipped into the sides, once it's erected, which means that no one can sneak underneath and get in that way. That flap is the only entry point.'

'Good gracious. I'm not sure how I feel about going back into the house now, with a murderer on the loose,' said Sarah, looking up at the windows glittering in the fading sunlight as they stood just outside. 'And surely they won't want strangers hanging around? Even if one of them didn't have something terrible on their conscience, they're a family in mourning. They'll want privacy.'

'Maybe. But people don't always get what they want, do they? You'll be perfectly placed to find out what's going on, especially as Charles is chums with them all. Look, it's crucial that I do well on this case. So please help me out, Aunty Sarah. Try and find out which one of them did it, will you?'

Sarah swallowed. It was a tall order. There must be a lot of resentment bubbling under this impressive roof at the best of times, if everyone was basically being paid to remain here. And now Mariella had more or less confirmed that one of the family was a murderer, too. This had the makings of a very dangerous undertaking.

Sarah hesitated at the front door, taking in the plush rugs underfoot in the gracious entrance hall, the lovely oil painting over the console and the gleaming grandfather clock ticking softly in the corner. For a moment, she wondered if perhaps it wasn't so bad to live with relatives you weren't keen on – if you could do it in a house this size, where you could all keep out of each other's way, and enjoy this sort of luxury while you were at it.

'Of course I'm going to help, Mariella. You can rely on me,' Sarah said, hoping she sounded more convincing than she felt. One of this family had been driven to kill, and none of the fancy trappings of the house seemed that enticing any more.

Mariella strode over to her team, waiting for her by the beautiful staircase, and started conferring with them in hushed voices. Sarah wandered back to the drawing room, puzzling again over the bouquet of flowers found under Madeleine Brett-Coates. What did that mean? Was the murderer trying, strangely and belatedly, to give the victim a floral send-off? Or was it something more sinister altogether?

What had the blossoms been again? Bluebells, tulips and foxgloves in wonderful shades of blue, yellow and purple, that was right. Foxgloves, she knew, were toxic – they contained digitalin, which could cause fatal heart arrhythmia. Was it possible they could have been the cause of death, if it wasn't strangulation?

Jonathan was an expert who seemed to know a lot about the poisonous properties of plants – was that just a strange coincidence... or could it be something more? She needed to try and get a word with him as soon as she could.

But all that went out of her head when she walked through the door and found Charles and Daphne at each other's throats.

FIVE

Both Daphne and Charles wheeled round as Sarah entered the room, and for a second she could hardly make out any words as each yelled their version of events at her. She held up a hand and said loudly, 'You two, stop it right now.'

Sarah saw that Helena Brett-Coates was watching her two friends with a sphinx-like smirk from the window seat. She turned to her. 'I'm going to ask an impartial observer. Helena here has had the dubious honour of listening to the whole argument. She'll soon tell me what's what.' With that, Sarah was gratified to see her grin disappearing.

'Oh, I wouldn't dream of getting involved,' Helena said, looking from one combatant to the other.

'In that case,' said Sarah, taking her at her word, 'let's change the subject entirely. Obviously tensions are running high this afternoon, as we've all had a difficult time,' she said glancing crossly at Charles and Daphne, who now sat at opposite ends of the sofa. Charles looked a little apologetic, but Daphne opened her mouth to speak. Sarah rushed to forestall her. 'It's been particularly hard for you, obviously, Helena. Losing your mother,' Sarah said.

Helena, who had been eyeing Daphne, now slumped in her seat and looked woebegone. Sarah was suddenly sure she was putting it on. Did she feel her mother's loss at all?

'You had a good relationship with her, did you?' Sarah asked.

At this, Helena bridled. 'What gives you the right to come into my home and ask me such impertinent questions?' she said, rearing up and pacing the room. She was getting into her stride, when the door opened and Bernard Brett-Coates stuck his head round. 'Hells. Seen Geoffrey?' he asked.

'No. Not for hours. Anyway, what do you care what he's up to? It's not like you want to spend time with him, is it?'

For a moment it looked as though Bernard was going to come into the room to argue the toss with his sister. Then he shook his head and closed the door instead. Outside, he could be heard calling out, 'Geoffrey? Where've you got to, old man?'

'Honestly. Bernard hates Geoffrey with a passion. I don't know why he's pretending they're so pally now.' Helena said with a sour expression.

'Sorry, who is Geoffrey?' Sarah asked.

Helena looked her over dismissively, and Sarah thought the question was going to go unanswered. Then the woman seemed to think better of it. 'My brother-in-law,' she muttered. 'He's married to Jonathan, the family's superstar,' she said, making ironic air quotes over the word. 'At least, he thinks that's what he is. Well, you met him earlier, didn't you? Geoffrey's no better. Says he's a historian and author, but that's just as tenuous, frankly.'

'Is that Geoffrey Brett-Coates, then? Who wrote *The Palladian Country House*?' Sarah asked. 'I suppose he took the family surname when he got married.'

'Good gracious, yes! Right on both counts. Geoff will be thrilled, finally someone who's read one of his dreary books. Don't tell me you're a fan.'

'Well... not exactly,' said Sarah, whose cheeks were growing a little pink. It had been her late husband, Peter, who'd been interested in architecture. Thinking of him now, with Charles in the room and indeed in her heart, she felt obscurely guilty. 'He must love this place, though.'

'Funny you should say that,' said Helena. 'He's tried for years to get Mother to agree to him doing a book about the house. She vetoed it last time he had a go, really let rip,' she said with a certain glum satisfaction. 'He's got a bee in his bonnet about one of our ancestors – Sir Bernard Brett-Coates. Something about the Battle of Culloden. I can't say the idea does much for me, and Mother was positively anti. She couldn't bear Geoff.'

Interesting, thought Sarah. There'd be nothing stopping Geoff writing his book, now Madeleine Brett-Coates was out of the way. Rather convenient for him, perhaps?

'What did Madeleine have against him?' Charles asked. 'I don't know Geoff well, but I met him at his and Jonty's wedding, of course. He seems a good chap.'

'Wait until you spend more time with him,' said Helena dismissively. 'Yes, their marriage will be when I last saw you. Was that after the treatment in Palm Springs? Did I have a tan?'

'Um, not sure I can quite recall... it was a few years ago,' said Charles apologetically, not wanting to say the wrong thing. 'And there were lots of people around that day. It all looked wonderful.'

'Yes, Mother was big on those family dos, even when she couldn't stand the actual family members involved. We had a marquee in the field, didn't we?'

'Yes. And there was a display of birds of prey, and a re-enactment by the Merstairs Militia. In the evening there was a guided tour of the roof and chimneys; it was splendid.'

'Geoff wanted all those touches. The family ghost is said to walk the battlements. He probably wanted to tempt it out of retirement,' said Helena.

'Ghost?' Daphne said, looking alarmed. 'Oh dear, it's not good to tinker with forces you don't understand.'

Helena looked at her quizzically. 'I shouldn't worry. It's all nonsense, of course. Apparently we got cursed after that Culloden fight went wrong yonks ago. Our most frequent visitor is the White Lady. She's supposed to be the faithless wife of a previous Sir Bernard. Tried to run off with a stable hand and her husband stabbed her with the old knife in the dining room, or so the story goes. Mind you, she only appears when a member of the family dies... Oh, I didn't think! Now that Mother's gone, I suppose she'll be walking tonight.'

Even though the room was warm and it was still daylight, Sarah felt a shiver up her spine. Was there really going to be a ghostly apparition here this very evening?

More sinister still was the way Helena was gazing out of the window, another half-smile on her face. For someone who had just lost a parent, she was bearing up extremely well. Was that because they hadn't got on – or could Helena have had something to do with the murder?

SIX

Jonathan Brett-Coates burst in, breaking the uneasy silence. 'I can't find him, I tell you, Helena. Where is he? What have you done with him? You've always hated him, haven't you?'

'You must mean Geoff, I suppose, Jonty. Where on earth do you think I've hidden him? Under my skirt? He wouldn't like that much,' Helena said with a cruel laugh. 'Have you tried Mother's study? That's my best guess. With her out of the way he can get on with his silly book project, can't he? He'll be rooting through her papers, or in the dining room eyeing up that dagger he's always going on about. Probably making arrangements to stick it on *Antiques Roadshow*. Not to mention covering up—'

'Shut up, Hells,' said Jonathan. He turned and registered the rest of them. 'What are you people still doing here? I thought the police had got rid of everyone.'

Jonathan Brett-Coates, with that mass of dark curls and those brooding good looks, was too restless and intense for something as mainstream as the news. But Sarah could just picture him with a spade in his hand, standing on a wind-blasted moor like a latter-day Heathcliff. Now he was directing all that slightly menacing charisma right at her, Daphne and Charles.

Before she could speak, Charles had sprung up. 'Steady on, old man. You've met Sarah and Daphne. Difficult day. My sympathies.' He clapped a suddenly much more amenable Jonathan on the back. 'Terrible loss.'

'I can't believe Mumsy is gone,' Jonathan said, passing a hand over his face and slumping, exhausted, onto the sofa next to Sarah. 'Sorry, yes, Charles, I remember your friends. But I'm not clear why they're hanging around?'

Charles looking embarrassed now, shrugged slightly at Sarah. *Over to you.*

'Um, Mariella, the detective on the case, asked us to come and sit with you all for a while. She thought Charles, as a friend of the family, might be of some use at a time like this,' Sarah said, thinking it sounded a bit thin.

'And of course I can get in touch with your mother's spirit, help her over to the other side,' said Daphne earnestly. Jonathan looked at her with distaste.

Sarah hoped they weren't going to get thrown out. She was keen to find out what Jonathan might know about the foxgloves under his mother's head. She was just framing a question, when Bernard stuck his head round the door.

'No luck yet finding Geoff, I take it? Where on earth can the blighter have gone? Jonty, you haven't had another row?'

'Shut up, Bernard,' Jonathan said bleakly.

'How long has he been missing, exactly?' Sarah piped up. The fact that a murder had occurred on the grounds, and now this Geoffrey had disappeared, was suddenly making her wonder if there could be a simpler explanation for the death of Madeleine Brett-Coates than the foxgloves theory involving Jonathan's expertise. What could be neater than Geoff committing murder, then fleeing rather than face the music? He could have learnt about poisons from his husband, after all.

'I haven't seen him all day. When I got up this morning he was already gone. His side of the bed was cold,' said Jonathan.

'Did he even come to bed last night?' Helena asked. 'I heard you arguing in the dining room last night. Maybe he's gone off to a hotel, or something.'

'It was just a tiff,' said Jonathan shiftily. 'It meant nothing. He'd have told me if he was leaving, even for a day. No, this is strange, completely out of character.'

'If you say so,' said Helena lightly. 'Well, I suppose that's one good thing about having all these police crawling round the place. They're bound to find him. Tell your policewoman to make sure they do a proper search,' she said curtly to Sarah.

'Um, I'm sure she's got the matter in hand,' Sarah said quickly before Daphne could object to her daughter being spoken of like some sort of lackey.

'The trouble is that it's such a big house. Hard to cover everything properly, from the attics to the cellars,' Charles said thoughtfully.

'Well, that's true. Except we all know Geoff would never in a million years go down to the basement. Not with his claustrophobia,' said Jonathan dismissively.

'Just a minute. Does Geoff by any chance have red hair?' asked Daphne, looking as though she'd had a flash of inspiration.

'Why yes, he does,' said Jonathan. 'What's that got to do with anything?'

'Someone whizzed past us when we were on our way here earlier in the car,' said Daphne. 'In fact, he nearly smashed into us, didn't he, Sarah?'

'Yes, that's right. He was driving at... quite a pace,' said Sarah, with some restraint. She remembered how shaky she'd felt after the encounter with that car, on a blind bend. It could all have ended very differently.

'Wait a sec, what time was this?' Helena asked.

Sarah and Daphne looked at each other. 'Just a bit before four, I suppose. What with one thing and another, it took us longer than it should have done to get here.' Sarah remembered all Daphne's faffing about with tins and scones at home. If only they'd left earlier. They would have avoided a near-death experience in the lane, and she wouldn't have been the one to find the body. Their scones might have been judged, too – though she knew that was not the most important thing, and it probably would have ended in disappointment for Daphne.

'I bet that was Geoff. What car was he driving?'

Again there was an exchange of glances. Sarah was used to being pretty much an expert witness, when it came to humans. With cars, it was a different story.

'I think it was a sort of navy—'

'Definitely deep purple—'

They spoke over each other, then caught each other's eyes. 'Honestly, what are we like?' said Daphne. 'It was a dark colour, anyway.'

'It was big and boxy – a Land Rover,' said Sarah.

'Ah! Yes, that's Geoff's. It's a midnight blue. That explains things, then,' said Jonathan, looking a lot happier.

'But don't you see?' said Helena to him. 'If that was Geoff running away... won't the police think he had a reason to? They'll say he was getting away from the scene of the crime.'

'Oh, don't be ridiculous, Hells. I know you can't stand Geoff but there's no way you can seriously think he did something to Mumsy. No, you were right first time. We had words last night, a silly disagreement about nothing. He's gone to cool off. Simple as that.'

'So why isn't he answering his phone? I'm assuming you *have* called him,' Helena went on, getting up from her seat.

'Obviously I have. He won't want to talk. Not until he's thought everything through. Once he's cooled off, he'll be back.'

'I think you're forgetting one thing, Jonty.' Helena said, suppressed emotion in her voice.

'What's that, Hells?' Jonathan settled himself down on the sofa more comfortably next to Daphne, and smiled at her happily. A weight had clearly been lifted from his mind, and he was now back in charming TV presenter mode. Sarah started wondering again if she could get him onto the topic of the flowers found under his mother.

But Helena hadn't finished with her brother yet. She pulled back the heavy coral silk brocade curtains to their fullest extent and pointed outside, past the wide lawns to the parking area beyond. 'Isn't that Geoff's car out there?'

SEVEN

Sarah and Daphne were immediately taken out by the police to see if they recognised the car. It certainly looked very much like the one that had almost forced them off the road, but Sarah couldn't say for sure.

Luckily, Daphne had no such qualms. 'This is it, officer, this is the one,' she said, addressing Constable Deeside as he scratched laboriously in his little notebook. 'I recognise it because I can still feel an evil emanation coming directly from the driver's seat. Yes, his aura is particularly poisonous, I don't mind telling you. Clouds of blackness oozing everywhere. You must be able to see it yourself?'

Here, Daphne directed a piercing glance at the constable, who looked at her, baffled, and then glared suspiciously at the car interior.

'There, I tell you, there! It's all around you now,' Daphne said, as the man stumbled about, looking behind him and then peering through the passenger window into the car. Sarah shook her head, her lips twitching, though there was little else that was funny about what had unfolded today.

'So, what would you like us to do now, officer?' Sarah asked the constable when he'd stopped chasing his tail. 'Are we free to go yet?'

'I don't know about that, Miss, er, Mrs, erm, Doctor... Sir. You'd better be asking the bigwig from Canterbury,' he said, finishing with a bit of a snigger. He soon thought better of it when he caught Daphne's eye.

'If you mean my daughter, then I'll thank you to use her proper title,' she said, and looked as though she was about to embark on a diatribe about hierarchy and respect, which was mercifully curtailed by the arrival of Mariella herself.

'You've identified the car? OK, Deeside, stay there until the SOCOs reach you, please. Mum, Sarah, can you come into the house with me?'

'I was wondering if we should get home, Mariella? Hamish could do with some dinner. He's been very patient, but I like to keep him in a routine,' Sarah said.

'And there's Mephisto, too. If he doesn't get his tuna chunks he could be quite upset,' Daphne put in.

'Hamish looks happy enough to me,' said Mariella, stooping to pet the little dog. 'He'll probably get on really well with the Brett-Coates's dog, Butler. He's an old black Labrador. And as for Mephisto, I'm sure that neighbour of yours can cope for a while longer, Mum. We're quite short-staffed on this one and I'd appreciate you sticking around with the family for as long as possible. I have a feeling you could pick up some useful titbits. I've arranged for CCTV to be installed all around the house and garden, so don't worry too much about anything else happening – I've got your backs.'

'Well, OK,' said Sarah, torn between a longing to get back to her little cottage and a feeling of pride, that Mariella was now trusting them with parts of the enquiry she couldn't quite cover herself. 'I suppose it makes it easier that Charles is a family friend, so we blend in a bit more.'

'And of course I never have any trouble making myself at

home,' said Daphne, swishing her scarf. 'As long as Mrs Jones doesn't mind looking after my kitty.'

'I'll check with her in a bit,' Sarah said. 'Is there any sign of Geoffrey yet, Mariella? Do you think the car is his?' she asked.

'It's definitely his car. The question is rather whether you saw him in it earlier – but Mum's said she's sure. Of course, he could always have turned round and come back, parked up and then got lost in this great big pile,' said Mariella, staring at the daunting façade of the house.

Just then, a gong sounded inside. 'What on earth do you think that is?' asked Daphne.

'I think it must be announcing dinner,' said Sarah. The front door opened a crack, and Charles stuck his head out.

'Ah, there you are, dear ladies. Bernard has invited us to join the family for supper. We'd better hurry up. Madeleine was always very pernickety about everyone being prompt, and I don't suppose anything's changed in the last few hours.'

Well, something has, Sarah thought. The lady of the house was no longer with them. But she said nothing, merely getting her phone out as they passed the mahogany box. She quickly texted Mrs Jones about Mephisto's tuna requirements. She was glad to get another thumbs-up, then hurried to rejoin the others. Charles proffered his arm, and she took it, with Hamish following at her heels.

The dining room was in the opposite direction to the drawing room, though again with a magnificent view out of three large windows. The walls were painted a deep navy blue, and the brocade curtains in this room were in a sumptuous old gold shade, swagged and held back with thick rope ties. The long shining walnut table was laid with crisp white napkins, glittering crystal glasses and porcelain plates with a pattern of blue and gold flowers on pristine white. If the meal lived up to its setting, this was going to be a very splendid affair indeed. Butler the Labrador was settled in a basket in the corner, and thumped his tail to welcome Hamish, who went over to make his acquaintance.

Bernard, Helena and Jonathan were all present. Bernard and Jonathan had found black ties somewhere and put them on, while Helena was wearing a dark grey crepe dress. Another woman was seated at Bernard's right hand. She didn't seem to have got the memo about sombre colours in a house of mourning, and was in a bright red dress which looked even more vivid against the almost yellow blonde of her hair. She was at least twenty years younger than Bernard. She had big round eyes, with a rather vacant expression. They were a wonderful shade of chestnut brown that reminded Sarah of Tinkerbell, the Chihuahua Charles shared with his ex-wife Francesca – the great love of Hamish's life.

'Ah, Charles, of course you have met my wife, Letitia,' Bernard said, introducing her. 'And these are Charles's friends, um, Mrs...?'

'Dr Sarah Vane and Daphne Roux,' Charles interjected smoothly. 'It's very good of you to have us here at such a difficult time,' he added courteously to Letitia, as they took their seats. Hamish curled up by Sarah's feet and seemed to realise it was time to show off his very best behaviour.

Once they were all sitting, Sarah realised the place at the head of the table remained conspicuously empty. This must have been the late Madeleine Brett-Coates's usual spot. Above the vacant chair hung a large portrait. It was rather dated in style, painted, Sarah imagined, forty or so years ago, and it showed an attractive woman with carefully arranged, light-coloured hair, and a smile which didn't reach her wide blue eyes. She was wearing a pale blue frock with a pretty white frill round the neck, but it might as well have been a suit of armour. She looked unapproachable, and rather frightening. It was also, Sarah realised, the face of the woman she had last seen dead in the tent.

'That must be your mother, I'm assuming,' she said quietly to Bernard, who was next to her.

'Indeed it is,' he said. 'Looking down on us all. As she tended to do in life,' he said with a sad smile as he helped himself to some rather dry-looking potatoes from a dish being brought round by a young girl Sarah hadn't seen before. She had blonde curly hair and protruding ears, and was wearing a pinafore with a red scarf tied at her throat. 'Thank you, Anna,' he said as he put the spoon back into the potatoes and the girl continued on her way.

It was a slow but stately method of serving food, which ensured the meal was cold by the time everyone had a full plate. As Sarah looked down at the pile of singed vegetables, the boulder-like potato and a single slice of chicken, she was thankful for the large jug of gravy that was now being passed up the table. Hopefully this would make everything a little more palatable. The kitchen staff must have had a terrible day, with the grim discovery of the lady of the house throwing everything into disarray, and the disappearance of another family member was no doubt contributing to the strained atmosphere. The wine, however, was excellent, and Daphne and Charles were both tucking in with appreciative slurps.

'Sorry about the grub,' Bernard said, raising his head for a moment. 'The standard's usually a lot higher than this. In fact, my mother would have had no hesitation in sending the whole lot back,' he said, spearing a burnt floret of broccoli and contemplating it without pleasure. There was a sob from the corner of the room, and the girl called Anna hightailed it out of the room in distress. Bernard half-rose to his feet, then seemed to think better of it.

'Honestly, Bernard,' said Jonathan. 'They're probably having a horrendous time in the kitchen.'

'Sorry. Didn't see her there. That girl has an unnerving habit of skulking in corners,' Bernard said.

Oh really? Sarah made a mental note to speak to Anna when she could. Who knew what the girl might have seen?

'I don't see why it's any worse for the staff than it is for us,' said Helena, pushing away her plate. 'It's not like their mother's died.'

'No, but they'll be worrying about their futures, won't they?' Jonathan said. 'Anyone can see things will change around here. We aren't going to want to stay here, now Mumsy's... well. Geoff and I will be moving out, as soon as everything is settled.'

'If by "everything" you mean the money,' said Helena, getting a cigarette out of her slim black moiré evening bag and lighting it up, 'then I wouldn't hold your breath.'

'What do you mean by that?' said Jonathan furiously, rounding on his sister. 'I've as much right to my share as you have.'

'Keep your curls on,' said Helena, arching her brows and blowing out a plume of smoke. 'I just meant probate and all that. It's a frightful bore. Winding up an estate can take months. Or years.'

'What would you know about it?' Bernard said. 'And put that damned cigarette out. You know how Mumsy feels – felt – about smoking.'

'That's irrelevant now, isn't it?' Helena shrugged.

'Well, I don't like it either and since I'm now head of the household—'

'Wait a minute, you're what?' Jonathan broke in.

'Yes, how on earth do you work that out?' Helena sounded amused – but at the same time, she ground out her cigarette in the centre of one of her potatoes.

'I'm the eldest, like it or lump it. And I'm an executor of Mumsy's estate. Might I also suggest, we should confine this type of discussion to times when we are alone?'

'*Pas devant*, and all that,' Jonathan laughed harshly. 'I thought Charles was one of your oldest friends.'

'He is,' said Bernard uncomfortably, as Charles studiously gazed at the view through the window. 'But all the same, we are in the middle of a, well, quite a situation here. Least said, soonest mended, and all that.'

'I doubt that's going to go down well with the police. They'll want us to spill everything. God, I wish Geoff were here,' Jonathan said, throwing his napkin down by his plate. 'This is all so wrong. I'm going to go back to the search.'

'Stay here, Jonty,' said Bernard. 'Let the police do their thing. We'd only be in the way. They're going through Mumsy's room at the same time – it's a muddle out there. We should all just get on and eat. If we can,' he said, looking round the table.

Sarah, who'd tried her best with the chicken, had been defeated by the potato and was now trying the vegetables. Daphne was munching without her usual gusto. Letitia, like her sister-in-law, had scarcely touched the meal. She seemed jittery, her pupils tiny in those glowing brown eyes. She was making little attempt to seem sorry her mother-in-law was no longer with them. 'Can I have a top-up, Bernie?' she said, waggling the stem of her glass and looking winsome in her flame-red outfit.

For a second, it looked as though he was going to ignore her, then he poured out a niggardly inch or so of wine, to her evident disappointment. 'I suppose we should get on with pudding,' he said gloomily, reaching for a phone on the mantelpiece and sending a text.

'I thought we weren't supposed to have mobiles in the house?' Sarah raised her eyebrows.

'Well, this is different,' Bernard said, with an on-off smile. 'Mumsy made an exception, as it makes things easier on the staff. We've moved on from the days when there would be a line of bells jangling away down in the servants' quarters, you see.'

'Yet we still have the servants,' said Jonathan.

'You say that like you disapprove, but I don't see you doing your own washing and ironing,' said Helena. 'Or moving out, for that matter.'

'I've told you we'll be going now,' Jonathan said. 'Obviously I couldn't leave when Mumsy was alive.' He stopped, seeming choked up.

Sarah realised with a shock that this was one of the few displays of emotion she'd seen from the family. Granted, Bernard was a bit tetchy, but none of them seemed touched by genuine sorrow. Perhaps it was a case of stiff upper lips hiding true feelings – or perhaps the rumours were true, and things had not been quite as they seemed in the Brett-Coates household.

'Anyway, pud will be coming. Until then, let's keep things civilised,' said Bernard heavily. 'Shame about the fair. The villagers will be disappointed. Have you been before?' he asked Sarah politely.

'Um, no. I haven't lived here long. But I'm told it's a wonderful occasion. Usually, I mean,' she said awkwardly. 'I did want to ask. There were some flowers found in the tent. I wondered if they had any particular significance.'

'Flowers? What flowers?' said Jonathan quickly.

'Oh, well it was a spring bouquet. Bluebells, tulips and, I think, foxgloves.'

'Foxgloves?' said Jonathan, electrified. 'There can't have been. Not foxgloves!'

'Yes,' said Sarah slowly, not sure what was provoking this reaction. 'Nice shades of purple, too,' she said.

'I don't believe you,' Jonathan shouted at her, rising to his feet and pushing back his chair so hard it fell over and toppled onto the lush carpet. Then he ran right out of the room.

EIGHT

Sarah, Charles and Daphne all looked at each other in astonishment. Then Helena and Bernard started laughing.

'It's quite absurd,' Bernard said. 'You had no reason at all to know this, but Jonty has the weirdest phobia about foxgloves.'

'Really? Why on earth would that be?' Sarah said.

'Oh, you see the portrait up there?' They all swivelled to have a look at the canvas that Sarah had already noticed. Madeleine Brett-Coates's unconvincing smile was wide. Behind her, Sarah noticed a large blue and white Chinese vase for the first time. It was filled with a profusion of foxgloves in delicious shades of pink, mauve and yellow.

'Oh yes. They're lovely flowers,' Sarah said.

'Trouble is, while the chap was painting the portrait – some fellow from the Royal Society of Fancy Artists, or some such – Jonty was running about. He was only a kid, you know, maybe three or four. Well, the flowers were brought in from the garden specially for the picture, and Mumsy spent forever arranging them. I dare say Jonty found that quite boring. No idea where Nanny was. Anyway, he managed to get up on a chair and start fiddling with them himself. Whether it was Mumsy yelling her head off at him, or a bee that had been in one of the foxgloves stinging him, we'll never know. But ever since then he's had a morbid dread of the things.'

'Quite ridiculous,' drawled Helena. 'Especially as he's supposed to be a plant guru.'

'Oh, come on, sis, you know you love his show. We watch it every week,' Bernard remonstrated.

'I have to admit he looks good, tossing those lovely curls of his. I wish I'd got his hair,' Helena said, running a hand through her straight dark bob.

'Oh, I think you've done OK,' said Charles gallantly.

Helena gave one of her feline smiles, then carried on. 'That show is just about him looking good in a pair of wellies. A real expert wouldn't get a completely illogical block against a certain flower.'

More importantly, thought Sarah, you couldn't murder someone with foxgloves if you were phobic about them. Perhaps Jonathan was off the suspect list after all.

'You're a bit harsh on the boy. He did study botany at uni,' Bernard said, sipping his wine.

'And got a third for his pains,' Helena said with a cruel laugh.

'That's still a degree, Hells, which is more than you have under your belt.' Bernard sniffed disapprovingly.

'Oh, I've got better things than that tucked away, believe you me,' said Helena.

Just then, the door opened. Sarah wondered whether it would be Jonathan, returning to the fray, but instead it was the put-upon Anna with a huge cut-glass bowl of trifle. The layers of custard, cream and fruit were sharply delineated and the whole creation shone like a jewel, topped with a scattering of toasted almonds. She hefted it into place on an ornately carved sideboard and scurried out of the room, giving Bernard a sidelong glance as she went.

'Thank you, my dear,' said Bernard heartily. 'That looks a lot better. Mrs Bunforth must have made it before all the ah, well, you know. The housekeeper,' he said, answering Sarah's unspoken question. 'We serve ourselves, I suppose.'

'It doesn't seem right to be eating. Not when Mother's lying there, out in the field, cold and dead,' said Helena, looking pained.

Bernard threw down his napkin. 'Well, that's killed my appetite. Thanks, Hells. Anyway, I think the, er, well, Mumsy... she's been taken away. Everyone, please ignore my sister and do serve yourselves.'

Sarah and Charles looked at each other. 'I wonder if one of us should go after Jonathan? Just to make sure he's all right?' Sarah said.

'What on earth makes you think you should get involved? He deserves privacy as much as anyone,' said Helena with a sniff.

'Well yes,' said Sarah. 'But the circumstances are quite unusual, aren't they? After all, his partner is missing – and someone did murder your mother. Maybe they put foxgloves in that bouquet in the judging tent deliberately, to cause Jonathan to have a reaction?'

Helena and Bernard looked at Sarah blankly. 'I hope you're not expecting an answer to that question. I, for one, am totally in the dark,' Bernard said.

'Same here. Listen, the house is swarming with police,' said Helena, shrugging. 'They'll keep an eye on him, surely.'

'Yes,' said Bernard, putting a large, meaty hand down on the table. 'Let's allow them to get on with their job. I only hope Jonty's not getting in the way. He's always been very highly strung, poor chap. I hope they find Geoff quickly. He's always been great at managing my brother's histrionics. The rest of us, well, we're a bit too down to earth to have much truck with that sort of thing,' he said, flicking his hand dismissively.

'That sort of thing' seemed to mean a normal human reaction to murder, Sarah reflected. Well, no wonder passions had seethed beneath the surface in this house, until violence was their sole outlet. After what Mariella had said about only family members going into the fateful tent, Sarah had to make the assumption that the culprit was one of the Brett-Coates clan. Yet could a member of staff, this Anna or the housekeeper, Mrs Bunforth, have been an accomplice? It wasn't impossible, and she needed to bear the possibility in mind, especially in view of Bernard's comment about Anna's habit of lurking in the shadows. Perhaps that was why the main course had turned out the way it had? Geoff, too, had to be a strong possibility, given his erratic driving and mysterious disappearance.

Bernard was still speaking ponderously. 'We just need to steer clear for the moment, until the police want to talk to us, of course. Give them the best chance to find this blighter. Must be someone loose in the grounds, maybe from over Merstairs way.'

'Oh, but—' started Sarah, on the verge of saying that surely a stranger wouldn't have known enough about the judging timetable to sneak in and kill Madeleine Brett-Coates. And strangers had been ruled out anyway by the sharp-eyed Neighbourhood Watch. She thought better of it, though. 'Excuse me, bit of a cough,' she said, patting her chest.

Daphne looked at her curiously, but Bernard carried on. 'I've heard there's been a lot of this sort of trouble in the villages round there lately. Anyway, dig in. Mrs Bunforth will be upset if we don't make inroads into that trifle. There's a jug of cream on the sideboard.'

'What sort of trouble? *Murder*?' said Helena, her eyes alight at the strangeness of what her brother was saying. 'I hardly think so, Bernard.'

Sarah wondered what Bernard was hinting at. 'Have you had burglaries recently? Or vandalism?' she asked.

'Ha! No,' said Bernard. 'Not the moment to discuss it, really, is it?' he said dismissively.

Sarah sighed inwardly. She wasn't going to get far if the family decided all her questions were unseemly. Perhaps they'd be more expansive after pudding. The food had been substandard so far, but the trifle really did look good. Daphne, returning to the table with quite a modest portion, gave Sarah a tremulous smile. 'I think this will help steady my nerves,' she said.

'Of course,' said Sarah. 'I'm sure it'll do the job.'

'I'll get you some, shall I?' said Charles, getting up gallantly to do the honours.

'Oh, yes please,' said Sarah.

'I can't wait till I'm your age and I don't have to worry about my looks any more,' said Letitia, looking askance at the portion Charles plonked in front of Sarah, as she returned with a scraping that wouldn't even have fed a sparrow.

'Letty!' said Bernard crossly. 'I wish you'd think before you speak.'

Letitia looked at him. 'You wish I didn't think at all,' she said with a pout.

'That's been pretty much granted, then,' said Helena under her breath, with a conspiratorial look over at Sarah. Sarah found herself warming to the woman for the first time.

Then, as Letitia sat down again with a swirl of her scarlet silk skirt, Sarah suddenly remembered with a jolt of horror where she'd seen that particular shade of red before. In the darkened tent, stuck between the buttons on the boucle jacket of the dead woman, Madeleine Brett-Coates.

NINE

Sarah put a hand to her chest, feeling her thumping heart calm to its normal rhythm. Then she turned to Letitia, who was toying with her smidgeon of trifle, pushing it round her bowl with the tip of her spoon. 'Did you enter any scones in the competition today?' she asked.

'Why would I do that?' Letitia seemed entirely baffled by the idea.

'I thought that might have been why you were in the tent earlier, with Mrs Brett-Coates.'

Bernard laughed heartily. 'You wouldn't be asking that, if you'd ever sampled Letty's cooking,' he said.

Surprisingly, Letitia seemed to find this almost as funny as Bernard did. 'Goodness! Can you imagine? They'd need to have the fire brigade on standby.'

'Not to mention the emergency room, to deal with the consequences if anyone was stupid enough to eat your creations,' said Helena with a sniff.

A little silence fell. 'Well, it's a good job Mumsy wasn't poisoned, otherwise you'd have more or less just accused me of murder,' said Letitia with a much less cheerful expression on her face.

'How do you know she wasn't?' Helena said quickly. 'The police haven't exactly been forthcoming with the details, have they? Unless you know something I don't? Come to think of it, the two of you weren't exactly best pals, were you? You were always at each other's throats. What was it Mother always called you? "Little Letty the leech", that's right.'

'Mumsy would interfere,' said Letitia in a sing-song voice, her eyes unfocused. 'I know what's best for Bernie, and she couldn't bear it.'

'That wasn't the problem, and you know it!' Helena said, her teeth gritted. 'She thought you were a conniving, gold-digging—'

Bernard broke in. 'Girls, girls. All this nonsense... it really doesn't help. Mumsy had some funny ways, but she didn't mean anything by them. Let's try and stay off the whole subject. I say, this is a very good trifle, isn't it? Definitely nothing wrong with *this*.' He took a big spoonful and they all watched it wobble, the light catching the deep crimson jelly around the fruit.

It was a brave attempt to change the subject, Sarah thought – but unfortunately Bernard had just reminded everyone of the possibility of poison, and that deadened appetites still further. Even Daphne dropped her spoon into her bowl with a clatter, though admittedly there was no trifle left in it.

'I'll call for coffee, shall I?' Bernard said sheepishly, tapping away on the phone. 'Charles, how's everything going in that shop of yours? I was thinking of you the other day, friend said he got some sketches going cheap down in Margate, could be just the thing for you. Probably Turners, don't you think?'

Daphne raised her eyebrows at Sarah. Charles had got excited once or twice before about daubings which, to Sarah's untutored eye, looked as much like works of art as the sketches she'd produced in the Merstairs Muses art group. And she'd be the first to admit she had absolutely no talent whatsoever. She was quite willing to discuss these pictures if they lightened the mood in the room, though – as long as they came nowhere near her little cottage.

'Watercolours, were they?' she asked with a polite smile.

'Oh, er, I think maybe acrylic?' Bernard seemed a little unsure. Since acrylic paint wasn't invented until more than a century after Turner's death, Sarah's willingness to believe these were lost masterpieces dipped even further. Luckily, Anna banged through the door at that moment with another loaded tray, this time bearing a coffee pot, teapot and pretty porcelain cups.

While everyone milled around by the sideboard, offering each other milk and sugar, Sarah realised one thing. Letitia, for all her apparently scatterbrained ways, had very neatly side-stepped the whole question of why a snippet of her dress had been tangled in the dead woman's buttons. Sarah went up behind her and studied the silky fabric of her frock carefully.

'Here, who's that, breathing down my neck?' Letitia said, spinning round on her three-inch heels. 'Oh, it's you!'

'Sorry, I was just eager to get some coffee,' Sarah said, stepping back and accidentally-on-purpose dropping a teaspoon from the pile near the sugar bowl onto the floor. She knelt down and, as she picked the spoon up, spotted a jagged spot on the dress where some material had been ripped away. Sarah knew exactly where she had last seen something very similar and so, judging by the horrified expression on her face, did Letitia.

'Bernard! This woman's trying to look up my skirt,' Letitia yelped.

'I certainly am not,' Sarah said, straightening up and looking round at the astonished faces of the group. 'I was just—'

'Got your shirt button caught, didn't you, darling,' said Charles, leaping to her rescue and giving her a meaningful look.

'Er, yes – that's right,' said Sarah, biting down the accusation that had been on her lips. Perhaps Charles was right to be silently urging caution. If Letitia had really been involved in Madeleine Brett-Coates's death, she was dangerous and it was far better to let the police deal with her. On the other hand, the woman seemed ditzy to say the least, and those tiny pupils were suggestive. Even if there had been bad blood between her and her mother-in-law, it was quite a stretch imagining her pulling off something like the murder in the tent.

Sarah sat back down, finding refuge in fiddling with the teaspoon. It had a little silver figure on the end of the handle. 'What a pretty thing this is,' she exclaimed.

'Ah yes. Mumsy's apostle spoons. Nice that we've managed to keep a few bits of family silver away from Geoff,' said Bernard heavily.

'Oh come now, Bernard. Not this old business again. You've always had it in for Geoff. He's an awful tick, I agree, but there's no way he's stealing from us,' said Helena.

'In that case, how do you explain all the bits and bobs that have gone missing since he arrived here on Jonty's arm?'

'What bobs?' said Letitia, licking her spoon dreamily with a small, pointed tongue, and glancing sideways at Sarah. Sarah looked away.

'Oh, you know full well, Letty. Why, you missed something yourself only last week. What was it? A picture frame or something?' Bernard poured himself more coffee and gestured round with the pot. Daphne got up to take some more.

'That's right,' Letitia said in her girlish sing-song voice. 'I'd forgotten. It was a picture of my ickle doggie, baby Fluffypaws. Poor Fluffy. I thought your mother had stolen it, Bernie, just to be mean. You know what she was like.'

Bernard eyed Letitia crossly but said nothing. It was left to Daphne to fill the silence. 'Chihuahua was it, your little dog?' she asked, spilling some coffee on the tray. 'Drat.'

Hamish stirred under the table, where he'd been having a snooze, and Sarah immediately thought of Charles's Tinkerbell.

'No, an Alsatian,' said Letitia. Sarah adjusted her mental image upwards and outwards.

'You don't seriously think someone's been pinching stuff in the house, do you, old man?' said Charles casually. Sarah inwardly blessed him for picking up the thread.

'Hard to see what else it can be. All these things can't go missing by accident. A snuff box, cigarette cases belonging to my late uncle, couple of candlesticks, even. It's someone who likes silver – or the money you can get selling it on,' said Bernard.

Just then the door opened again, and a tall, austere-looking woman with iron grey hair arranged in a complicated bun came in, her high-necked, long-sleeved black dress alleviated only by a blindingly white apron tied around her thin waist. Her eyes were very red, in an otherwise colourless oval of a face. She had a pained expression and was holding a tray under her arm. 'I just wondered if I could clear the last bits away, Mr Bernard,' she said, managing to radiate disapproval at everyone in the room. 'I've sent Anna off to bed. She was very upset.'

'Oh, er, of course, Mrs Bunforth. Thank you so much,' said Bernard, ushering her in. 'We'll get out of your way. Drawing room, everyone?'

There was a general scraping of chairs as they all got to their feet, only for Mrs Bunforth to speak again. 'I just wanted to say, Mr Bernard, ladies and gentlemen, I'm so sorry for the main course. I wasn't myself tonight. I was so upset about my lady passing, I asked Anna to do the cooking. I wish I hadn't.' Here she lifted the corner of her apron to her eyes and wept.

'There, there, Mrs B. Awful day for you, and, um, the rest of us, of course. We know how close you two were,' Bernard said, avoiding the woman's eyes and obviously hoping she would shut up so they could all sidle out.

'Twenty years I've been here, if it's a day, and always with Mrs Madeleine showing me the way,' said Mrs Bunforth, really getting into her stride now.

Bernard looked pained, then stepped forward reluctantly and took the woman in an extremely awkward hug. The rest of the group shuffled past, Letitia in front. She evidently felt no need to console the sobbing woman, even though her status as wife of the eldest living Brett-Coates seemed to indicate she'd have the most to do with the housekeeper from now on.

'Thank goodness we've got away from her,' she said loudly as she opened the drawing room door and flung herself down on the sofa, the little ruffles on her dress billowing prettily. 'Bunny gives me the creeps sometimes. Could someone get me a brandy? It's been quite a day.'

Charles went over to the drinks cabinet and did the honours. 'Can I get you something too, ladies?' he said to Helena, Sarah and Daphne. Helena also asked for a brandy, but Sarah and Daphne were content to take their seats and start a slightly desultory chat about what a good boy Hamish was being – always a useful gambit in sticky moments, Sarah felt.

The dinner had been grim enough, but at least they'd had the food to keep them occupied. Now it was over, there seemed to be almost no justification she could think of for lingering on like this. It seemed a terrible imposition, as the family was – or should be – grieving. But she remembered Mariella's words. If they could pick up anything, no matter how small, it could be incredibly useful for the investigation. She wondered if Mariella knew that, according to Bernard, Geoff was rather light-fingered. That, plus the fact he was still missing, had to be of interest. Could he have been caught out by Madeleine Brett-Coates? That would be a strong motive.

Charles was just pouring himself a whisky, when Bernard strolled into the room and spoke up. 'Oh, do you think you ought to, old man? It's all the same to me, but what with wine at dinner, won't you be over the limit for driving back? They're devils for a breathalyser around here.'

'That's a point,' said Charles, putting the heavy cut-glass decanter down. 'I suppose I should err on the side of caution.'

'That's if the police let you go at all,' said Helena darkly.

'What do you mean, Hells?' Bernard asked, pouring himself a measure and swirling the dark liquid round in his glass, before sipping appreciatively. Charles looked on rather sadly.

'Haven't you worked it out yet? The police have planted them here, to listen to the three of us – four, if you count Jonty, wherever he's got to – yammering on and incriminating ourselves.'

Bernard burst out laughing. 'Oh, don't be ridiculous, Hells. I've known Charles since I was eight years old. You've known him since you were six, come to that.'

'True, but who are these women he's brought with him? Sarah keeps asking very pointed questions, and was virtually looking up Letty's skirt earlier—'

'Yes, I told you,' said Letitia eagerly, while Sarah blushed and opened her mouth to protest.

'—And this one's daughter is a DI in the Canterbury police force.'

'Goodness! Really?' said Letitia, looking at Sarah and Daphne as though they were something Fluffypaws might have dragged in.

'Now, I can vouch for both these lovely ladies, no need to get excited,' Charles said firmly to Helena. Sarah felt a warm glow at his words, but, as far as Helena was concerned, it was like pouring kerosene on a naked flame.

'How dare you tell me what to do? Can't I feel safe and unobserved in my own home, after losing my mother? This is the worst day of my life, and having spies around us is making it ten times worse,' Helena yelled.

Sarah couldn't help but feel she had a point. 'I'm so sorry,

Helena, and all of you. The last thing we want to do is make you feel uncomfortable. I really feel it's time we left.' She stood up, urging Daphne to do the same.

'Be seeing you soon, old boy. Sympathies and all that,' said Charles, clapping Bernard on the shoulder as he passed. The trio made it as far as the door, when it was flung open.

Deeside stood there, a slightly wild look on his face. 'Nobody leave the room,' he said, glaring round at them all. 'Which one of you owns this bag?'

With that, he upended a battered leather holdall onto the ottoman between the two sofas. There was a crash and a tinkle as metal objects cascaded out – sugar tongs, a small bud vase, what looked like a christening cup and a pair of candlesticks. They lay there, gleaming, as the firelight flickered over the astonished faces of the family and their reluctant guests.

TEN

'Good grief! This is... this is Mumsy's silver,' said Bernard, stepping forward.

They all looked at the beautiful shiny objects, each one a collector's item. The whole haul must have been worth a tidy sum.

'Where did you find all this?' asked Sarah.

'Never you mind,' snapped Deeside.

'I must insist on knowing,' said Bernard quickly. 'This is my family's property, after all.'

'Well, all right then, I suppose it can't do any harm,' said Deeside, shuffling from foot to foot. 'The holdall was wedged into the compost heap, behind the outbuildings in the garden. It was one of the other coppers who came across it by accident, like.'

'What sort of accident could have sent them to inspect the compost heap?' Sarah asked.

'If you must know,' Deeside said shirtily. 'He was looking for somewhere to have a bit of a nap out there. We've been on duty for ages, and he needed to, um, rest his eyes.'

'I suppose the real mystery is what it was doing there,' said

Charles slowly. 'Could someone from the fair have slipped into the house and made off with all this?'

'A villager, you mean?' said Bernard. 'Those blighters.'

'You said earlier that you suspected Geoff of having, um, a tendency to pocket things?' said Sarah. 'I wonder if it could have been him.'

'My goodness. I always thought you were making it up about Geoff, Bernard. I suppose you were right all along,' Helena said. She walked over to the ottoman. 'Mother's favourite little vase. She always had it on her dressing table with a single flower in it. Poor Mother.'

'You're right, of course. It must have been blasted Geoff,' stormed Bernard. 'Where on earth is Jonty when we need him? He won't be able to carry on pretending Geoff is innocent now. The man has clearly been pilfering from us for years, just as I always said. He must have thought someone was onto him and scarpered, I suppose.' Bernard was now pacing up and down in front of the fireplace, getting redder and redder in the face.

'I'll need to take statements from you all about this,' said Deeside, looking rather smug about his discovery.

'Well, we don't know anything about it,' said Daphne. 'So we might as well go. Right, Charles and Sarah?'

'Yes, I agree,' said Charles. 'It's about time we got out of your hair.'

Sarah nodded. She would have liked to help Mariella out more with the investigation – but this new development did seem to clear things up. Although something was nagging away at her... why would Geoff have hidden all this swag, and then not taken it with him?

'Not so fast,' said Deeside quickly, moving so that his bulk blocked the doorway. 'You two were the ones who saw this Geoff in his car earlier, right?'

'That's right, constable,' said Sarah patiently. 'But we did explain all that to Mari— I mean, your boss, earlier.'

'Even if you've explained it before, you'll just have to go over it all again. We didn't know the significance then, did we? Now we know this Geoff was planning his escape... probably right after offing your mother,' he said to Bernard, who recoiled. 'No offence, like.'

'Erm, none taken, I suppose,' said Bernard, looking at Deeside as though he were a particularly irksome specimen of the villager type. 'Well, carry on, then.'

Sarah, Charles and Daphne glanced at each other. Daphne sighed. Sarah felt for her. She'd been so looking forward to getting back to her cottage and checking up on Mephisto. 'Hopefully this won't take too long,' she said comfortingly.

'It'll take as long as it takes,' said Deeside sternly. 'I want you all to form an orderly queue.'

'I say,' said Bernard. 'Is that really necessary? We can all just sit down here in comfort while you ask your questions – if you really must.'

'Oh, ah,' said Deeside. 'I suppose that would be acceptable. Well then, sir, we'll start with you. Where did you last see Mr Geoff Brett-Coates, and when?'

Bernard sat down rather heavily in one of the fireside chairs, and stirred the embers with a poker. 'Well, let me see,' he said.

Daphne slumped on the sofa, and Sarah wondered how long they'd be there now. Charles strode over to the window and drew the curtains. It was dark and cold outside, but being here in this snug, warm room didn't bring Sarah any comfort. It was what was inside the house that was the problem.

Sarah was sitting there, the frown between her brows growing bigger and bigger, when Helena interrupted Bernard's lengthy explanation of where he'd last seen Geoff. She got to her feet. 'Well, this is simply ridiculous. I refuse to sit here all night waiting my turn. I'll be in my room when you're ready for me.'

With that, she grabbed the doorknob – just as it was being

opened from the outside. Mariella came in, with a very sombre look on her face. She glanced at the silver still glinting on the ottoman. 'I'm afraid I'm going to have to ask you to be seated,' she said to Helena.

'Why should I?' said Helena, drawing herself up to her full height. 'Who are you to tell me what to do?'

'I'm the detective in charge of a double murder investigation,' said Mariella. 'I regret to inform you all that we've found another body.'

ELEVEN

Sarah had never much liked cellars. It was a combination of the rich, rank smell of rot and the uncertain lighting. The basement at the Brett-Coates house had both in spades. She was currently holding Mariella's police-issue torch above her head to give the policewoman the best view possible, as they both crouched over the mortal remains of a thin, red-headed man – Geoffrey Brett-Coates.

'Oh, Mariella,' said Sarah. 'This is so dreadful.'

'You can say that again.' Mariella sighed. 'I wasn't expecting this in my first couple of months in Canterbury. Tell me what you see, Aunty Sarah, before that pathologist gets here.'

'Dr Jarvis again? Right,' said Sarah. The thought of how much the young man would enjoy this was rather revolting. 'Well, as you can see, poor Mr Brett-Coates is lying in what I would describe as a foetal position, arms wrapped round himself and knees drawn up to the chest. He appears to have almost squashed himself into a ball.'

'Yes, yes,' said Mariella. 'But what do you make of his eyes?'

Sarah shone the torch onto the man's face, and his bulging, bloodshot, terrified eyes gleamed like those of an animal in the headlights. His mouth was open in a silent scream. It was most unsettling. 'He looks absolutely scared witless, doesn't he?'

'Yes,' said Mariella. 'But that's the thing. He's just facing a blank wall. What can have frightened him so much?'

'I suppose that's what we've got to find out,' said Sarah. 'It's all very odd. What was he doing in this godforsaken corner of the place anyway?'

The cellar, as befitted a house of this size, was large. There were quite a number of separate rooms. Some were used for wine storage. There were a couple that were full of miscellaneous rusting garden furniture. One small room underneath the front door area was still half-filled with coal, from pre-central heating days. Although there was some mains lighting, it didn't reach into the far corner, which was where Geoffrey Brett-Coates had been found.

'Goodness knows what he was up to. Was he looking for something?' Mariella asked, standing up now and putting her phone on torch mode, sweeping it around, making eerie shadows on the walls.

'I doubt it. Jonathan said he suffered terribly from claustrophobia, and this was the last place he'd be,' Sarah said. 'I think someone must have lured him down here.'

'I was hoping you wouldn't say anything along those lines,' said Mariella, running a dusty hand through her hair. 'Can't it be a natural death for once?'

'You sound like your mother,' said Sarah with a tiny smile. 'Well, I suppose we won't know until there's a post-mortem. There's one thing that's peculiar, though.'

'What's that?' Mariella looked at Sarah in alarm.

'Do you see the faint lines around the body, look, here and, um, over there?' Sarah said, letting her torch swing over the area. Sure enough, there were thin marks on the dirty floor where something had recently stood.

'They form a square, or rather a sort of oblong, all around

him. How strange,' Mariella said. 'It's almost as though... well, as though he was in a kind of box.'

'That could be why he's rolled himself up like that.' Sarah nodded. 'I think you need to look for something that could make those marks. And I'd say it's probably still down here. That would be the easiest for the murderer. They wouldn't have to drag anything upstairs and through the house, then.'

'*Murderer*, drat that word,' Mariella said, almost with a wail. 'OK then, let's have a look around and see what we can find.'

'I think the lumber rooms are the best bet. Over here,' said Sarah, leading the way through the gloom to one of the areas full of old garden paraphernalia. 'There's some metal benches over there, but they wouldn't leave a line like that. This is tricky,' she said, looking at the mess in front of them.

'What about this?' Mariella said, diving in and indicating what looked like a three-foot-high stack of metal mesh. 'I wonder what it was used for?'

'I think it might have been a dog crate, once upon a time. They collapse quite easily and don't take up much space. Some owners swear by them, for training puppies and helping dogs feel secure.'

'Hmm,' said Mariella, shining her torch onto the bottom of the mesh. 'It's not so dusty here. I think it's been moved recently.'

'There are no signs of it having been pulled across the floor, though,' Sarah said, playing the light across the path from the lumber room to the place where Geoffrey lay so still.

'It isn't heavy to lift,' Mariella pointed out. 'I'll get the forensic team down here, just to check it out, but I think your theory might be correct. What would they do that for, though? Put a cage around him. He looks like quite a fit man, for his age. Surely he'd just knock it over and go about his day?'

'Perhaps. Unless someone wanted to use his fear of confined spaces against him.'

'But claustrophobia couldn't have killed him, could it?'

'You know, it's not impossible. Say he was enticed down here, briefly immobilised, then enclosed like that, in pitch blackness. Get Jarvis to check his head for bumps. Someone might have knocked him out, just for long enough to assemble the cage, then left him to it. Waking up in the crate might have brought on a panic attack, causing him to hyperventilate and possibly lose consciousness, or could even have triggered a heart attack. It's a profoundly cruel thing to do.'

'Yes,' said Mariella. 'Cruel – and evil. It suggests the culprit knew him.'

'Well enough to exploit his weaknesses to kill him. So it looks like we've worked out how,' said Sarah, without satisfaction. 'That still leaves us with the most difficult questions, though – why? And, of course, who? You know, I was pretty sure for a while back there that Geoff was the killer himself – he had a motive. If Madeleine Brett-Coates had caught him stealing, then silencing her would have been in his interests.'

'We don't know that she did catch him, though, do we?' Mariella said.

'No, we don't. And I think the bag proves he didn't kill her either. If Geoff had stolen all those little silver knick-knacks, and stashed them to take to a jeweller's – then why didn't he do just that when he had the chance? Daphne and I saw him driving away from the house, a little before four. The time fitted in perfectly with Madeleine's murder. But if Geoff killed her and then zoomed off in his car, then why on earth would he return here, bringing the silver back into the house, too? Were those really the actions of a killer who was determined to sell the family's treasures and escape? It just doesn't make sense.'

'Well, we know now. He wasn't the killer at all,' said Mariella. 'That just leaves us with the little problem of finding out who it really is.'

TWELVE

By the time Sarah returned to the drawing room, it was quite late. Everyone was flagging. Daphne's head lolled as she sat in a comfy chair in the corner of the room, Hamish and Butler curled at her feet. It would have been a rather peaceful scene, except that the family was now mourning two of its members. Jonathan, who'd been tracked down in his bedroom and had chosen to come and sit with his brother and sister, had his head in his hands, tears trickling through his palms and onto the expensive upholstery, while the others looked shell-shocked.

Charles shot to his feet as Sarah came in. 'Ah, there you are. I'm thinking we should make a move now, leave you folks to, er, get on with things,' he said, as though they had a few tiresome forms to fill in, instead of a full-scale double murder investigation cranking up around them.

'Oh, Charles, old boy. Don't dash off yet. I've been thinking...' Bernard was scratching his head.

To Sarah, this sounded a little ominous, but she sat back down with Charles and waited.

'Look, it's like this. We don't really want the police here, interfering and badgering us, morning, noon and night,' Bernard said gruffly.

'Good grief, no thank you,' said Helena with a shudder, almost more horrified at this prospect than she had been by the deaths themselves.

Letitia yawned widely. 'Surely it won't take them long to sort it out, Bernie? It's bound to be someone your mother got on the wrong side of. You know what she could be like. She was simply awful to me from the moment I got here.'

'Oh, don't be so ridiculous, Letty. Mumsy could be a little forbidding, but she meant well.'

Letitia laughed harshly. 'Did she? She was constantly telling me I was "no better than I should be" when you were out of earshot. It was awful. Well, if it wasn't someone who hated her and Geoff, maybe it was a villager? Half of them are on drugs these days.'

Bernard brightened up at this, but then his face fell again. 'But how could a villager have got into the house to kill Geoff?'

'Exactly,' said Helena. 'The place is crawling with police. There's no way they could have sneaked in and murdered him in the basement. And calling Bernard "Bernie", I ask you,' she snapped.

'He loves being called Bernie, don't you, Bernie-boy,' said Letitia, swaying over to him in her floaty dress, and trying to run a hand through his hair, to his intense embarrassment.

'Not now, darling,' he said through gritted teeth.

'Later, then, Bernie,' she said with a wink, flouncing back to her seat.

Helena mimed being sick, while Bernard stared fixedly out of the window.

'In any case, Letty, I'd have thought you'd be beside yourself with terror,' Helena said. 'What if the killer decides you're next on the list? He might hate that shade of red almost as much as I do.'

'I told you, it's some rando from outside. Nothing for us to worry about,' Letitia said, examining her nails, which had been painted with white daisies featuring red centres. 'Drat, I've got a chip,' she said dreamily. 'I'll have to get them done when the salon opens on Monday.'

'However will you manage till then? Maybe the murderer will help you. They're quite the artist, judging from the way they arranged those flowers behind Mother's head,' Helena drawled.

'Did you see the bouquet?' Sarah asked.

'I bet you wish I had. Or better still, picked the blooms myself and positioned them. But you're out of luck, Sarah. I'm only going by what you said earlier,' said Helena with a gleam in her eye. 'Anyway, didn't you lot say you were making a move?'

'Ah, that's what I wanted to discuss,' said Bernard. 'As I said, we're stuck with the police, but I'm not sure I've got much faith that they're going to get to the bottom of things quickly. I was wondering...'

'Oh, for goodness' sake, Bernard, just spit it out,' said Helena.

'I'd like you two, Charles and Sarah—'

He was interrupted by a loud snore from the armchair. 'Who? What?' said Daphne, rubbing her face with her hand.

'—Um, and Daphne, to stay on here and look into things for us. Charles here says you have a bit of a reputation as a sleuth,' he added, nodding at Sarah.

'Are you crazy?' Helena jumped up and bounded towards him. 'It's bad enough having those plods here pawing through everything. You surely don't want more spies in the camp?'

'Listen, Hells, as I said earlier, you've known Charles forever. Better him than a stranger, and if Sarah and Daphne can speed things up too, well, isn't that all to the good?'

'I think it's bats,' said Helena succinctly. 'But I get no say, as usual. I suppose they do bulk up the numbers, and if it gives the murderer a few more bodies to get through before they reach me, well, that's no bad thing. In any case, I've had quite enough for one day. I shall be locking my bedroom door tonight,' she said, glaring at everyone as she left the room.

'I'm not sure I like the idea of being cannon fodder for a killer,' said Daphne, looking extremely worried.

Sarah pressed her hand. 'Don't forget, there are police everywhere. No one in their right mind would try anything, don't worry.' She was glad no one had mentioned the fact that the second murder must have taken place while the house was full of oblivious officers.

'So, what do you say, Charles? Sarah? Are you in?' Bernard was speaking in hearty tones, as though proposing a jolly adventure.

Sarah raised her eyebrows, but looked at Charles, who seemed to be waiting for her to agree. Daphne was reaching down to pat Hamish, avoiding everyone's eyes. She was, Sarah was willing to bet, dying to leave. But would it be fair to abandon this stricken family in its moment of need? Sarah looked at Letitia's vacant, pretty face and Bernard's anxious eyes behind the jocular smile, and felt she had no choice.

'Of course we'd be happy to stay.'

As soon as she'd said it, though, Sarah realised 'happy' wasn't the right word at all – not with a double murderer on the premises.

THIRTEEN

It was a terrible night. Sarah tossed and turned, trying not to remember the stuffy tent with its dead occupant, or the rank cellar either. Instead she saw a horrible collage of scones, foxgloves and bunting every time she closed her eyes. She wondered how Charles was getting on, but didn't want to be caught by a policeman wandering around the place at night.

It felt as though she had only just nodded off when she woke up with a violent start. Someone was shrieking outside her door. For a horrible moment, she feared it must be the threatened visitation from the Coates House ghost, the White Lady, provoked by the deaths in the family. But then she recognised Letitia's shrill voice. She threw her duvet back groggily, gave Hamish, curled up in an old bed of Butler's, a few reassuring strokes, then cracked open her door. Sure enough, there the woman was, in a gossamer-thin sugar-pink nightdress, her mouth a wide O of distress.

'Letitia, what's the matter?' whispered Sarah. Just then, Bernard came down the stairs from his room on the upper level.

'Ah, if you don't mind, Sarah, can you let me deal with this?

She's still asleep, you see. She gets these night terrors... It's a long-standing thing, nothing to do with, er, yesterday's events.'

'Oh, I see,' said Sarah, brought up short. She'd heard of such cases, of course, but never seen anyone in the grip of this syndrome before. She could have sworn the girl was conscious, her wide eyes staring, but presumably Bernard knew better. As she watched, he enfolded Letitia in a hug.

'Come on now, Letty, that's enough, don't wake anyone else up,' he said in a low voice, and led her gently back up the stairs, with a backward glance at Sarah. 'Thanks,' he murmured.

'No problem at all,' said Sarah, shutting her bedroom door. Her heart was still hammering after the rude awakening. She was beginning to wonder about Letitia's strange behaviour. And Hamish was now convinced it was time to be up and about. He scratched at the door, an unmistakable sign that he had needs which must be taken care of.

'Oh, for goodness' sake,' Sarah sighed. One of the many troubles with having to stay at Coates House was that she'd been forced to borrow a nightdress and had no slippers or dressing gown with her. Mrs Bunforth had provided the night-wear, looking extremely disapproving as she did so. Sarah hadn't wanted to ask too many questions about its provenance – but judging by the wonderfully fine linen and lace trims, she suspected it must have belonged to the late Madeleine Brett-Coates. She shrugged her coat on over the nightdress and put on her outdoor shoes, then felt her way down the wide oak stair-way, with only a delighted Hamish for company. Once she got to the hall, she found her phone in the box and set it to torch mode with a sigh of relief.

To say the house was creepy at night was a massive under-statement. In daylight a very comfortable mansion, it was terri-fying in the dark. Shadows leapt up the walls as Sarah made her way around, and all the alcoves and niches that made the place so charming were now filled with gloomy blackness. Sarah's certain knowledge that a murderer lurked somewhere within these walls did nothing to make the experience more enjoyable. The promised constable on watch was Deeside, who was slumped in a chair by the door, sound asleep and looking as though not even a troupe of White Ladies dancing past him would ever wake him up.

By the time she'd reached the imposing front entrance, she had thoroughly spooked herself. Trying to get the massive oak door open proved impossible; she really should have guessed it would be firmly locked up as a matter of routine, and even more so after recent events.

She was just casting about, wondering whether she and Hamish could get out through a window, or whether she could somehow persuade the dog that his pressing need was purely psychological, when there was an ominous creak behind her.

Sarah must have jumped about a foot in the air, and swung round breathlessly to confront whoever had crept up behind her, ready to use her phone as an almost entirely useless weapon against the potential assailant.

Thank goodness, it was only Daphne, carrying a large mug of what smelt deliciously like hot chocolate.

'Oh, are you up too? Goody, I was getting bored on my own,' she said.

'Shh,' said Sarah, clutching her heaving chest and conscious of the sleeping Deeside, not to mention the family upstairs. 'I need to take Hamish out for a quick you-know-what,' she said. 'And this door seems to be triple-locked. Is there a back door in the kitchen?'

'I wasn't looking,' said Daphne. 'Let's check.'

Daphne led them through a servants' passageway running behind the dining room and drawing room, ending in the large, echoing kitchen. It was a square room with a stone-flagged floor, a range of units running around two of its walls, and a big scrubbed pine table in the centre, which must be where most of the food preparation took place. Bunches of dried herbs hanging from the mantlepiece above the range cooker scented the air. Sarah spotted a door in the corner of the room which must give onto the garden, or at least a courtyard, which would do at a pinch for Hamish. But when Sarah rattled the doorknob, she got the same result as before. It was locked.

Hamish whined slightly, and Sarah leant to pat him. 'I'm so sorry, boy, I'm not sure what we do now. Everything seems to be bolted shut.'

Suddenly the kitchen was flooded with light. Sarah blinked, then realised Mrs Bunforth was standing with her hands on her hips in the doorway, looking very tall, pale and cross.

'I'm so sorry to have woken you, Mrs Bunforth,' Sarah said. 'I'm afraid my dog needs to go out.'

'Right,' said Mrs Bunforth, looking grimly at Hamish. The Scottie put his head on one side and more or less crossed his paws, and the housekeeper unbent a little. 'Well, we can't have the poor thing getting distressed. I'm glad he didn't just widdle on the floor. Mrs Letty had one which did that all the time, and it was no end of trouble.' Mrs Bunforth shook her head. 'At least our Butler's well behaved,' she sniffed. The old black Labrador, lying in a large fleecy basket to the side of the door, heard his name but didn't trouble to get up, just wagging his tail once or twice before going back to sleep. While she was speaking, Mrs Bunforth fished a large key out of her pocket, then drew back bolts at the top and bottom of the door. At last it opened and they could all smell the tang of the cold fresh air. Hamish pricked up his ears and barked happily.

'All right, Hamish, don't wake up the whole house. Here we go. And it's not walkies, remember, we're just doing the essentials and then everyone can go back to bed,' Sarah said, crunching outside onto the gravel.

She found herself in a small courtyard, blocked off on two sides by outbuildings, which she guessed in years gone by must have been stables and sculleries. Now they appeared to be garages. Her phone torch was running low, but the sky, which had been deepest black, was now streaked with gentle fingers of grey, as dawn crept over the horizon towards them. Hamish, more than delighted to be out, wanted to get a bit further from the house before stopping. Sarah inched cautiously across the gravel, conscious that her steps were crunching unnaturally loudly in the silent space.

Suddenly there was a loud crack from the direction of the kitchen. She wheeled round, only to see Daphne silhouetted in the doorway – with the dark shape of a tall man looming behind her.

FOURTEEN

Sarah couldn't help it – instinct took over. She dropped Hamish's lead and ran back towards Daphne. 'Watch out,' she yelled. 'He's behind you!'

As she sprinted across the gravel, she watched Daphne turn, as though in slow motion. Then, as quickly as it had appeared, the shadow was gone. By the time Sarah panted up to her friend, there was no one in sight.

'Did you see who it was?' said Sarah, holding her side.

'No-no,' stuttered Daphne, looking white and clutching the neck of her nightdress. 'Are you sure there was someone there?'

'As sure as I'm standing here,' Sarah replied with a shiver. She was certain that the person had not had Daphne's welfare in mind. She heaved to get her breathing under control, and then decided not to worry her friend further. 'Well, maybe it was a trick of the light. Drat, Hamish has run off now. Come with me and we'll track him down.'

'I don't know whose slippers I'm borrowing,' said Daphne, following meekly, which was not at all like her. 'But they're going to get wrecked.'

'I'd say that's the least of everyone's worries,' said Sarah, pulling Daphne along by the arm. 'Hamish ran off through this gap between the outbuildings. I hope he hasn't gone too far.'

'He'd never usually do anything like this, I wonder what's come over him?' said Daphne, peering at the bushes as they followed the path, which opened up to reveal the large formal garden they had been looking out on last night through the drawing room windows.

'He's been cooped up all afternoon in a strange house, and then had to sleep here for good measure. He's a bit discombobulated by it all, I should think. Plus the atmosphere is bound to be getting to him.'

'I'm not surprised. It's all getting a bit too spooky for my taste – and spooky is basically my job,' said Daphne, now clutching Sarah's arm.

'The sun's coming up now, though, Daph. Nothing looks as bad in broad daylight,' Sarah said bracingly – then they both jumped a mile as they met someone coming the other way.

Once they'd got their breath back, they realised it was Bernard. 'Good grief, ladies, I wasn't expecting to run into you two. Heard a dog barking out here, thought I'd come and look,' he said.

'Oh, I'm afraid that's probably Hamish. He's usually such a good boy, but he got out of the kitchen...'

'Door should have been locked. I'll have words with Mrs Bunforth later.'

'Oh, please don't,' said Sarah. 'We got her to unlock it for us. It's entirely my fault. As you know, I was woken up by Letitia, then Hamish wanted to spend a penny. How is your wife now?'

'Letty? Oh, she's fine. Often does that sleepwalking thing. It's not a big deal.'

'Right,' said Sarah, who thought it was very unusual. 'Might be a good idea to run it past your GP?'

'Oh, no point taking a slot from someone who really needs

it. She's fine. Bit highly strung, maybe,' said Bernard. 'But perhaps it's understandable at the moment.'

'Well, that's certainly true. These are difficult times for your family,' Sarah said, as they continued to walk around the grounds. There was no sign of her little dog, and she was beginning to get worried. 'I wonder where on earth Hamish can have got to?'

'Wait, is that him over there in the bushes?' Daphne was pointing straight ahead, past the formal garden and over to a stand of shrubs that partially concealed the field which yesterday had been used for car parking, and still contained a few vehicles. Sure enough, some of the foliage was moving, as though being inspected by a small but determined creature.

Sarah bounded towards the bushes, glad the mystery was solved – but then a lean young fox burst out, took one look at her, and streaked away towards the fringe of tall trees on the edge of the grounds, his orange brush flaming behind him.

'Oh no,' she said. 'I really thought that must be him. Oh Hamish, where are you?'

'Tried whistling for him?' Bernard said, frowning slightly.

'I can't whistle, to tell you the truth,' Sarah confessed. 'I've always been very lucky before, he's usually so good and never runs off. I hope he hasn't got stuck anywhere.'

'There are a few rabbit holes around,' said Bernard, doing nothing to allay her fears. 'Perhaps we should leave him to it for now and have another look when it's fully light.'

'I certainly don't want to keep you,' Sarah said. 'Please do go back to bed. You too, Daphne. But I wouldn't be able to sleep a wink. I'll just have another look around,' she finished. If Hamish was really missing, she didn't quite know what she'd do.

FIFTEEN

'Well, if you're sure you'll be all right,' Bernard said immediately. 'Shall we go back, then, Daphne?' He held out an arm to her.

Daphne shook her head. 'No, I'll keep Sarah company. I know how I'd feel if my cat ran off,' she said, scanning the horizon for any sign of the little dog.

'Thanks, Daph,' Sarah said as Bernard walked back to the house. 'I'm really not sure where to look. These grounds are so big. Hamish is only used to my tiny cottage garden.'

'Don't worry,' said Daphne, putting a comforting arm around her friend. 'Let's do what you're best at, and think about this logically. The whole place is new to Hamish. Where looks the most fun for a small Scottie to explore?'

The rising sun helped them out, displaying Coates House in all its glory. The formal garden, with its parterres and occasional rose bushes, really offered nowhere for a dog to hide. To each side were the shrubberies. Then the park unfolded like a green scarf, running all the way to the field where the fair had taken place. It really didn't look as though there was much scope for hide and seek.

Just as Sarah was beginning to get anxious, she saw a small black blob on the horizon, coming from the direction of the car park. Was it? Could it be? She couldn't stop herself from running forward, and Daphne did the same.

There, bounding up to her, looking totally unrepentant, was Hamish, his coat damp with dew but otherwise unscathed.

'Oh, you naughty boy,' she said, picking him up and hugging him close. 'Now where on earth have you been hiding all this time?'

Hamish opened his shaggy jaws, almost as though he was laughing at her, and Sarah saw a flash of red. 'What's that you've got in your mouth? Give,' she said sternly, and Hamish let his tongue unfurl. On the end was a sodden piece of red fabric – silk, Sarah was willing to bet.

'What on earth is that?' said Daphne. 'That's a very odd thing to eat.'

'I don't think he was trying to swallow it. I think he was bringing it to me. Weren't you, boy?' She had the snippet on her palm now, and put Hamish back on the ground. 'Can you show us where you got this?'

'Oh, I was thinking we could go back to bed,' yawned Daphne. 'It's quite chilly out here.'

'That's fine, if you'd rather go and sleep,' said Sarah immediately. 'I feel I ought to follow this up, though.'

'Well... I suppose I've been up half the night now,' said Daphne. 'Might as well crack on. Show us, then, Hamish.'

Sarah pressed Daphne's arm gratefully. Even though Hamish was back, there was still a murderer lurking in the vicinity. She had a strong feeling the culprit was tucked up in bed, but you never knew. Hamish was pretty good with his teeth when the situation called for it, but there was safety in numbers.

'All right, boy. I'm not risking you taking off to who-knows-where again, so I'll have to use something as a lead – Daph, can

I borrow your scarf?' Daphne passed over the flamingo-pink number she was wearing with her nightie and Sarah quickly tied it through the dog's collar. 'Now show us where you were.'

As though he understood every word, Hamish gave Sarah's hand a quick lick and then plodded off across the grass, the scarf stretching out as he lolloped over the tufty lawn. Sarah and Daphne followed behind, helping each other over the tussocks as they got further from the house and the grounds became less manicured. Soon they were at the perimeter of the lawns, marked by a low hedge of what looked like yew. Hamish jumped over this, and waited expectantly on the other side for his mistress.

Not feeling she was quite up to leaping, after only a couple of hours of sleep, Sarah clambered carefully over and then gave Daphne a hand to do the same. The dew had almost evaporated from the grass now, and a dawn chorus of birds was beginning to tweet merrily. They both glanced back at the house, which looked truly majestic in the early morning, the first rays of spring sunshine making the mellow brick glow. On top of the highest chimney, the weathervane caught the light. She noticed for the first time that it was in the shape of Old Father Time, with his scythe over his shoulder, and she couldn't help but shiver. The only other figure usually shown like that was Death.

'What a sight,' said Sarah.

'Yes. Beautiful place. Shame it's chock-full of nutters,' said Daphne. 'Oh, and look!'

She was pointing to a section of the hedge.

Wedged into the dense yew was something that looked completely out of place. Hamish sat on his haunches and panted, happy that his mistress was finally up to speed.

'But that's incredible,' said Sarah. 'What on earth is that doing there?'

Daphne ran forward and, before Sarah could stop her, she had plucked another scrap of red silk right out of the hedge.

'Daph! Think of the forensics,' Sarah wailed, and Daphne immediately stuffed the material right back where she'd found it. 'That won't help,' Sarah said, really wishing she could roll her eyes but knowing her sensitive friend would be crushed.

'Oh, they'll have my fingerprints already, they can just eliminate them,' Daphne said. 'The important thing is, we found it. Er, what is it, exactly?'

'It's another piece of Letitia's red dress. There was a bit of it entwined in the buttons on Madeleine Brett-Coates's suit when she was found. I was trying to have a look at it last night and, um, it didn't go too well, if you recall.'

'Oh yes, Letty thought you were trying to sneak a look at her pants,' Daphne giggled. 'Do you think she came this way, after bumping off Madeleine?'

Sarah straightened up and looked around dubiously. 'I'm not sure I see her as a scampering-through-hedges sort of person, do you?'

'Well, there's no telling what she might do, if she'd just murdered someone. That could make her behave in a way that was totally out of character.'

'That's very smart, Daph. But something doesn't quite stack up... even that bit of material caught in Madeleine's buttons. The bits of the dress that are flouncy are all around the skirt, not at the top. Why would she have had the skirt right up near Madeleine's chest, where the button was?'

'Maybe they had a fight,' said Daphne. 'Maybe Letty shoved Madeleine down on the ground, and was kneeling on her... Oh my goodness, I can't keep on picturing this, it's making my third eye go all squinty.'

'That's good thinking, too, though. They might well have had a fight. Letty seems quite up and down emotionally, to say the least, and everyone says Madeleine Brett-Coates was a toughie. It's well known Madeleine was pretty mean to Letitia. Maybe she lost her temper and flew at her? Or fell over and

Madeleine pulled at her dress? I admit, that seems a bit unlikely, she was an old lady. And any fighting would probably have left bruises, which should show up in the post-mortem. We'll mention it to Mariella, though, and she'll need to get someone out here to, erm, retrieve that bit of fabric too.'

'I suppose I'll have to tell her I touched it?' Daphne said, clearly hoping Sarah was going to contradict her.

'Afraid so, Daph. Right. Shall we carry on looking? I wonder if there are any more scraps around?'

'Ooh! Look, just over there, a few yards away. It's a splash of red again. Come on, Sarah.'

This time, Daphne was careful to keep her hands behind her back, and they both studied the tiny piece of silk, caught on one of the banks of shrubs at the end of the garden.

'It's the same fabric. It's almost like someone wants us to find things, isn't it?' said Daphne, scanning the horizon.

'That's the third brilliant thing you've said this morning,' said Sarah approvingly. 'This could easily just be a false trail someone's laid.'

'What would they be hoping to achieve?'

'Well, it's keeping us busy, for a start. And I suppose they'd be planting the idea that Letty committed the crime, then went haring off across the fields in this direction.'

'If she's not a hedge-scamperer, then she's definitely not a cross-country person, is she?' Daphne wrinkled her nose.

'Well, again, as you said, people behave differently under stress. If she'd just killed Madeleine, then I suppose she might.'

'But she was back at the house later, wasn't she?' Daphne said, pulling a weed out of Hamish's fur. 'Wouldn't she have tried to run off?'

'You'd have thought so. Unless she didn't think anyone would suspect her? We can suggest Mariella checks all those timings for Letty's comings and goings,' said Sarah. 'If you're right, and this is a false trail, then that rather suggests we need to be looking over the other way – in the opposite direction from these bits of fabric.'

'You mean, back towards the house?' Daphne asked.

'Yes. An inside job. And you know what that means.'

Daphne looked at Sarah, horror on her face. 'Don't say it.'

'Keeping quiet about it won't make it go away, Daph. I don't think there's much doubt about it. Someone in Coates House is responsible for two deaths.'

Daphne was already shivering when, as they watched, the front door was flung open. Someone staggered out, waving their arms and shouting.

'Who's that? And what are they saying? I can't make it out,' Sarah said, screwing her face up with the effort.

'It looks like Mrs Bunforth,' Daphne said. 'Oh my goodness, did you hear that?'

'No, it's just indistinct yelling from a blob. I must get my eyes sorted out,' said Sarah in frustration. 'And probably my ears, too!'

'Well, you're not going to like this,' Daphne said, breaking into a run.

'What? What is it, tell me quickly,' Sarah said, gripping her arm and jogging along by her side.

'She says Charles has gone missing.'

SIXTEEN

All was pandemonium when they reached the magnificent entrance of Coates House. As well as Tweedledum and Tweedledee, there were three new police constables. They were all wearing high-vis jackets, milling around, gabbling into their walkie-talkies and, to Sarah's eye, achieving nothing.

When Mariella burst out of the drawing room, Sarah hailed her. 'What's this about Charles? Is he really missing?'

'Well, no one's seen him yet this morning.'

'It's not even seven yet... Maybe he's still asleep?' said Sarah, frowning.

Mariella patted her arm. 'It looks like his bed wasn't slept in last night. Do you, ahem, know anything about that?'

'No,' said Sarah, looking thoughtful. 'We were both so tired, we just went to our allocated rooms. Then Letty woke me up around five or six, Hamish wanted to go outside, we bumped into Daphne and, well, we've just been for a little walk...' She looked meaningfully at Mariella, who then beckoned both her and Daphne back into the drawing room, where Sarah handed over the snippet of red silk.

'I'm afraid I did touch it, darling,' said Daphne apologetically. 'But there's another piece still in the bushes. I wondered if it might be a false trail incriminating Letty.'

'It sounds as though Madeleine was thoroughly unpleasant to Letitia,' Sarah said. 'So she does have a motive.'

'Thanks, Sarah. Hopefully this will be useful. This case... It's turning into a nightmare,' Mariella sighed. 'And I really want to prove myself, show the Canterbury lot I'm cut out for the job.'

'Don't worry,' said Daphne, giving her daughter a hug. 'We're here to help you. We'll have it solved before you know it – even without Charles.'

'Well, I hope it's going to be *with* Charles. The last time someone went missing in this house it didn't exactly end well,' said Sarah anxiously.

'We'll find him,' said Mariella. 'Look, I know I asked you for help, but just be careful, won't you? Don't go poking any hornets' nests. I can't stress this enough – there's someone dangerous here. In fact, if you want to go, then that would be great too.'

Sarah and Daphne looked at each other. 'I'd love to leave,' said Sarah. 'But actually, now we've sort of promised Bernard we'd stay.'

Mariella gazed at both women. 'That doesn't have to be binding. If you feel uneasy at all, you can leave with my blessing. And Mum, you could go and Sarah could stay.'

'Of course I would do no such thing,' said Daphne, outraged.

'No? Well, be careful. Now it's back to the fray for me,' said Mariella, opening the door and plunging into the scrum of police. She gave a few terse orders, then there was the sound of purposeful movement, and a silence eventually fell.

'Well, what are we supposed to do now?' said Daphne listlessly, once they'd got dressed in yesterday's clothes and come downstairs to the drawing room. 'Mari didn't seem all that interested in the red fabric, the family are like clams when we're around, and we can't even think of leaving while Charles is missing, can we?'

'No, we can't, Daph. So let's make the most of these lovely comfy sofas and work out what we're going to do next.'

'Mari's just told us to be careful. You heard her.' Daphne flumped down on the sofa and sank into the cushions.

'Yes, but when have we ever taken any notice of that?' Sarah said. 'What's the worst she can do, if we do come up with an idea?'

'Well, arrest us,' Daphne said, but a little more quietly. She'd arranged a pillow under her head and had made herself a nest, kicking off her shoes. Hamish was curled at her feet, and they both looked very happy in a patch of sunlight. Sarah, too, was tempted to have a nap – she'd had an awful night's sleep – but how could she even shut her eyes, with Charles missing? She needed to do as she'd just said, and think this through calmly.

Charles hadn't said where he was going last night, when they'd shared a very satisfactory kiss out in the corridor. She was pretty sure she'd even heard his door click when she'd gone into her own bedroom. But his room had not been slept in – which meant something had happened shortly after they had parted.

Had she heard any other noises in the corridor last night that might give her a clue? She racked her brains to remember. The bedrooms, like everything else at Coates House, were beautifully decorated and very comfortable. She'd headed to her ensuite bathroom after saying goodnight to Charles. Then, once she'd sorted out Hamish in his little comfy corner on the floor, she'd got into bed, planning to read a chapter of the paperback she'd found on the bookshelf by the window, to try and take her mind off the events of the day. Instead, she had rapidly fallen into an uneasy sleep. She had woken up again for the first time almost immediately – but why?

Hamish had been barking, she suddenly remembered. What had disturbed him? At the time, she'd dismissed it as a request from the Scottie to go home immediately, which she'd dealt with by giving him lots of reassurance and settling him back into his bed. But what if he'd woken up because Charles had been padding along the corridor?

What could Charles have been doing, prowling around the house after everyone was asleep? Did he have a hunch about the deaths he wanted to investigate? It was so reckless, attempting to go it alone. Sarah skipped over the fact that she'd done this herself, several times. She really hoped *he* hadn't been foolish enough to try it, in this well-upholstered house of death.

Sarah levered herself off the sofa and went over to the window. She looked out, beyond the plush curtains, and saw a couple of the PCs touring the perimeter of the property, beating at the hedges with sticks. They must be looking for more fabric.

Just then, one of the PCs shot a hand up into the air, and his colleague ran towards him. They both leant towards the hedge, careful not to touch anything. What were they looking at? Sarah couldn't make it out, but saw a pair of binoculars on the windowsill, for birdwatching, she supposed. She snatched them up and, once she'd got used to the strong magnification and managed to point them in the right direction, she could see everything clearly. The taller of the two constables was putting on latex gloves and was freeing an object from the middle of the hedge. Even at this distance, she could see how unyielding and stiff the close-packed yew was. Eventually, he succeeded, and dropped the item into the plastic bag being held out by his colleague.

Sarah rocked back on her heels. Suddenly there was a noise right behind her, and she wheeled round to see Bernard peering over her shoulder. How had he got in here so quietly? She looked down, and saw he was wearing old-fashioned carpet slippers.

'What are they up to? Did they find something?' His voice was sharp.

'Yes, it looks like...'

'Looks like what?' he snapped.

SEVENTEEN

Sarah was a little taken aback, but after the last twelve hours it wasn't surprising Bernard was on edge. 'Well, I'm afraid it looks like a crisp packet.'

Bernard rocked back on his heels. 'Oh! Oh, I see. It'll be one of the villagers. They drop litter everywhere.'

Sarah noticed how pale he was and saw his hand tremble slightly as he put it rather heavily on the back of a chair. 'You must be exhausted,' she said. 'All this has been a terrible strain.'

'You can't imagine,' he said, shaking his head. 'The annual fair is a burden at the best of times, but Mumsy always insisted it had to go on. "There's been a fair at Coates for as long as the house has stood," she'd say. What she based it on, I have no idea. There aren't any records of fairs much before the nineteenth century.'

'Still, that's a pretty long period in itself. It's rather nice that she wanted to uphold the tradition,' Sarah said.

'Harrumph. Well, not when other people had to do all the hard work to make it happen. And by other people, I mean me. Since Helena's been back, all she's done is stir up trouble. Jonty's no good to man nor beast, always obsessing about that silly telly show of his. Geoff, God rest him, well, he was as much use as a chocolate teapot.'

'What about Letitia? She must be a support,' said Sarah, keen to know more of the dynamics of this unlikely-seeming marriage.

'Letty? Hum. Well, you've met her, so how much help do you...? Oh, what's the use. It is what it is, as people will say nowadays. Anyway. Time for a bite of breakfast, if you can face any.'

'Breakfast?' Daphne sat up bolt upright from her position on the sofa, and Hamish looked from face to face, wagging his tail.

'Oh, didn't see you there,' said Bernard, eyeing Daphne rather disapprovingly. 'And your dog, too.' His face relaxed a little and he bent down to pat Hamish. 'Never could resist a pooch. Letty's not keen on another after poor Fluffypaws, unfortunately, so I'm not sure what we'll do when Butler goes.'

Butler, hearing his name, stuck his nose round the door at this point, making them all smile and improving the general mood in that special way only dogs can.

'Well, I'd better investigate what Mrs Bunforth has in the way of snacks for Hamish,' said Sarah, gathering the little dog up. 'Then we should probably all join the search for Charles, whatever Mariella says.'

'Charles? What's happened to the old boy?' Bernard raised his brows.

'Haven't you heard?' mumbled Daphne through her yawns. 'He hasn't been seen since last night.'

'But that's ridiculous!' Bernard thundered. 'We can't have people going missing left, right and centre. Place has turned into an absolute madhouse. And as for what happened to Geoff...'

Sarah shivered. What would she do, if the same fate had befallen Charles? It was unthinkable. She hoped Mariella would have some news for them soon.

The little group trooped along the corridor to the dining room, where they found a huge meal already laid out for them. Mrs Bunforth certainly wasn't having any truck with the idea that grisly events destroyed the desire to eat. After that rather dismal dinner last night, produced by Anna, she had taken back control and was on top form. Everything looked and smelt delicious, and nor did she seem to be adjusting her catering to suit the diminishing numbers in the house.

There was a row of dishes covered with silver domes on the sideboard which, when Daphne peered under them, revealed scrambled eggs, bacon and grilled tomatoes. A neat stack of sourdough bread stood next to a toaster, and Thermos flasks of coffee and tea were lined up with mugs, plates and cutlery. Cut-glass jars of marmalade, raspberry jam and blackcurrant preserve caught the light, each one with a silver spoon on a dish in front of it. As they admired the spread, Anna scurried in with a platter of sausages, and arranged them on the rather crowded sideboard. She was wearing the same navy pinafore and red scarf as last night. Sarah wondered if it was some kind of uniform.

'Thank you, Anna,' Bernard said absently. The girl's smile lit up her rather spotty face.

'This is like a five-star hotel breakfast, only better,' said Daphne, clapping her hands.

Sarah found Butler tucking into a bowl of kibble, with another, smaller helping next to it, which luckily he hadn't got round to demolishing yet. Mrs Bunforth had remembered Hamish without being asked. The little dog certainly didn't need a formal invitation to join the old Labrador, and was soon happily noshing away.

His mistress was not so easily distracted. Sarah stood listlessly with her empty plate, as Bernard and Daphne heaped theirs up. Letitia drifted in not long after, wearing beautifully cut beige trousers and a sleeveless blue silk top. She gazed around with those strangely unfocused eyes and put a spoonful of scrambled egg on her plate.

'Any coffee left?' Helena asked, walking into the room a few minutes later. She was wearing a chic linen dress in a grassy shade. Sarah sighed mentally, knowing that on her the garment would have been as rumpled as an old paper bag in minutes. If Bernard was serious about them helping out, then she and Daphne would have to go home to get some fresh clothes at some point. There was nothing wrong with her hyacinth-blue cotton blouse and trousers, but she hadn't expected to be wearing them for two days on the trot, all while spending time with women whose clothing budgets seemed limitless.

She was trying to make conversation with Letitia about the weather, a subject which the younger woman couldn't seem to grasp at all, when the door to the dining room was flung open. Charles stood there, a beam on his handsome face.

'Breakfast on the go? I call that excellent timing,' he said, smiling round at the faces gawking at him. 'Oh, and I found this on the doorstep, Bernard, old thing. I think it's for you,' he said, putting a wreath of foxgloves and bluebells on the table. A note fluttered down from it and fell to the floor, in the dead silence that followed.

EIGHTEEN

'I thought I'd drop my car at home last night and get the early bus back this morning. How was I to know you'd think I was dead?' Charles was saying, a tinge of colour in his cheekbones, as Sarah stood facing him five minutes later with quite a glare on her face.

'Oh, for goodness' sake, Geoff disappeared in exactly the same way yesterday, and turned up as a corpse in the cellar,' she all but yelled at him.

'But that was totally different,' he said, palms out. 'Surely you must see that? Though from the way you're raging at me, it sounds like you wish I was a goner anyway.'

At this, Sarah turned away and sat down. They were 'having a chat' in the dining room, though the chatting had mostly been done by Sarah at high decibels. She was exhausted now, after her sleepless night and morning full of worries.

'Well, if you can't understand that it would have been helpful if you'd explained what you were up to, so we wouldn't all think you'd been murdered, then I'm wasting my breath,' she said, closing her eyes briefly.

At this, Charles seemed to reconsider his stance. 'Look, I'm really sorry,' he said, taking a seat. 'It didn't occur to me you'd think I'd been bumped off too. I just thought it would be handy if I went and collected a few things for everyone. Who knows how long we might have to stay here, and we can't go on wearing the same togs day after day. I brought Hamish's favourite biscuits, too.'

As Charles was now wearing a hangdog expression to rival the Scottie's best efforts, Sarah really had no choice but to give him a loving smile. He'd been trying to do something useful, after all. Even if that had meant abandoning Sarah and Daphne for the night in a house with a potential double murderer on the loose. She couldn't deny she was longing to get changed. Apart from anything else, the weather had done a swift about-turn, as it so often did during an English spring, and it was now rather chilly.

'Thank you, that's great. I could definitely do with a jumper.'

'Oh, er – not sure I packed those,' said Charles doubtfully.

Sarah began to wonder what he had brought, but then realised it was not the most important thing on the agenda. 'Just to bring you up to speed, we found some red fabric in the grounds,' she told him.

Charles was peering at the mantelpiece. 'What? Oh really?' he said, then stared at it again.

'Is anything wrong?' Sarah asked.

'Not exactly,' Charles said, frowning. 'That is, I could have sworn... Oh well, never mind. You were saying?'

'We found snippets of red silk... like Letitia's dress,' Sarah said.

'Heavens,' Charles stared at her. 'So you think little Letty might be involved? I'd be surprised, though, wouldn't you? Would she have the physical strength to do away with Madeleine and Geoff?'

'Well, we don't quite know what happened to Geoff yet,

though he was probably immobilised somehow...' Sarah said. 'The thing is, she and Madeleine didn't get on at all. Madeleine thought she'd married Bernard for his money, and kept saying as much, too. It sounds quite a toxic situation.'

'But Madeleine was strangled with her own bunting, wasn't she? Not easy for a slip of a thing like Letty to kill someone like that, even if she was maddened by all the jibes. Terrible way to go,' said Charles with a shudder.

'Well, Mariella would probably be cross with me for saying anything, but no, strangling wasn't the cause of death. They are thinking some sort of poison was administered to Madeleine first. The bunting was just window dressing,' said Sarah.

'Oh, I see,' said Charles. 'That does make a difference.'

'Indeed. Even a "slip of a girl" can administer poison,' Sarah said, raising an eyebrow.

'I say, though,' said Charles. 'Surely Letty—'

Just then, the door flew open, and Letitia Brett-Coates stood there, swaying slightly. 'I really don't feel well,' she said, taking a few tottering steps into the room. Then she collapsed, and fell full length on the luxuriously thick carpet.

* * *

'Letty, darling!' squawked Bernard as he burst into the drawing room and rushed over to the sofa. Letitia was now lying down with her shoes off. A cold compress Sarah had fashioned out of a napkin rested on her forehead.

'No need to panic, Bernard. She's going to be absolutely fine,' said Sarah in matter-of-fact tones.

'What's going on? Is she ill?' Bernard lifted his head and looked at Sarah in anguish.

'I think she just fainted, probably because of the, er, rather stressful situation in the house,' said Sarah, who actually had other ideas about Letitia's condition, but didn't want to air them until she was more certain of her ground.

'My poor darling,' crooned Bernard.

Charles turned his face away and Sarah walked over to the window, to give the couple a bit of privacy. Considering they had barely acknowledged each other's presence up until this point, it was a surprisingly touching scene of marital devotion.

'Perhaps we should give you some space,' Sarah said after five minutes of smooching noises from the sofa. 'Come on, Charles, let's go and see what Daphne's up to.'

Charles agreed wholeheartedly, and they were soon out in the corridor gazing at the closed door.

'I'm not sure I can work that couple out,' Sarah said. 'They didn't seem very lovey-dovey yesterday, or this morning, come to think of it.'

'Bit odd,' said Charles, looking thankful to have escaped. 'Right, shall we check on Daph?'

'Actually, would you mind doing that, and making sure Hamish has a little walk? I might see if I can run Mariella down,' said Sarah, looking rather determined. 'But before I do, what was on the note attached to that foxglove and bluebell wreath you gave Bernard earlier, did you have a chance to see?'

'Oh, ah, yes! I knew you'd want to know. So I memorised it for you,' he said with a boyish grin. 'It was rather cryptic. "*Sorry for your loss, and you'll be sorry for it too.*" Sinister, I thought. I'm not sure that's what I'd write on a wreath for a bereaved family.'

'Thanks, Charles,' said Sarah, touched at his efforts. 'Hmm, I agree, that's really strange.'

'Are you sure you want to tackle Mariella? She's rushed off her feet. And you know how she gets when we try and, um, help,' Charles said.

'It won't take a minute. And I think it's the kind of information she might find useful,' Sarah said firmly.

'All right, then. I'll see you in a bit,' Charles said, ambling off in the direction of the dining room.

Sarah watched until he was out of sight, and then made for the main staircase. The huge bouquet of flowers on the table by the door had been changed. The gorgeous purple tulips and agapanthus that had looked so spectacular yesterday had been swapped for an arrangement of early roses in pristine white, with lots of trailing ivy – sombre, and more fitting for a house in mourning. There was no sign of the wreath with the odd message, though. Had Mrs Bunforth spirited it away, for reasons of her own? The housekeeper could easily be another member of the household with something to hide.

Sarah wondered where she would find Mariella. She hoped she was still on the premises. Just then, there was a crash from upstairs. Well, it sounded as though Tweedledum and Tweedledee were around, at any rate. Sarah grabbed the bannister and puffed her way up. She was soon swinging back the door on what looked like the master bedroom.

The place was a riot of peachy tones – a plush carpet on the floor, wonderful apricot curtains swagged and looped at the windows, and resplendent in the centre of the room, a giant four-poster bed with a frilly canopy. It was a little over the top. Granted, in the pictures and photos around the house, and even in the pink suit she'd worn on the day of her death, Madeleine Brett-Coates had gone for feminine choices, yet there was something about the set of her jaw that suggested she was no pushover. But Sarah supposed people's fantasies – of one sort or another – came out in the boudoir. Standing by the bed was Tweedledee, holding the remains of a rather beautiful blush pink alabaster vase. There was a large chunk of it on the floor, as well as a muddle of pink roses. There was a similar vase on the dressing table, this time filled with tall foxgloves in purple and pink hues.

'Oh dear,' said Sarah, darting forward to help. 'What a shame.' Between the two of them, they put the shards of the vase carefully in a wastepaper basket and mopped up the water, which had gone everywhere. They left the roses in the basin in the ensuite bathroom, accessed through a small doorway behind the bedstead. The bathroom was like a spa, with piles of fluffy towels and flacons of expensive lotions and potions lined up by the tub.

Once order had been restored, Sarah turned to Deeside, who was looking shame-faced. 'What happened, to make you drop that vase?'

'Oh, er, well, I can't really...'

'And don't say you can't remember. It was five minutes ago,' said Sarah sternly.

The PC went a bit red and shuffled his feet. 'I should probably tell the boss,' he said.

'No harm in discussing things beforehand,' said Sarah rather slyly. She knew it was a touch naughty, but she was very keen to leave this house. Anything speeding up her investigation – and the police's – was good news in her book.

'Well, I'd just been searching the bathroom, as per orders. And then I saw it, out of the corner of my eye, like. It gave me a right turn. I banged into the bedside table, and the flowers went flying. Stupid place to put them,' he said mulishly, keen to blame the whole debacle on a bunch of innocent blooms.

'What was it you saw?' Sarah was asking, when the door opened again. This time it was Mariella, striding into the room with a cross look on her face. Sarah inwardly winced.

'What are you two doing? You look like you've been caught with your hands in the cookie jar,' Mariella said, looking from one to the other. 'What, neither of you wants to speak up? That's a first. You're usually chatty enough.'

Sarah cleared her throat. 'I came in because I heard—'

'This vase just fell off,' Deeside said at exactly the same time.

Mariella gave them both a headmistressy glare, stepped round to inspect the wet patch on the carpet, spotted the roses in the basin in the bathroom beyond, and rolled her eyes. 'Any useful finds in here?'

Sarah couldn't help looking towards Deeside, and willing him on. Now was the moment for him to divulge what had caused his little accident. But to her surprise, he went rather pink, and shook his head. 'Not so far,' he said.

Mariella looked at Sarah, who shrugged her shoulders. 'All right. No reason for you to be in here, Aun— erm, Sarah. Off you go, back with the others.'

'I did just want to make sure you knew about the cryptic message that came with the wreath this morning,' Sarah said.

'Of course. Ideas about what it means?' Mariella tapped her foot.

'Um, not just yet. And Mrs Bunforth seems to have got rid of it, which could be significant. I wanted to have a word about Letitia, too. It's possible she may be exp—'

'Well, it's going to have to wait,' said Mariella. 'I must get on now. Downstairs, please.'

'Um, I think I'll pop along and get changed first,' Sarah prevaricated as she went through the door Mariella was holding open.

'Fine,' said Mariella, giving her a steely look. 'But then go straight down and sit with the others. I need you to get the inside track from the suspects. I've got enough people tramping around the house looking for physical clues, I don't need another, thanks.'

Sarah had no choice but to nod. Mariella's mood was probably to do with her officers bagging things like crisp packets instead of evidence, rather than anything personal. But Sarah couldn't help chafing at the summary dismissal. If she was downstairs, she'd have no chance of bumping into Deeside again and finding out what he'd really seen in Madeleine Brett-Coates's bedroom. Whatever it was, it had to be pretty extraordinary. After all, he had just lied right to Mariella's face about it. That could only mean one thing – he was trying to protect someone. But who?

NINETEEN

Downstairs with the Brett-Coates clan was every bit as much fun as Sarah had anticipated. She had changed into some of the clothes Charles had kindly brought. Unfortunately, it looked as though he'd packed in the dark, with his eyes tightly shut for good measure, and the lilac blouse and emerald slacks she was wearing was the best combination she'd been able to come up with. Helena looked up as she entered the room and her eyebrows said it all. Daphne seemed more than happy, though, in the leopard-print harem pants and orange top he'd fetched.

The changeable Letitia had now sunk into an impenetrable gloom. Her brief lovey-dovey moment with Bernard was over. He was sitting as far from her as humanly possible and did not once look in her direction. Instead he gazed sternly out at the lawn, as though willing it not to grow.

Helena, by contrast, was doing her best to flirt with a rather flummoxed Charles. From what had been said yesterday about Charles and Bernard's school days, it was evident they'd all known each other for years, so this seemed an odd moment for Charles to have suddenly become irresistibly attractive to her. But Helena was doggedly hanging on his every word, laughing uproariously at the least thing and gazing at him with her extraordinarily green eyes.

Sarah, by now rather used to Charles being the object of other women's attentions, looked on with some amusement. She was pretty sure he would have flirted back if they'd been alone – he was a polite man, and it was his default way of communicating with the opposite sex – but now he was squirming every time Helena put a hand on his sleeve or batted her eyelashes coquettishly at him.

Sarah tried to keep herself busy by engaging Bernard in conversation, but it was rather like swimming through treacle with all your limbs tied together.

'Your family must have been here for years,' was her opening gambit.

'Ah. Yes,' said Bernard cautiously, as though she was trying to prise state secrets out of him.

'Since when, exactly?' she persisted.

'Oh. Um. Sixteenth century. Geoff was the one to talk to about this stuff, knew more about our family tree than any of us.'

This was quite unhelpful, Sarah thought. Geoff was obviously well beyond such a conversation. And surely Bernard knew more about his own background than someone who'd only married into the family? Nevertheless, Sarah persisted. 'He took an interest, did he?' she said politely. 'How nice.'

Suddenly Jonathan threw the magazine he'd been leafing through aside. 'Nice? Nice. That was the one thing Geoff wasn't. He was an honest man, unlike... oh, never mind. You wouldn't understand.'

Hunched up in a corner chair, he seemed incredibly on edge. But then he was a performer – maybe some of this was put on? He was the only member of the family who knew anything about poisonous plants. Could he have killed his mother, and then got rid of Geoff, too? Perhaps Geoff had suspected him, even accused him of murder? Jonathan said Geoff had disappeared before Madeleine met her fate in the tent, but no one else had corroborated that. It was worth thinking about. On the other hand, his reaction to even the mention of foxgloves suggested he wouldn't have been capable of arranging that bouquet behind his dead mother's head, let alone ordering the foxglove wreath. But maybe he was a better target for her conversational gambits than Bernard?

'Try me. Tell me about Geoff,' said Sarah, turning to face Jonathan, but he shot to his feet and stormed over to one of the huge windows.

'To think, this time yesterday they were still with us. Both of them.' His shoulders heaved and he seemed to be trying to contain his emotions.

Daphne got up and kindly put an arm round him, but he shook it off and rushed over to the door. 'I can't do this, can't sit here with you lot, not saying anything about what's been happening, pretending everything's normal. I won't, I tell you!' With that, he slammed the door behind him.

'What's got into him?' said Helena languidly, searching Charles's face as though the answer was somewhere there.

'To be expected, I would have thought. He lost his husband yesterday,' Sarah pointed out mildly.

'Yes, but it's not as if— Oh well. You know what I mean, Bernard,' Helena said.

'Not a clue, old thing,' said Bernard, avoiding her gaze and staring fixedly at the lawns. 'Oh look, there's Peabody.'

Helena and Letitia perked up at this, and Letitia even got out of her seat and went to join her husband. 'Oh, thank goodness. Something's going right at last,' she said, watching the figure now striding purposefully across the lawn.

Sarah got up and stood with them. Sure enough, there was a tall, muscular young man advancing across the lawn, longish fair hair bouncing as he went. Dressed in jeans and a hoodie, he appeared to be in his twenties, and was conspicuously good looking. As he neared the house, someone intercepted him from the kitchen pathway. It was Jonathan Brett-Coates. After a heated discussion, the man followed Jonathan somewhat reluctantly the way he'd come, away from the group silently watching.

Letitia turned away from the window with a despairing gesture. 'That's that, then,' she said, flinging herself down again in the chair and inspecting her manicure stonily.

'Probably for the best,' said Helena, her elegant brows arched.

'In what world?' snapped Bernard.

Sarah and Daphne looked at each other. Not for the first time, Sarah thought it would really be quite useful to have some kind of guidebook to the Brett-Coates. A lot of what they said and did was totally incomprehensible to her. She peered at Charles, hoping he might have an idea of what had just transpired, but his face was blank and expressionless. A shame. Jonathan, being so closely linked to both victims, had to be a key suspect. The more information she could gather on him, the better.

When Mrs Bunforth burst in a few moments later with a wild look on her pale lozenge of a face, even the notion that there'd been another tragedy seemed like a welcome interruption to the charged atmosphere.

'It's gone, I tell you. Gone,' she shouted.

TWENTY

'Bunny, do calm down,' said Bernard immediately, rushing to Mrs Bunforth's side and manoeuvring her into the nearest armchair. 'Everyone's a bit overwrought at the moment, only natural you should feel the same. Someone get her a cup of tea,' he said over his shoulder to the rest of them.

Letitia and Helena stared at each other. 'But Mrs Bunforth's the one who makes tea!' Letitia blinked, as if she'd been asked to pull off a moon landing single-handedly.

'Oh, fine, I'll go and sort it out,' said Daphne, getting up with a shake of her scarves.

'That's very good of you,' said Sarah, although she resigned herself to quite a wait for a cuppa. 'Would you mind taking Hamish with you? It's probably time he poked his nose outside. Don't let him run off, though.'

'Of course. Come on then, boy,' Daphne said, leading the little Scottie out.

Mrs Bunforth, meanwhile, was hyperventilating in her chair, with Bernard's hand pressing heavily on her shoulder.

'If you wouldn't mind giving me some room,' said Sarah, going into doctor mode, 'I'll just see what the trouble is.'

Bernard moved away reluctantly, resuming his stance by the window. Sarah knelt at Mrs Bunforth's feet, and took her wrist in a loose clasp to assess her pulse. Hmm, it was racing. She'd clearly had quite a shock. Her usual pallor had been replaced by a hectic flush and there were beads of perspiration standing out on her brow.

'Close your eyes, Mrs Bunforth,' Sarah said, noting the way the woman was darting restless glances around the room while her thin chest heaved up and down. 'I want you to start counting up to ten, very slowly, just in your head. That's it, no rush.'

Gradually, as Sarah watched, the woman's breathing became less laboured. Charles was looking on with concern while Helena, appearing faintly disgusted, had moved over to stand with her brother and had temporarily lost interest in flirtation.

'I suppose this means lunch will be delayed,' Sarah heard Helena saying crossly to Bernard.

At this, Mrs Bunforth's eyelids fluttered open. Sarah gave her a sympathetic smile, and she rapidly closed them again. A couple of minutes later, she seemed to gather her strength and sat up straighter. 'I feel much better now,' she said in a faltering voice. 'I'd better be getting back to the kitchen.'

'Wait a minute, Mrs B,' said Bernard, swivelling away from the window. 'When you came bursting in, you were shouting about something. What was it?'

'Oh yes,' said Mrs Bunforth, the colour mounting to her cheeks again. Sarah, worried she'd have another panic attack, leant towards her, but the housekeeper waved her away. 'It's just that, well. I was in the dining room dusting, and I couldn't see it. I dare say it's just got misplaced, though.'

'What? What's been misplaced?' said Helena impatiently. 'Come on, Bunny. It's not like you to make such a big drama out of things.'

'Well... That dagger on the mantelpiece. It's... it's missing,' Mrs Bunforth said, as she looked from Helena to her brother and back again.

'Good grief! You can't mean the Coates dagger?' Bernard took a step forward, looking aghast.

Mrs Bunforth nodded, and swallowed miserably. 'It was there last night, that's all I know, Mr Bernard.'

Bernard turned away, and rammed his fist into the wall. Sarah blinked in surprise. It was a curiously violent action, and must have hurt him a lot. Indeed, he immediately started rubbing his knuckles and shaking his head.

Letitia rushed to his side. 'Are you all right, darling?'

He shook her off brusquely. 'Yes, yes of course. Just frustrated, you know. That blasted thing, the dirk, it's been in the family for centuries.'

Sarah's mind was whirring... Was this why Charles had seemed so confused in the dining room earlier on? He'd been looking at the mantelpiece. She glanced over at him and he nodded his head imperceptibly. Aha.

'One of my ancestors brought it home from Culloden in 1746. A souvenir,' Bernard went on.

'Culloden... in Scotland?' Sarah frowned to dredge up memories of distant history lessons.

'Yes of course,' Bernard snapped. 'We put down the Highland rebellion. Got cursed by the locals for our pains, would you believe it? Some guff about the dirk bringing misfortune to our house. Well, that's absolute nonsense, as you can see,' he said, glaring at them all. 'Geoff was the one who could have told you the ins and outs of the whole business – mind you, if he'd still been with us, he'd be the first person I'd suspect of running off with it.'

'Bernard, honestly,' said Helena. 'Poor Jonathan. Thank goodness he's not here to listen to you.'

'Don't pretend it didn't cross your mind, Hells. You know

perfectly well what Geoff was up to. What about that bag of silver we found only last night? He had all those contacts in the antiques business. He was clearly trying to flog it.'

'Ahem,' said Charles. 'He never approached me.' He sounded rather hurt; Sarah knew how sensitive he was about his dusty curio shop on the esplanade at Merstairs.

'Of course he wouldn't try and palm things off on you, Charles. You would have told me immediately,' said Bernard.

'So, given that it couldn't have been Geoff, who do you think might have stolen the dagger?' said Sarah.

'Not a clue,' said Bernard glumly. 'But it's not just the fact that it's gone. No one would get so much as a fiver for it down at a bric-à-brac stall in the market, I'm sure. It's what it stands for that's the problem.'

Helena turned to him suddenly. 'You don't think...? No, surely you can't believe that old rot.'

Letitia sat bolt upright. 'What? Not that old nursery rhyme again? You're obsessed with it, darling.'

'I'm not obsessed. And it's not a nursery rhyme, either,' said Bernard angrily. 'It's on our coat of arms, for one thing.'

'What is all this, old boy?' Charles asked languidly. 'Some sort of family motto?'

'If you want to call it that,' said Bernard. 'Here, follow me, I'll show you.'

They all trooped out with him. Mrs Bunforth, who was back to her usual sepulchral paleness, made her excuses and was returning to the kitchen when she met Daphne and Hamish with her cup of tea. She took it, looked at it in dismay, and hurried off, probably to throw it down the sink. A beaming Daphne joined the others as they entered the dining room. Bernard led the way over to the wonderful old carved wooden mantel, and stood in front of it, almost to attention. Now that they were facing it, Sarah realised that there was a small stand in the centre that was now empty. This must have been where the dirk had been displayed. Had it been there during dinner last night? She really couldn't remember. Bernard didn't seem interested in the gap, though. He was pointing at the wood carving behind it.

Sarah looked at the fine engraving more closely. She could see that the ancient oak had been fashioned into a crest. Underneath it was a scroll which she had dismissed as blank. But when she looked really hard, she could see traces of words, which the smoke of many a fire over the centuries had darkened and dulled. Now Bernard followed the curved script reverently with his fingertips, whispering the motto as he did so.

Dreich the day the dirk does go,
To them that steal it false steps and woe,
Until an heir untouched by horror,
Drives the devil from this door.

TWENTY-ONE

Despite herself, and in direct contravention of all her years of scientific study and rationalism, Sarah felt goosepimples springing up on her arms. She looked at Daphne, who was backing away from Bernard, and even Hamish whined a little and scampered over to his mistress for reassurance.

'What does that m-mean, exactly?' stuttered Daphne. 'It sounds like the Highlanders were bringing down a curse on anyone taking their dagger.'

'What, and then tripping them up? Oh goodness me,' said Bernard, chuckling heartily. 'Of course it's not meant literally.'

'Yes, take no notice of it,' said Helena. 'My mother was always threatening to have that crest thing removed. A lot of our ancestors have fallen off things or missed their footing here or there and she didn't like the reminder.'

'Really?' said Daphne, clasping her hands together. 'So it is a curse. I thought I could feel some strange vibrations.'

Bernard gave her a sharp look, then addressed himself to Helena. 'If you're talking about our great-great-grandfather taking a wrong turning off the top of the Matterhorn, anyone could have done that in a snowstorm.'

'What about Mother's second cousin, then? He got into a lift without looking and plunged right down the shaft. Then there was our great-uncle, who fell over at the late Queen's coronation in 1953...'

'He didn't die, though, Hells, did he?' Bernard said crossly.

'No, but it was a total embarrassment. Mother certainly felt it would have been better if he had.'

'I'd say this inscription dates right back to the Battle of Culloden itself,' said Charles, stepping forward and making as if to touch the design.

'Don't,' said Bernard, grabbing Charles's arm. 'Sorry, old man. Not a good idea.'

Charles stared at his old friend in confusion. 'Oh. Of course. My apologies.' He stood back and looked rather sheepish.

'It's just that it's rather, um, fragile,' Bernard said. 'Helena's always dismissing the Brett-Coates heritage. It suits her modern ways,' he said, with a sharp look at his sister. 'But we're a rather ancient family, when it comes down to it. That phrase may mean nothing, but it's been up there a long time, and I for one want to keep it intact. Now, where's Mrs Bunforth when we need her? I bet we could all do with a cup of tea, couldn't we?' he said heartily.

'If not something stronger,' said Helena, with a longing glance towards the drinks trolley, groaning with bottles of whisky, gin and sherry.

'A bit early, even for you, Hells,' said Bernard firmly.

'Hardly,' said Helena. 'Anyway, Bunny's having a fit of the vapours. We'd better not disturb her.'

'Oh, stuff it, I'm having a gin,' said Letitia, drifting over and pouring herself a stiff one. Helena quickly followed in her footsteps and was soon sipping from a large glass, looking a little more composed.

'There was a man who passed the window earlier, before

the, um, dirk issue was raised. Peebles, I think he was called?' said Sarah.

'Do you mean Peabody? I wonder why he caught your fancy,' Helena smirked. 'He's our gardener. Mother wasn't entirely a fool.'

'Hells! Please. I don't know what you're suggesting. Poor Mumsy doesn't deserve to be made the butt of your foul insinuations,' said Bernard, sitting down again. Letitia patted his shoulder, giving Helena a frosty look.

'Oh, give over, Bernard. We all knew what was going on. Don't pretend you weren't wise to it.'

Sarah looked at Bernard with interest. Was Helena implying a relationship between her mother and the gardener? The age gap must have been immense. But would it have seemed so extraordinary if the roles had been reversed, and Madeleine Brett-Coates had been a man? Sarah's head was swimming.

Bernard was staring into the middle distance, his face unreadable. There was no clarity to be had there. But even if the dead woman had been having a fling with a man much less than half her age, would that have been a motive for murder? Only, Sarah imagined, if it had meant she was planning to change her financial affairs to reflect the relationship...

The door opened suddenly, and Mrs Bunforth poked her head round, looking much more like her usual pallid self. 'Mr Chivers is here, sir, with his clerk. Shall I send him in?'

'Yes, yes, and if you're better, can you bring us some tea?' said Bernard, suddenly looking tired. 'For those of us who haven't hit the bottle already. Chivers is Mumsy's solicitor,' he said to Charles. 'I wonder what he's after?'

'Surely it'll be about Mother's will. Not much mystery about that,' said Helena dismissively. 'And we all know what was in it anyway. She told us often enough.'

'Oh, er, we'd better make ourselves scarce...' Charles said, gesturing towards the door.

Sarah groaned inwardly. She'd have much preferred to keep quiet and see if they could stay for this potentially fascinating meeting. But to her relief, Bernard wouldn't hear of them leaving.

'No need, old boy. As Helena says, we all know the score. You might as well stay. Ah, there you are, Mr Chivers. Do take a seat.'

A man with a pronounced stoop entered, together with a lanky-looking clerk in his twenties, holding a large black leather briefcase. The man snapped his fingers at the clerk, who handed the case over. 'Wait outside, Jenkins, please,' he said, hobbling gingerly forward. 'Bad back, you know,' he explained. 'I had to bring the boy to carry the paperwork. My apologies.' He was almost certainly younger than Sarah, but his grey hair and ashen complexion made him look like something out of a black and white film.

'First, let me say, I am so sorry for your grievous loss,' said Mr Chivers, wincing as he shook hands with Bernard. 'What a shock. Your mother was a wonderful woman.'

'Yes, yes,' said Bernard, passing a hand across his face. 'It's been horrendous. You can't imagine.'

Behind him, Letitia gave a small sob and reached for a tissue. It was the first sign of distress she'd really shown, and it elicited a very tender look from Mr Chivers. 'Appalling for you all,' he said.

'Indeed. Do sit down,' said Bernard, pointing at the comfortable sofas. Chivers shook his head, clutching the small of his back, and chose a spindly wooden chair in the far corner of the room. It was the most uncomfortable-looking item of furniture Sarah had yet seen at Coates House. He eased himself down and placed his briefcase lovingly on his lap. There was a bang at the door and Anna appeared, red scarf jaunty at her neck, as she lugged a large tray bearing a teapot, coffee Thermos and a plate of biscuits.

'Oh, thank you, Anna, my dear,' said Mr Chivers.

Everyone milled around for a while, offering each other the delicious shortbread. A dry cough reminded them to take their seats again. There was an expectant hush as everyone turned to face the solicitor. With a snap that was close to a magician's flourish, he opened up the briefcase. Then he looked around again.

'Ah. Mr Jonathan is not with us,' he said, looking concerned.

Bernard could barely conceal his impatience. 'He's not, no. My brother is doing what he does best, having a hissy fit in his room. Don't worry, we'll tell him exactly what you've said when he finally deigns to show his face.'

'I'd rather he was present,' the solicitor said, frowning heavily.

'Well, he's not. And he won't come down. Believe me, Helena and I have both tried often enough in the past. Leaving him be is the only way.'

'He's just lost his husband, Mr Chivers. I think we should allow him a little slack,' said Helena, sounding quite reasonable for once.

Mr Chivers looked at them both again, gave another small dry cough, and made a decision. 'Very well, then,' he said.

Bernard had been adamant that they all knew the contents of Madeleine Brett-Coates's will, but still one could have heard a pin drop as Mr Chivers took a long envelope from the briefcase. He then slid a few sheets of thick white paper out and studied them, as though for the first time.

Helena's drawling voice cut through the silence. 'Oh come on, Chivers. Spit it out. It's not as if we don't know the drill by now. One third each to us children, a life interest in the house for me and Jonty, and Bernard's noble line to inherit it in perpetuity. Blah, blah, blah,' she said, feigning a yawn.

'Well, indeed, Miss Helena, if I may call you that. The will was precisely along those lines, I don't mind telling you,' Chivers said mildly.

Helena pounced. 'Wait a minute. "Was", you said?'

'Well exactly, Miss Helena. I was coming to that. Your mother, that is, Mrs Brett-Coates—'

'I know who my mother was, you idiot. Now what the hell did she do?' Helena screeched.

TWENTY-TWO

When Mr Chivers looked up from his nervous reading of the last will and testament of Mrs Madeleine Brett-Coates a few minutes later, there was stunned silence. His hand was shaking as he put the papers down, but Helena remained tight-lipped. After her initial outburst, she had subsided sulkily back onto the sofa, and confined herself to glaring at Bernard and the solicitor.

The contents of the will had turned out to be relatively straightforward. Instead of dividing her estate into three as expected, Madeleine Brett-Coates had, for reasons of her own, decided to give everything to Bernard, barring a £10,000 legacy for Mrs Bunforth. There was nothing for Peabody, the gardener, which made Sarah think that Helena had just been winding Bernard up earlier with her insinuations. And there was no longer a life interest in the property for Helena or Jonathan, or any bequest either, which meant they were now effectively homeless and quite probably penniless too.

Jonathan was still absent, which meant he hadn't yet heard the news. Helena seemed to be absorbing it slowly, and not finding it to her liking one little bit. Indeed, she looked a lot more stricken now than she had been when she was informed her mother had been murdered. Bernard seemed baffled.

'I had no idea Mumsy had gone and changed things,' he said candidly – but he didn't look as though the idea of inheriting everything was exactly unappealing. Letitia sat quietly, in her own little world as usual, but with a smile playing on her face.

Sarah was feeling acutely uncomfortable at witnessing this reversal of fortunes, but Daphne was swivelling her gaze between Helena and Bernard as though she were at a tennis match.

Finally, Helena spoke. 'So when, exactly, did Mother make these changes? And who knew about it?'

Mr Chivers glanced nervously at Bernard before answering. 'Mrs Brett-Coates came into the office three weeks ago. She rang me beforehand. I offered to come here, but she always preferred to visit me in town. I haven't been to the house for, oh, ten years now. When she arrived, she was very clear-cut about things. I did venture to explain this would put you and Mr Jonathan in a tricky position, Miss Brett-Coates, but your mother was set on her path.'

'Did she say *why* she did it?' Helena asked, her eyes now glittering with unshed tears.

'She did not,' said Chivers. 'And nor was it my place to ask her that question. I did, however, point out what I saw as the obvious pitfalls... but my views fell on deaf ears. I'm afraid I can't tell you any more than that.'

With that, the grey little man got to his feet.

'You're not planning to leave, now that you've wrecked our futures? I think you owe us more of an explanation than that,' Helena said furiously.

'I have given you the particulars of your late mother's visit, and read you her last wishes. I'm sorry if you find either inadequate,' Mr Chivers said, courteous to the last. 'Well, if that is all...'

'It is not *all*, not a bit of it,' Helena screamed, letting go entirely now. 'I hold you responsible for this, this abomination. And as for you...' She picked up a glass paperweight from the little desk and hurled it straight at Bernard's head. He ducked, in the nick of time, and it thudded into the wall by the fireplace, shattering on impact. Shards of glass flew everywhere and Letitia, Sarah and Daphne leapt up. Hamish whined and Sarah gathered him into her arms.

Even Butler woke up for a second, looked around in surprise, then subsided into sleep again. There was some glass on his coat, which Sarah carefully brushed out. She gave Helena a furious stare, but the woman didn't take a blind bit of notice. Mr Chivers took advantage of the lull in hostilities to clasp his beloved briefcase to his chest and hobble to the door, without a backward glance at the family.

Helena, now quivering from head to toe, broke into sudden sobs. She was standing by the windows giving onto the lawn, and for a worrying moment Sarah wondered if she might throw herself through them, not that the drop would have done her any harm, it couldn't have been more than a foot or two. Then she ran for the door. She fumbled to get out, then burst into the hall. The last they heard was her taking the stairs two at a time.

'My goodness,' said Letitia, laughing behind her hand. 'I think she's a tiny bit upset.'

'So would you be,' said Bernard gravely. 'Honestly, I can't think what Mumsy was up to. For as long as we've been able to walk and talk, she drummed it into us that we were like the Three Musketeers, united in keeping the Brett-Coates name alive and the house and grounds in one piece. And she made us stick around, too, for all these years. This is really extraordinary, what she's done.'

Sarah looked at him closely, and was surprised to see how stricken he looked. She'd thought he had very little time for either his brother or his sister, but he seemed genuinely thunderstruck by the news.

'Do you know why she might have changed her mind like this?' Sarah asked quietly.

'Me? I haven't the first clue. But I imagine that display you've just witnessed may have had something to do with it. Helena has always been volatile. Now she's more or less out of control.'

'Oh, you know that's not true, Bernie,' said Letitia. Helena's outburst seemed to have brought her back to earth. 'She used to be way worse. What about when she lived in that commune in California? Or when she ran off with X-Ray, the rap star? Granted that was a few years ago, before she lost her looks,' she added. 'Your mother was beside herself about that. But she straightened herself out and came home, all so she could share in the inheritance. And now this. No wonder she's lost it.'

It was Letitia's longest speech to date and, for once, Sarah found herself agreeing with the gist of it. If Helena really had been promised a hand in running the estate after her mother had gone, then this was a dreadful wake-up call. She could be put out of the house by her brother, any time he felt so inclined. And she had no financial cushion to fall back on, either, after living what sounded like a charmed life. She had no job, probably no savings, and nowhere to go. On the other hand, she did have a lot of green outfits and an attitude that took no prisoners.

As for Jonathan, he at least had a career. But where on earth was the man? After meeting Peabody in the garden, he seemed to have vanished – as thoroughly as his husband Geoff, it seemed. In this house, with two murders already uncovered, that could not possibly be a good thing.

Mind you, there was one other person who obviously benefitted from the changed will, apart from Bernard. If Letitia had known about the new bequest, she would have an excellent motive for murder. And, given that there was no love lost between her and Madeleine Brett-Coates, this now had to seem like a distinct possibility.

Sarah wondered what Mariella was up to. It was all very well, leaving her and Daphne to find out more from the family, but they needed to know what was going on from the police's point of view, too. Were there any clues to the diabolical caging of Geoff? Could Letitia have done that? Had the post-mortem on Madeleine revealed what poison had actually stopped her heart, since it hadn't been the savage use of the bunting? And had the police traced whoever had sent that strange wreath this morning – or had Mrs Bunforth destroyed it somehow? These were all questions Sarah was burning to have answered.

She was just trying to think of a form of words that would get her out of the room so she could go and find one of the officers on the case, when the door opened again. This time, it was Mariella standing there, with an accusatory look on her face, and a tall pink vase of foxgloves in one hand.

TWENTY-THREE

Mariella, now sitting on the sofa flanked by Sarah and Daphne, had plonked the flowers in their vase on the mantelpiece. After fussily finding a coaster and arranging the bouquet on it, Bernard had remained on his feet, and was now glowering down at them all.

'In answer to your question, officer, yes of course I do know the name of those flowers. But the real expert on plants is my brother, Jonty. If you find him, I'm sure he'll give you a full run-down on the dratted things. Now if there's nothing else, my sister stormed out of here a while ago and I think I should go and check that she's all right.'

'Wait a minute,' said Sarah firmly. 'We all know those are foxgloves and that Jonathan has an aversion to them. He reacted very oddly to them yesterday and you told us he hated them. He might have been stung by a bee in a bunch of the flowers when he was little, you said.'

'You've got a good memory,' said Bernard grudgingly. 'Well yes, they weren't his favourite. But despite that, Peabody always grew them for Mumsy,' he said, gesturing to the vase. 'She was very fond of them,' he said.

'It isn't just this vase of foxgloves,' said Mariella. 'There was also a wreath delivered to the house this morning. Who knows anything about that?' She looked around, at uniformly blank faces. 'Well, it's funny that you've all got amnesia. Because they were ordered by someone in this house, using the landline phone. A very strange voice, the florist said, almost a whisper. They couldn't tell if it was male or female. And the order went on the usual account, so there were no payment details to help identify the person.'

'You're kidding,' sniggered Letitia. 'I wonder what Jonty would make of that.'

'Oh, he'd do what he always did, make a big fuss to Mumsy,' said Bernard wearily.

'Wait a minute,' Daphne piped up. 'I'm very sensitive to these things. You just referred to Jonty in the past tense. Do you... sense his disappearance from this mortal plane?'

Bernard ran his hand through his greying hair and glared at Daphne. 'Of course not. I wasn't referring to Jonty. I was talking about my mother. Who is, very sadly, dead as of yesterday. I know we as a family asked you lot to stay on to help, but I'm really not sure how useful it's proving. Anyway, as I said, I'm going to check on Helena. If that's all right with everyone here?'

The request was put in a voice dripping with acid, and he stalked out before anyone had time to answer.

Daphne was left looking at Mariella. 'Well! I don't think this is doing much for Bernard's manners. All that breeding, and he goes spiky at the first sign of stress.'

'That's my husband you're talking about,' said Letitia with a giggle. 'Though it'll be the first time he's shown much interest in Hells since he got back.'

Daphne clapped a hand over her mouth, having evidently forgotten the woman was still in the room. 'Oopsie, my dear. No offence meant, I'm sure. I forgot myself for a second. I think I've got low blood sugar. I might just have one of those biscuits,' she said, making for the plate that had been left rather neglected during all the hoo-hah over the will reading. She put her hand to the teapot. 'Hm, still warm. Anyone want a cup?'

Soon everyone was sitting with a cup of tea or coffee and a biscuit, and a sort of peace had descended on the room. Sarah quickly filled Mariella in on the stipulations of Madeleine Brett-Coates's new will, and the varied emotions this had given rise to.

'Should someone check on old Bernard, too, I wonder?' said Charles mildly, biting into a piece of shortbread. 'He's been gone a while.'

'If he's trying to calm Helena down, he could be at it for weeks,' said Letitia, who looked on with envy as Daphne polished off a stack of the biscuits. 'I wish I could eat those,' she said wistfully.

'I'm sure you could,' mumbled Daphne through a mouthful of crumbs. 'It's really not that hard. You just take one, like so, and have a nice, big bite,' she said, ably demonstrating with a fresh piece of shortbread.

'Oh, not for me. I couldn't end up— Well, Bernie wouldn't like it,' Letitia finished with another girlish giggle.

'Plenty for him, too,' shrugged Daphne.

Mariella cleared her throat. 'I came in here to ask everyone about foxgloves. As Bernard's, um, busy elsewhere, maybe you can enlighten me, Mrs Brett-Coates,' she said, looking at Letitia.

Letitia carried on gazing vacantly ahead, then gave a start. 'Oh, you mean me? I always think people mean Madeleine when they say that, I forget we have the same name, so silly,' she tittered. 'Sure, if I can help, I will,' she added, making the prospect seem extremely unlikely. 'Bernie did just say that Peabody grows the flowers, though,' she pointed out carefully, as though speaking to a child.

'Yes, but where? There aren't any in the beds around the house,' Mariella went on.

'And it's a little early in the season for them to be flowering so beautifully,' Sarah put in.

'Oh, that's easy. They'll be from the hothouses. Just go through the kitchen door and turn right past the outbuildings. You can't miss them. The Victorians loved that sort of thing, didn't they? I believe they grew pineapples there at one point.' Letitia looked down at her manicure.

Mariella stood up. 'Well, thank you all. I'll be calling you out for individual interviews as soon as I can, Mrs Brett-Coates. If you see your husband and sister-in-law, please make that known to them.'

'What? Oh, me again,' said Letitia, her eyes huge. 'Yes, whatever.'

As Mariella left the room, taking the vase with her, Sarah slid out behind her and called her back as she was striding along the corridor. 'Mariella? Could I just have a quick word?'

Mariella stopped and almost shook her head, but then seemed to have second thoughts. She gestured to Sarah to come with her, as she mounted the stairs and went into Madeleine Brett-Coates's bedroom. The sun shone through the window, falling in golden shards onto the four-poster and the peachy carpet. Mariella shut the door carefully, replaced the vase of flowers on the dressing table, and swung out the small chair there for Sarah to sit on, while she perched on the bed.

'What's on your mind, Aunty Sarah?' she asked with a tight smile.

'I know you're rushed off your feet. I'll try not to take up too much of your time. There are two things, really. The first is that Deeside was acting really oddly in this room earlier. I came in when I heard him drop that vase – you remember, there was water everywhere. But he was really shifty when I asked him how he came to tip it over.'

'Ah, I think I can explain this. He came clean to me earlier. He saw a packet of cigarettes in the bathroom, and made the assumption, goodness knows why, that they belonged to Dumbarton. They were the brand he usually smokes. He thought Dumbarton would get told off for leaving them in a murder victim's bedroom, so he reached out to pocket them and knocked the vase at the same time. It turns out that Madeleine Brett-Coates, who ruled her children with a rod of iron and forbade them to go near cigarettes, wasn't averse to a crafty puff herself when she was on her own.'

'Oh! I suppose that explains it. I was hoping it was some secret that was going to blow things apart – wishful thinking. Nice of Deeside to try and cover for his partner, however wrong-headed.'

'Yes,' admitted Mariella. 'Now I don't have to work with them every day, those two don't seem nearly so bad. But you said you had two things to discuss. What was the other?'

'Well,' said Sarah. 'It's just that Letitia really had a grudge against Madeleine Brett-Coates. Apparently the woman was a terrible bully, always making nasty digs. It must have been very hard to live with. If Letitia knew about the will being changed in favour of her and Bernard, that would be a sizeable motive. She'd be getting her revenge, and the money as well.'

'But even if the will hadn't been changed, she and Bernard would have been getting a third of the money,' Mariella said. 'The red fabric is suggestive, but when we tried to measure up the pieces you found against Letty's dress, they weren't a match.'

'That's peculiar,' said Sarah. 'I could have sworn they were silk, too. Unless...' Her voice tailed off and Mariella got to her feet.

'Right, I'd better get on,' the detective said.

'Just a second,' said Sarah, reluctant to let her go just yet. 'I also wondered why you brought those foxgloves into the drawing room just now? It seemed, well, like an odd thing to do... Were you trying to stir things up, get someone to say something unwise?'

Mariella shrugged. 'Maybe this is all making me go a bit loopy. Wouldn't be surprising, would it? My first few weeks in a new job and I land one of the worst murders in the Vanstone area for about five hundred years, and no sooner do I get here than we find another body. I've got the chief constable breathing down my neck, wanting an update every five minutes. I used to think DI Brice was the limit.'

Sarah, who was no fan of Brice, the man in charge of the police force in Merstairs, could only give Mariella a deeply sympathetic smile. 'I'm sorry, it must all be awful. Then again, I suppose you've got a real chance to prove yourself, if you can get this straightened out.'

'That's a big "if", Aunty Sarah. There are clues, all right, but they're pointing all over the place.'

'That brings us back to the foxgloves,' said Sarah shrewdly. 'I know you, Mariella. You weren't showing them to us just for the sake of it. And, as Madeleine Brett-Coates wasn't actually strangled, I have to ask... do you think those flowers play a part in her death?'

TWENTY-FOUR

Mariella looked very seriously at Sarah. 'You know I wouldn't normally bring you in on something like this, don't you?'

Sarah nodded mutely, conscious that a word out of place now could send the detective scurrying back to the safety of protocol and a strict no-civilians policy.

'The thing is, we're under time pressure. The chief wants this wrapped up in the next few days.'

'Is there some deadline coming up?' Sarah asked quietly.

Mariella hesitated. 'Not exactly... To be frank, it's because he's going on holiday and he doesn't want this hanging over him.' She looked at Sarah, and didn't quite roll her eyes, but Sarah certainly got the picture.

'Anything I can do, you only have to ask. You know that,' Sarah said earnestly.

Mariella paused for a moment. 'You've had some experience with poisons,' she said.

They both thought back to recent events in the little town of Merstairs. 'You're asking whether I think Madeleine Brett-Coates was killed that way?' Sarah said, her head on one side. 'I'd certainly say it was likely.'

'It wasn't the bunting that finished her off, that much is clear. I just need to know what else could have done it.'

'Hmm,' said Sarah, thinking hard. 'As you know, every home in the country is filled with substances that can be fatal. Eye drops, oven cleaner, you name it, we have cupboards stuffed full of lethal potions. But you're thinking of something more obvious, aren't you?' she added softly. 'Something that keeps cropping up.'

Both of them now raised their eyes to a photo of the dead woman, hanging close to the bed. Again there were flowers in a vase by her side, including some foxgloves. She really didn't seem to care a jot about her son's phobia.

Sarah wrinkled her brow. 'Surely you'll be getting the toxicology reports back from the lab soon? There won't be much doubt then.'

'In the normal way of things, that would be the case. But there's a problem with the lab.' Mariella squeezed her eyes tight shut, almost as though she was in pain.

'A problem?' Sarah had a brief vision of a shortage of test tubes or a white coat famine.

'Yes. The last batch of tests they did was contaminated. Thank goodness, they weren't connected with this case, but as a result we've been ordered to find another lab to do the processing, and as you know, that can take time.'

'My goodness. Are you serious?' Sarah was stunned.

'Never more so, unfortunately.' Mariella's face was glum.

'How long do you think the delay will be?'

'I don't know... obviously I'm only familiar with the Merstairs lab. There are various other firms that are being checked out. But it's all going to cause a time lag that we really don't need right now... And we have to be extra-careful as any defence team would be able to drive a coach and horses through the chain of custody if the samples hang around too long or get mishandled. That's if we ever catch the perpetrator.'

Sarah had rarely seen Mariella looking so fed up. 'We'll get them, don't you worry,' she said, with more confidence than she felt.

'Let's hope so, or I might break the record for the shortest career ever in the Canterbury police.'

'Is there anything I can do to help on that front?' Sarah asked, pretty sure the answer was going to be no. But to her surprise, Mariella gave her a tired smile.

'I think we're going to have to treat this case in an old-school way, just getting a feel for the culprit and then hopefully forcing a confession. And, let's face it, Aunty Sarah, you're rather good at that,' Mariella said, looking at Sarah frankly.

'Oh,' said Sarah, suddenly feeling the pressure too. It was all very well to bumble along as, she hoped, a talented amateur, getting to the heart of things while the police did the donkey work. It was entirely different to know those in authority were looking to her to sort things out, with no safety net. She swallowed, then squared her shoulders. 'All right then. Let's look at what we've got.'

Sarah stood up, and went over to the photo. 'As you know, foxgloves are extremely toxic. That's every part of the plant – leaves, flowers, seeds, stem, possibly even the roots, I'm not sure. They are used to make drugs that control irregular heartbeat and even heart failure. But as well as treating these conditions, they can provoke them in otherwise healthy patients. There's been a lot of focus on foxgloves so far – Jonathan has his well-known aversion to them – yet they are grown in the hothouses here so they're in full bloom already. He has a degree in botany and presumably knows their qualities. They feature in the portrait downstairs as well, and were found in the tent, under the dead woman. They were in the strange wreath delivered this morning, too. So everything points to Madeleine Brett-Coates dying of digitalin poisoning, and I expect that's the result you were expecting from the post-mortem samples.'

Mariella looked at Sarah intently. 'Yes, absolutely. Hang on, though. From the way you're saying all this, it sounds like there is a big "but" coming. What are you getting at?'

'Just this,' said Sarah, her head on one side. 'Even though Jonathan is the only one with a qualification in the subject, I'd say it's well known that foxgloves are toxic. *But* foxgloves aren't the only poisonous plant in this photo, or in the bouquet found under Madeleine's head.'

'Really? You're kidding,' said Mariella, walking up to the picture and staring at the flowers in the vase. 'What else is there that is as poisonous? Not tulips, surely? Or those pretty daisies?'

'Flowers can be very misleading, can't they?' Sarah said, peering up too. 'Such a pretty arrangement. You'd never know which ones are deadly.'

'You're teasing me now, Sarah. Which is toxic?' Mariella looked at her rather crossly.

'The bluebells,' said Sarah simply. 'They look so innocent, with that beautiful colour and the dainty cloche shape. But they contain glycosides, which can cause vomiting, diarrhoea, slowing of the heartbeat and, ultimately, death.'

'My God,' said Mariella. 'All this time, we've been concentrating on the foxgloves. The SOCOs have gone to town on those hothouses. Meanwhile, there are bluebells everywhere on this estate. They run along the edge of all the perimeter hedges, and they're in the wooded wilderness area... They're in full bloom at the moment. You're telling me they could have just as easily been used to drug Madeleine, and that would have allowed the killer to drape her in bunting?'

'I'm afraid so. There would have been obvious signs that she was suffering the effects of glycoside poisoning – she would have been suffering terrible stomach cramps and would have felt nauseous. And she would have had to have ingested quite a lot of the plants. But there are ways round that, I'm sure. A bluebell bulb is about the same size as a spring onion. If I were you, I would be asking Mrs Bunforth what everyone ate before the fair opened.'

TWENTY-FIVE

Mariella scribbled some notes down in her little book, while Sarah waited patiently. Eventually, the detective looked up, with a 'You still here?' look on her face. 'Maybe you should be back down there with the family? Gathering as much information as you can?' she said.

Sarah accepted the dismissal, then turned back. 'Listen, Mariella, Jonathan has been missing for a while now. Shouldn't everyone be combing the grounds for him?' she said earnestly.

'What makes you think they're not?' Mariella asked.

Sarah nodded towards the window. Outside on the perfect lawn, Tweedledum was sharing a cigarette with one of the Canterbury constables, and laughing uproariously at something that had just been said. Mariella strode over and rapped sharply on the pane, and the two men split up and tried to look extra-busy. The PC peered under the ornate wrought-iron garden furniture, while Dumbarton started prodding a topiary peacock. Mariella shook her head.

'I'll have to go out and bang their heads together in a minute. OK, before we both get on with our tasks, is there anything else you think I should know?'

Sarah thought for a moment. 'Well, nothing you won't have noticed, I'm sure. I'm more and more worried Letitia could be addicted to a drug of some sort. I'm not sure whether Bernard is aware or not. Either that, or her strange state is, um, something else entirely. Helena on the other hand seems to be hitting the bottle quite hard, and both Jonathan and Bernard seem to like a drink too – though that's not perhaps surprising given the stressful situation.'

'Good grief,' said Mariella. 'It sounds like we should get them a block booking at the nearest rehab – the moment we've arrested one of them for murder, that is.'

'I know. It's not what you'd expect, in a wonderful place like this. The worst thing is, I keep thinking I've already seen the answer to it all out of the corner of my eye. Do you ever get that feeling?'

'Not nearly as often as I'd like,' said Mariella. 'Right. I'd better get on.'

With that, the young detective swept out of the room. Sarah was thoughtful. This case was getting more and more complicated by the minute, and she didn't like it at all. She went back to her bedroom and stood by the window, looking out on the police who were now rushing around as busily as ants, searching for a list of items that seemed to be growing by the hour.

Her reverie was interrupted by the sound of the lunch gong. It was such an old-fashioned summons, and suited Coates House, which in many ways seemed straight out of the 1950s. But as soon as you started looking a little deeper, it was clear there were distinctly modern tensions and vices at play. When there were this many secrets beneath the surface, everyone was an unreliable witness. There was one question that was now uppermost in her mind, though. Where was Madeleine Brett-Coates's place in all this? Was she the traditional chatelaine, representing a dying, well-heeled mode of life? Or was she a more sinister figure altogether, whose abuse of her family had led one of them, ultimately, to become a murderer?

Sarah hurried down the stairs and trooped in behind the rest of the gang as they took their seats in the dining room for lunch. Mrs Bunforth and Anna had laid the glistening mahogany table, and the sideboard was heaped with covered dishes of what looked like salads and quiches. Sarah resolved to keep a good lookout for spring onions – or anything resembling them. Though the cook seemed devoted to Madeleine Brett-Coates, she'd had plenty of opportunity to poison her – and could have enticed Geoff down to the basement too. She was certainly an excellent planner – there was a bottle of Chablis lined up with crystal glasses, as well as tea and coffee in Thermos flasks for later. Here was catering on a lavish scale, produced at regular intervals, even with half the local police force on the premises and a murderer on the loose.

Hamish, who'd been lolling in Butler's basket, was thrilled to see Sarah and settled contentedly at her feet. She took a chunky wedge of asparagus and salmon quiche and was looking forward to tucking in.

Daphne sat next to her, and immediately set to work on her own meal. It was a somewhat depleted gathering; Helena and Jonathan were still missing. Letitia was present but looked absent, and only picked at the few leaves she'd plonked on her own lovely porcelain plate. Bernard peered at the others somewhat grudgingly and seemed disinclined to chat.

'Mrs Bunforth has come up with the goods, all right, with this delicious lunch,' Charles said, valiantly trying to get a conversation going.

Letitia completely ignored him, Bernard merely shrugged, and it was left to Daphne and Sarah to murmur polite and inconsequential phrases about the quality of the quiche. All the while, Sarah was thinking. Who would have had reason to wreak such havoc on this family?

'Mrs B's a treasure all right,' said Bernard eventually, after chewing through a mound of lamb's lettuce. 'Shame she'll have to go.'

'What?' said Letitia, turning to him very slowly, her eyes like saucers. 'You can't think I'm going to manage this place without Bunny.'

'Of course not, darling,' Bernard said, with a somewhat insincere smile. 'Heaven forfend that you'd actually have to do some work. No, I mean we're going to sell the place.'

Letitia dropped her knife and fork with a clatter. Even Sarah and Daphne looked at him in surprise.

'I say, old boy!' said Charles. 'The ancestral home, and whatnot? Surely the place has been in the family for...'

'Five hundred years, yes, do you think I don't know that?' Bernard was suddenly looking choleric. 'All this history, bearing down on me every day, the pressure to do as well as my forebear at Culloden fields,' he said, waving an arm at the empty spot where the dagger was normally displayed. 'Well, I'm a modern man. I'm not suited to vanquishing Highlanders. As you can see, even keeping my nearest and dearest in check is beyond me. No, a nice little flat in town, and somewhere in the country maybe... a cottage. Easy to run, cheap to heat, what could be nicer, eh, Letty?'

Letitia, now more alert than Sarah had ever seen her, had her mouth open. 'But I thought you loved all the stuff about your glorious past?'

Bernard looked at her, not unkindly. 'I did. In a way, I still do. But I don't want to be its prisoner any more. Mumsy was the worst, much as I loved her. Always going on about the splendours of yesteryear.' He passed a hand over his forehead. 'I feel as though I've wasted my youth, chasing dreams of my ancestors' glory.'

'Not just your youth,' said Daphne, raising her eyebrows.

'I'm sorry, old chap. Thought you were proud of the heritage.' Charles looked embarrassed. 'But I understand.'

'It's a burden. And the sooner I'm shot of it, the better, frankly,' said Bernard.

Letitia looked stunned. 'I think we could have discussed this, Bernard. I was looking forward to opening the annual fair here, not to mention the Christmas market. I've bought new hats and everything.'

'Well, you can send them right back. If you think I'd ever host another event in the grounds, after what's just happened to Mumsy, you're even crazier than I thought,' Bernard said dismissively.

Letitia threw down her napkin, scraped back her chair, and made for the door, sobbing as she went.

There was a painful silence. Poor Letitia, Sarah couldn't help thinking. She was a strange one, for sure, but she didn't deserve such public humiliation. And Sarah strongly agreed that Bernard should have talked over such a huge decision with her in private, rather than springing it on her in this way. Perhaps this was the kind of treatment that could push a woman to drastic action? All right, the red fabric wasn't from her dress, but Letitia did still have a motive. With Madeleine, her persecutor, out of the way, Bernard would inherit – and Letitia would get a sizeable slice in any divorce settlement if she decided she'd had enough of him. If she'd known about the new will in advance, leaving out everyone but her husband and Mrs Bunforth, her motivation would have been even stronger.

'Come on, everybody, we don't want all this good food going to waste,' said Daphne, trooping up to the sideboard for another piece of quiche.

Sarah looked down at her plate, wishing she could think of something to say that would break the tense silence. Then she stared harder. The pattern on the border of the fine porcelain, which she had admired as being pretty and nothing more, was, she now saw, a little coronet of entwined foxgloves. It seemed a peculiar choice of dinner service, given that Jonathan Brett-Coates had such a problem with the flowers. Maybe it was his mother's way of toughening him up? A way, perhaps, of rubbing his phobia in his face at every mealtime? Or even a not-so-gentle hint from Mrs Bunforth or Anna in the kitchen that they could do away with them all at any moment, just by adding a pinch of something special to their food. That reminded Sarah to check with Mariella on the women's background, as both were well placed to have dosed Madeleine Brett-Coates without arousing suspicion.

Just then, there was a rattle at the door, and Jonathan himself stuck his head round. 'Ah, I hoped lunch would still be on.'

Looking none the worse for his unexplained absence, Jonathan helped himself to a heaped plate and a large glass of Chablis, and sat down. 'What have I missed?' he said nonchalantly.

'Apart from the entire police force searching for you, you mean? I should have known you'd breeze in without a word of apology,' snapped Bernard.

'I'm not sure why I'd have to say sorry to you, I'm not accountable to you unless something has changed drastically,' Jonathan said, forking up his rice salad as though he hadn't eaten for days.

'I'm the head of the family now,' Bernard said reprovingly.

'Oh, get lost with all that,' Jonathan said, hunkering down over his lunch and swigging back his wine. 'As soon as I get my share of the dosh I'll be out of your hair.'

Charles, Sarah and Daphne looked at each other.

'Ah,' said Bernard slowly. 'That reminds me. You didn't show up earlier for the will reading. And I dare say you haven't been checking your messages, either.'

'Excuse me if I haven't been glued to my phone. I'm grieving. I was with Geoff's parents down the road in Deal, if you must know. I thought they deserved to hear about... what happened... from me. They're devastated. We said some prayers together. It helped.'

'I didn't know you were religious these days,' said Bernard.

'I'm not, generally speaking. But as you know, Geoff was quite devout. It's one of the many reasons he loved this place. There used to be a chapel in the grounds here, you know,' Jonathan explained to Sarah and Daphne.

'Oh really? I didn't realise that,' Sarah said.

'No reason why you should. It was deconsecrated in Grandfather's lifetime. Mumsy didn't bother to restore it and it ended up being demolished. Sad.'

'I wonder whether they'll rebuild it, when the place is sold,' said Daphne, finishing the last of her salad.

'Sold? Oh, I think you've got something wrong there. This place will never go on the market,' Jonathan said with a confident smile.

There was another charged silence. 'What? What did I say?' Jonathan looked around the table, baffled, then turned to his plate.

Bernard cleared his throat. 'Jonty, if I could have a word? In the study? Right now,' he said gruffly.

'I'm eating,' Jonathan said, head down.

'Jonathan! Now,' said Bernard, threat in his voice.

'Oh, for goodness' sake.' Jonathan threw down his napkin and followed Bernard out of the room.

'I wonder how he's going to take the news?' Daphne raised her eyebrows.

They heard shouting from next door, then a terrifying thud and, finally, an awful scream and a door slamming almost off its hinges.

'I think that rather answers your question,' said Sarah, as they all got to their feet and ran out.

TWENTY-SIX

Sarah reached Madeleine Brett-Coates's study just in time to see Jonathan disappearing upstairs. There was a groan from behind the door. She opened it cautiously. Bernard was sprawled on the floor.

'Oh my goodness,' said Sarah, rushing forward. There was a cut along his cheek, and it was oozing blood. 'Daphne, could you get a couple of napkins from the dining room, please? And the jug of water.'

'No need for all this fuss,' said Bernard, his hand clasped to the side of his face as Daphne scurried out. On the floor was the large bust of Napoleon that had stood on Madeleine Brett-Coates's imposing desk, clearly the cause of the injury.

'Just lie still,' Sarah said, but Bernard struggled to his feet, then swayed in place.

'Here, old boy, sit yourself down,' said Charles, helping him to the large, padded chair behind the desk.

'Oh, that's better,' said Bernard, looking pale and shaken.

Daphne came in with the napkins and Sarah soaked one in water from the jug and attempted to clean up the wound, but Bernard pushed her away. 'I'm fine, I tell you.'

There was a muffled shriek from the stairs, then Letitia hurtled in. 'Bernie!' She rushed to his side. 'Jonty pushed me. He can be so rude. Did he do this? You must do as the doctor woman tells you.' She looked distraught, and firmly back in loving wifey mode.

'As if you ever take a blind bit of notice of medical advice,' grumbled Bernard, but he let Sarah take a closer look at his head.

'I don't think you'll need stitches,' said Sarah. 'Just put some ice on it for now and take paracetamol if it's throbbing. You'll have a fine bruise by the morning. What brought all this on?'

'Don't pretend you don't know. There are no secrets in this house any more, not with all these eyes and ears on our every move,' said Bernard bitterly.

'Well, you did ask us to hang around, old boy,' said Charles.

'I expect Jonty didn't like being left out of the will,' said Letitia. 'Getting nothing, while Bunny pockets ten grand. Now he'll have to stand on his own two feet at last.'

'Not difficult, surely?' said Daphne. 'After all, he's a telly star. He must be making tons from that.'

'I think Geoff had expensive tastes.' Letitia shrugged, as though that wasn't a problem she suffered from.

'The thing is, Jonty's had a shock. Not surprising he'd lash out, I suppose,' said Charles. 'But he could have brained his brother with that statuette.'

'Yes indeed,' said Sarah. 'Bernard, you were very lucky. It's quite a weight; solid marble. In fact, I'm only surprised it didn't do more damage.'

'I'm going upstairs to lie down,' said Bernard weakly.

'Oh, could you go with him, Letitia? It's not a great idea to sleep straight after a head injury. Just in case,' Sarah said quickly.

'I suppose so.' Letitia followed Bernard out of the room, not looking particularly enthusiastic about being pressed into service. Once again, Sarah wondered what lay behind her changeable nature.

'You don't think Bernard should get checked out at the hospital?' Charles asked.

'I think he'll be OK. His pupils are not dilated, he didn't lose consciousness or seem disorientated, he can speak normally. I think he's got off lightly,' she frowned.

'Jonathan was out of order, doing something like that. Goodness knows where he's hared off to now,' Charles said.

'Well, he was heading for the bedrooms. I wonder if it's worth seeing what he's up to? And trying to have a word with Helena, too. After all, we're supposed to be gathering as much information as we can,' said Sarah.

'Disturbing them in their bedrooms is a bit much, Sarah,' said Daphne. 'Poor things, they're all dealing with a lot – poverty, the deaths. Let's give them a break.'

'I suppose you're right,' sighed Sarah. 'It might be a bit unseemly. Though if Geoff was running through Jonathan's earnings, we should consider whether that gives Jonathan a motive. Sounds like he'll be better off without his husband around – particularly if the man was stealing from the family.' She thought for a moment. 'Actually, I ought to take Hamish out. He could definitely do with an airing. And Butler, too. He's a good old boy. I'm pleased the pair of them are getting on so well.'

'A lot better than any of the humans,' said Daphne. 'Well, apart from us. Come on, then. Let's go for a walk.'

'Yes, and we can see if there's anything else to find in the gardens. According to Mariella, that red fabric didn't come from Letitia's dress after all, so let's keep our eyes peeled and see if we can find any more of it.'

'It's not Letty's? Really? It looks the same colour.' Daphne seemed doubtful.

'If it's who I think it was, it's surprising they were out in the gardens,' said Sarah.

'What do you mean?' asked Daphne with a frown.

'Well, can you think of anyone else around, apart from the family, who's consistently been wearing red?'

TWENTY-SEVEN

There was still a SOCO team at the site of the fateful marquee, and there were police vehicles drawn up on the gravel circle outside the house, but otherwise there was little outward sign of anything amiss at Coates House. Its mellow, creamy stone glowed in the spring sunlight, and the sweeping cedar trees bowed low over the lawn as they had done for a century. The path to the formal gardens beyond seemed to beckon them.

Sarah felt as though she could breathe easily for the first time in ages, away from the increasingly oppressive house. Hamish obviously felt the same, zooming here and there, enjoying being off the lead and inspecting all the hillocks and tufts with admirable thoroughness.

'Have you ever seen the folly, Daphne?' Charles asked as they wandered along.

'No, never,' said Daphne. 'I've only been here for the fair, not as an honoured guest, like you. There are usually signs everywhere telling people to keep out.'

'Oh, well, let's take advantage of this moment. It's magnificent, though a bit dilapidated. The trees have grown up around it so you can't see anything until you're almost upon it,' said Charles.

'You'd think the family had enough space, with that huge house. Why on earth did they need a folly as well?' Daphne crinkled her nose.

'Maybe it was just a way of showing off their wealth,' Sarah said as they strolled along. 'A slightly pointless building must have been quite a status symbol in those days.'

There didn't seem to be any more snippets of red. But as they got closer to the low hedge where they'd been found, they met Peabody and two policemen walking the other way, swinging an evidence bag.

'What's in that?' Daphne asked, turning round to stare.

'It looks like... yes, it's a syringe,' said Charles.

'Goodness me. Drugs, I suppose,' said Daphne in shocked tones.

'Interesting that Peabody seems to have found it,' Sarah noted thoughtfully. The gardener, after all, must have plenty of plant lore at his fingertips. Even if he hadn't been involved with Madeleine, he had a link with Jonathan. They'd argued earlier, and had gone off into the gardens together. On the other hand, Peabody wasn't mentioned in the will, and Jonathan didn't benefit from his mother's death either. In fact, he'd been impoverished by it... though he hadn't known that beforehand. Oh, her head was spinning now. 'I'm surprised there's any kind of drug problem so far out of London,' she said, keen to take her mind off the suspects for a minute.

'It's all this county lines stuff you hear about these days, I expect,' said Charles.

'There's an alternative, of course. That syringe could have been used by Helena or Letitia. Letitia often seems pretty out of it, and Helena has been very open about going to various rehabs. There's a third possibility, too.'

'I dread to ask... but go on, do tell,' said Daphne.

'Well, whatever was used to subdue Madeleine Brett-Coates could have been administered by syringe, before someone threw all that awful bunting over her.'

'Ugh. That's given me the shivers,' said Daphne. 'Come on, let's get a bit further from the house, the place is beginning to give me the creeps.'

They were now entering the woods. Hamish bounced along, flattening a carpet of bluebells without a second thought, and for once Sarah didn't call him off. She couldn't help looking askance at the flowers. They appeared so innocent, their intense blue popping against the murky green background. Yet they could easily have been used to poison Madeleine Brett-Coates. Sprinkling the chopped-up bulbs over a salad would have been an easier way to administer the glycoside than via syringe. She wondered if Mariella had had a chance to check the fair day menu with Mrs Bunforth yet.

As they wound their way deeper into the woods, where it was dark and quiet, they saw pale patches of mushrooms poking their way through the soil. Every now and then the undergrowth rustled, as though small creatures were watching from afar. Then through the branches Sarah spotted the distinctive terracotta colour of brickwork. 'Look! That must be it,' she said, pointing ahead.

'Yes. It's surprising how close you can get without seeing it,' said Charles, pushing aside a branch, which swung back and nearly knocked little Hamish over. 'Sorry, boy,' he said.

'I'll pick him up,' said Sarah, bundling the dog into her arms. 'There are loads of nettles here. I'm not sure if they sting dogs but let's not take the chance.'

'Look,' said Daphne, pausing a few steps ahead. 'Lots of these weeds have been flattened, over here and, yes, there.'

Sarah stopped and took stock. They had walked through the thick of the forest, and were now in a small clearing. The folly was ahead of them, visible suddenly in all its rather mad nineteenth-century glory. It had a circular tower, rising up to a mass of red-brick crenelations and turrets.

'Gosh, it's quite a creation,' Sarah said, craning to take the whole thing in. It was like the castle in 'Sleeping Beauty'. But instead of lying undisturbed for a century, someone had waded through these lush banks of greenery very recently. The sharp scent of crushed leaves lingered in the air.

Sarah was beginning to get a bad feeling about this. First the bluebells, which now seemed so sinister. And then the folly, which should have lain peacefully neglected. Who had been traipsing around here – and to what purpose?

Daphne, having paused for a moment, went galumphing on through the nettles. Luckily her leopard-print harem pants covered her from ankle to waist, so she was undeterred. But Sarah couldn't let her go a step further.

'Daphne, no! We have to ring Mariella. Stop where you are.'

'Yes, listen to Sarah,' Charles chimed in.

'What? Why?' said Daphne, turning round and gaping at them. 'It's only nettles, it's really not a police matter.'

Sarah wasn't so sure. 'Mari's on the premises, Daph. She won't mind coming over. If this place hasn't been searched by the police yet, well, it probably should be, don't you think? Anyone could have used it, maybe stored things in it...'

Daphne gasped and took a huge step back, almost tripping on a tree root. 'You think the murderer has been here, don't you?' she said, looking over her shoulder comically as though a sinister shape was about to loom up and overpower her at any second.

'It's just a possibility,' Sarah said, trying to allay her friend's growing panic. 'But we don't want to take any chances,' she said in jolly tones.

'I know what it means when you use that voice,' Daphne said. 'You think there's something terrible going on in there. Just admit it! Is it another... another, *you know what*? Tell me it isn't!'

Sarah put Hamish down and took her friend firmly by the arm. 'Listen, I just think it might be useful for the police to check the place for, er, fingerprints. Anything they find could make a difference.'

While they were talking, Sarah and Charles were leading Daphne quickly back through the woods, retracing their steps until they came out on the wide lawns flanking the beautiful old house. Hamish bounded off across the grass, and Sarah saw, to her relief, that he'd spotted Mariella. That was going to save her a phone call.

'I tell you what, Daph, perhaps you and Charles could take Hamish and ask Mrs Bunforth to get some teas and coffees going? Maybe even a cake... It's not long after lunch, but people might be peckish. What do you think?'

'Yes. Yes of course,' said Daphne, taking a deep breath. 'You're right. That will keep me nicely occupied. And it will distract everybody else, too. Giving you and Mari time to go and discover the body in the folly.'

TWENTY-EIGHT

Sarah had told Daphne firmly that a corpse was the last thing she was expecting to find in the Coates folly – but when she and Mariella fought their way back through the last few clumps of nettles, she was feeling a little flustered, and it wasn't just from the exertion.

'I've taken photos of the pathway through these weeds, so the SOCOs will have something to go on if we do... if there is...' said Mariella, not bothering to finish her sentence. 'They'll be along in a minute or two.'

'Should we wait for them before we go in?' asked Sarah, rather hoping the answer might be yes. She'd been very matter-of-fact with Daphne, but she thought the chances were very high that there was something quite nasty lurking in the old building. 'I wonder if it's even structurally safe?'

Mariella gave her a quizzical look. 'You can stay out here if you wish, Aunty Sarah. But if you do come in, for once in your life, you can put on gloves and shoe protectors. Here you go,' she said, handing Sarah two sets of flimsy blue covers.

With her feet now whispering at every step, Sarah followed Mariella through the old oak door. It had been intricately carved with patterns of flowers, now sadly decaying after years of neglect. Her fingers in their thin latex gloves traced the design of bluebells and roses as she stepped over the threshold into a dim, musty interior.

Once inside, she was in a perfectly round room with a fireplace at one end and a wrought-iron spiral staircase at the other. She didn't want to think about what might be up those stairs. Helena, that haughty, beautiful woman, had been missing from the house for hours now. And what about Jonathan? He seemed to flounce off whenever he felt like it. Was this where he hid out?

Those swathes cut through the nettles had shown one thing clearly – someone had trampled their way through here today. There were marks on the dusty floor, too, and parallel lines scored through the dirt and leaves. Sarah wasn't a betting woman, but she'd have put all her money on those tracks having been made by a pair of inert feet being yanked along in the wake of a very determined, and seriously dangerous, person unknown.

'I suppose there's nothing for it,' said Sarah, gazing up at the spiral staircase.

Mariella, standing close by, shrugged slightly and grasped the metal bannister. 'Don't worry,' she said, somewhat unconvincingly. 'These things are never as bad as they seem.'

Sarah thought back over a few recent incidents where she'd stumbled upon things that were much worse than she could have imagined. But it was hardly the time to say so. She planted a foot on the metal step and trudged after Mariella.

Once at the top, she was relieved to see nothing but another dusty room, with narrow windows and rich swags of spiders' webs providing a sinister echo of yesterday's bunting. But, oh no, there were the familiar drag marks and smudged tracks again, leading to a second spiral staircase.

'I didn't realise there were two upper floors,' said Sarah worriedly, a little out of breath after the first climb.

'Nor me,' said Mariella, not puffed at all but looking at Sarah with concern. 'Are you sure you're all right to go on up?'

'Oh, absolutely,' said Sarah with an enthusiasm she certainly wasn't feeling. Who in their right mind would want to progress further up rickety stairs into a creepy, deserted building which might, just might, still contain a double murderer and their latest victim? But she plastered on a smile which she hoped suggested she'd been looking forward to this, if not all her life, then at least a decent portion of it. 'I've been meaning to ask you,' she puffed. 'Did you sort out what the menu was for the family's lunch before the fair opened? That seems the most likely time for the poison to have been administered to Madeleine.'

'Right. Yes, I made some enquiries,' Mariella said, hurrying on. 'Let's talk about it as we're going up. We shouldn't waste a second,' she said, making for the next handrail. 'Take care here, this feels a bit shakier than the last.'

Excellent, thought Sarah drily to herself. 'No problem,' she said, following in Mariella's wake as the detective made her way up the stairs.

'They ate chicken with mushroom sauce, potato salad and green beans. Fresh fruit and cream for pudding. And before you ask, yes, there were spring onions in the potato salad.'

'I see. The kitchen staff presumably deny having anything to do with it?' Sarah said, trudging upwards.

'However did you guess?'

'And sprinkling bluebell bulbs on Madeleine's portion would have been the easiest way to dose her up with glycosides,' said Sarah thoughtfully. 'I suppose you're checking into Mrs Bunforth's background? And Anna's?'

'Of course,' said Mariella. 'Mrs Bunforth's been at the house for ages, but Anna only came a couple of years ago.' She reached the top, and steadied herself. Then she gave a sudden gasp and dashed forward.

Sarah, coming out onto the second floor, still holding the handrail, saw immediately what had shocked Mariella. There was someone lying spreadeagled on the filthy floor. Instinctively she ran towards the body, her feet in their slippery forensic covers skidding on the dust and dirt.

She got down on her knees and stared. It was Mrs Bunforth, the housekeeper, looking paler than death. She reached out a hand.

Mariella immediately moved to try and block her. 'Sarah! You know not to touch.'

'Yes, but she's still alive, Mari,' Sarah said urgently, and pointed to the woman's chest. As they watched, it moved slightly. 'Get on the phone, we'll need help getting her out of here.' Sarah grabbed the woman's wrist. The pulse was faint, but unmistakable.

'Do you know what's wrong with her?' Mariella said, grabbing her phone and dialling.

Sarah moved to hover over the woman's face, brushing away her hair very gently. The eyes were heavy-lidded, the face as pale as death. She sniffed. 'I think it's a type of poison, maybe,' she said.

'Drat it,' said Mariella, looking at her phone in disgust. 'There's no signal here. I'll have to go outside and see if I can call from there. Will you be OK?'

There was no other answer to that question but yes, so Sarah nodded briefly, bending back to her charge as Mariella trampled down the stairs at top speed, the old metal clanging with every footstep. Then Sarah was alone in the tower, the sound of Mariella crashing through the nettles fading away. This woman's fate was entirely in her hands.

TWENTY-NINE

Sarah cursed the gaps in her medical training. Seven years, and yet they'd spent so little time on toxins. She watched poor Mrs Bunforth. Each breath seemed a little more laboured than the last, while the pulse under her fingers was getting harder and harder to detect. She took off her cardigan and tucked it over the woman's thin shoulders. If the housekeeper had been in better shape, Sarah would have tried to get her to vomit, in the hope it would purge her system of whatever she had taken. But she was in no condition for that. It was awful feeling so helpless. Sarah cast around, but there was nothing in this godforsaken tower that would be the least use in stabilising the woman's condition. Her life depended on Sarah holding her nerve – and Mariella getting help in time.

The sunlight coming through the narrow windows seemed to change in quality, then rain began to drum against the old window panes. Sarah felt hope starting to ebb away. Mrs Bunforth's pulse was barely perceptible. Her chest was hardly rising.

'Come on, hang on in there. Help is on its way,' Sarah said desperately to the inert woman. Just then, she thought she heard something – a muffled shout, a twig snapping. Was this salvation, someone lost in the woods – or something more sinister?

Sarah waited on tenterhooks. Then there came the steady, purposeful sound of people wading through the nettles, and the brief static of a walkie-talkie springing to life. Thank God!

What seemed like a few moments later, the still, grim scene in the turret room was replaced by action and purpose, as two paramedics clambered up both flights of stairs with a stretcher and a portable drip. A frail-looking Mrs Bunforth was covered in a blanket, strapped to the back board, had an IV line inserted to give her fluids, and was declared stable enough to move. Sarah almost wept with relief.

'You kept her alive. Well done,' said one of the paramedics as they retreated carefully, manoeuvring the stretcher down the narrow stairway with difficulty. Sarah followed, feeling she didn't deserve the thanks at all. What had she done but watch and cross her fingers? But at least Mrs Bunforth hadn't been alone.

She stumbled down the rungs of the old staircase, the fast descent making her dizzy, until they reached the ground floor. Then they were out again in the green world of the forest. Mariella was waiting and Sarah collapsed into a hug for a second, drawing strength from the detective's comforting pat and then pulling herself together.

'Thank goodness. Is she going to be all right?' Mariella asked her.

'Long term? Quite honestly, I couldn't say. It will depend on what she's taken, and when. But she's still alive and they've got her stable.'

'"What she's taken"? Do you actually think it's possible she's done this herself?' Mariella frowned.

Sarah frowned. 'It was just a turn of phrase – but are you

thinking she killed Madeleine and Geoff, and then felt remorse? That would be tidy, at least.'

'Yes...' Mariella sounded a little doubtful. 'Maybe too neat. Has anyone suggested a motive for her?'

'Well, if she knew ten thousand pounds was coming her way, that would be a strong incentive. I'm not sure why she would have killed Geoff, though. And in such a cruel way, too.'

'We've had the results back from his post-mortem, now, and they show no toxic substances in his system. It was a heart attack,' Mariella said.

'So he really did just die of panic. How horrific,' said Sarah.

'Perhaps he saw Mrs Bunforth do something to Madeleine – administer the bluebells to her food, for example. So then he had to be got out of the way,' Mariella suggested.

'Mrs Bunforth would constantly be serving food and drinks to Madeleine. I'm not sure how anyone could have told accurately whether there was poison in them or not.' Sarah was unconvinced.

'Hmm,' said Mariella, unwilling to let it drop. 'Maybe it was the *way* she served something.'

'With a sinister cackle, you mean?' Sarah said drily. 'And if she is our murderer, then who's done this to her?'

'Let's think,' said Mariella. 'Is there anyone who'd want to kill her?'

'It's hard to imagine any of the children doing it. They depend on her entirely. I doubt the three of them working together could assemble a decent sandwich to save their lives. I think they see her as a useful appliance, rather than a human being. I'm not sure they care about her enough to kill her, if you see what I mean. Maybe we should be asking who she'll be leaving her legacy to? Someone could be after that,' said Sarah.

'Hmm,' said Mariella. 'Yet another thing to check up on. OK, I'll add it to the list.'

'Oh, and by the way, we saw the policemen with the syringe

when we were on our way to the folly. Presumably that's getting tested? It could have been used to administer something to Madeleine – or to Mrs Bunforth.'

'We're on it,' said Mariella. 'Let's hope we get some results soon.'

Sarah patted her shoulder consolingly. 'It's a lot, I know. Listen, I could do with getting back to the house. I'm filthy and I'd like to make sure Hamish is OK.'

'Of course, Aunty Sarah. Listen, I don't mind you discussing things with Charles and Mum, but don't say a word about what's happened here to the family, will you?'

'I'll keep quiet about it, don't worry. Are you trying to see if anyone gives themselves away by knowing too much?' Sarah asked.

Mariella shrugged. 'Well yes, I suppose so. At this point, any little crumb of a clue would be handy. We don't have many advantages over whoever's doing this, so we need to maximise the few we have. If anyone does seem to have the slightest inkling of what's happened to Mrs Bunforth, I'm relying on you to note it.'

'OK, but I'm going to have to sort myself out first,' said Sarah, pulling a piece of foliage out of her hair.

'You do look as though you've been through a hedge backwards,' Mariella said, her concerned expression taking the sting out of the comment.

When they finally made it out of the woods and back onto the wide expanse of lawn, the ambulance was long gone. Sarah hoped all was going well inside it. A black speck hurtling towards her resolved itself as Hamish, as thrilled to see his mistress as though they'd been parted for years. Daphne wasn't far behind.

'Thank goodness you're all right!' she said, panting and holding her side. 'I was so worried when I saw the ambulance. No one would tell us anything. Charles is beside himself.'

Charles, who'd been sunning himself in a deckchair, threw down his paper and ran across the lawn towards them the moment he caught sight of her.

'You're all right,' he said, embracing her while Hamish jumped up to try and make it a group hug.

'You're all very sweet,' Sarah said, slightly breathlessly as she disengaged herself from the huddle. 'But it's Mrs Bunforth we should be worrying about.'

'You're joking!' said Daphne. 'It was Bunny in that ambulance? That's so awful. The poor, poor woman.'

'I know. Thank goodness we went to the folly. If we hadn't... Well, let's hope we weren't too late,' said Sarah.

'Who could have harmed her? I would have said all the Brett-Coates kids adore her.' Daphne looked shocked.

'That might be a bit strong, Daph. As far as I could see, everyone treated her like part of the furniture.'

'Isn't that the highest praise, for a servant, um, I mean a member of staff?' said Charles. 'She's one of the family.'

'Well, this particular family seems hellbent on killing its members off,' said Sarah wryly.

Daphne raised a hand to her mouth in horror as a thought struck her. 'What about dinner tonight? What on earth are we going to do then?'

'I'm sure we'll manage, Daph,' said Sarah. 'We must be careful not to mention any of this in front of the family, though. Mariella is hoping someone will give themselves away.'

'Of course,' said Daphne. 'This is all so dreadful.' Then she looked up. 'It's no good if everyone gets hungry on top of being anxious and upset, though. So I might go and see what's what in the kitchen, and ask Anna if she needs any help. I could even put something together for tea this afternoon.'

'Great idea,' said Sarah. 'We'll give her a hand, and then gather everyone together to eat. It will be a good way of asking everyone what they've been up to today.'

'Checking everyone's alibis. I see. Very clever,' said Charles. 'Hopefully someone will crack.' But then his face fell. 'Not a game, though, is it? In fact, it's an awful business. Friends I've known since childhood. What on earth makes people go to pieces like this, and do such dreadful things?'

'Money, usually,' said Daphne succinctly. 'Will you take Hamish, Charles? We can't really have him in the kitchen.'

Hamish, feeling slightly affronted, was mollified only when Charles proposed another nice walkies all around the grounds. 'You never know, I might find a new clue,' Charles said, giving the ladies a mock salute as he walked off with the little dog in tow.

'That's got the boys out of the way. Now you can tell me what you really think,' said Daphne, taking Sarah's arm as they marched towards the kitchen.

'It's just as I said,' Sarah replied. 'We've got a jumble of clues. They're all tangled up, just like the bunting round Madeleine's neck. Even that was a ruse, since she wasn't even strangled – sorry, Daph. But it's a question of sorting out what's real, and what's been thrown in to put us off the scent.'

They were now at the kitchen door, and Sarah paused before turning the brass knob. 'I think this might be our most difficult case yet, you know, Daph.'

As soon as she saw the state of the kitchen, she realised just how right she was.

THIRTY

Flour and pasta were heaped all over the floor, and broken china had flown everywhere, as though plates had been hurled around the room. Food was spilling out of the fridge, and, a sight that made Daphne cry out in pain, an entire sponge cake had been thrown into the fireplace.

'Oh my goodness! This is such a tragedy,' Daphne said, scampering up and down and causing clouds of flour to fly this way and that.

'Careful, it's also a crime scene,' Sarah said, grabbing Daphne as she ran past. 'Plus you're going to make me sneeze,' she said, rummaging in her pockets for a tissue. 'We'd better go back outside and flag down one of the constables and let them know what's happened... but let's have a quick look around first. There's plenty here that can be salvaged.'

'But not that cake!' said Daphne, pointing to the cream and jam oozing out onto the logs in the fireplace.

'Maybe not that. Honestly, I feel you're more upset about this than you were about the murders. Or me finding Mrs Bunforth.'

'What an awful thing to say, Sarah,' said Daphne, absent-mindedly picking up a spoon and scooping up some jam from a pool on the table.

'Don't touch anything!' Sarah said sharply. 'And be careful with that jam. It could have glass in it, if the jar has been broken,' she added.

Daphne threw her spoon into the sink with a clatter. 'We're going to need a hand clearing this lot up when the police have finished with it. Where on earth is Anna?'

'Good question,' said Sarah, frowning. Then she spotted something else on the table. It was a white envelope, now sprinkled with wholemeal flour and what looked like cooking oil. It said 'The Family' on it in rather crooked lettering.

Using a tea towel, Sarah picked it up. 'We need to give this to Mariella,' she said. 'I'm dying to see what it says, aren't you?'

'Ooh, we really shouldn't open it, should we?' said Daphne, coming over and standing close to Sarah. They both stared at the envelope. Sarah turned it over. Here and there, the oil splashes had made the paper transparent.

'Can you read that writing, Daph?' Sarah asked, squinting.

Daphne held the envelope in its towel about a foot away from her nose. '"I hereby give my notice",' Daphne read out. 'Oh my goodness! Did Mrs B write this and then try and kill herself, do you think?'

'It doesn't look like her writing, you can see it in that recipe book,' Sarah said, pointing to a handwritten folder thrown on the table. 'I think this must be from Anna.'

Daphne sighed. 'Well, it explains why she's not here. We're on our own with all the cooking, then. Gosh, this is pretty serious. Do you think she trashed the place as her last act?'

'I think she'd just had enough of the atmosphere. Who can blame her? And with Mrs Bunforth gone, she'd have to work morning, noon and night from now on.' Sarah was thoughtful. 'I think whoever put Mrs Bunforth in the tower made all this mess. Thank goodness, there's Mariella.'

The detective was passing the kitchen window, deep in conversation with one of the constables. Sarah walked over, scooting round the mounds of spoilt food, and hailed her. Mariella poked her head round the kitchen door.

'Look at all this! Do you need to get the SOCO team in here?' Sarah asked. 'And here's a resignation letter – from Anna, it looks like.'

'Believe it or not, the SOCOs have already been and gone. Thanks for this,' Mariella added, putting the letter in an evidence sachet. 'No news from the hospital yet, but I'll keep you posted. Don't forget – not a word to the rest, mind.'

'Of course,' said Sarah, watching her go and then sighing. 'Well, I suppose it's down to us to sort this out, then. You scout around for a dustpan and brush, and I'll see what's in the larder.'

'Where do you think the cleaning stuff is kept?' Daphne stood in the centre of the kitchen looking a bit overwhelmed.

Sarah glanced around and spied a built-in cupboard. 'There,' she pointed. 'Try that. Looks big enough to have a hoover in it, which would be great.'

Daphne crunched over the dropped pasta, crushing myriad shells and fusilli shapes into oblivion, and flung open the cupboard door. Immediately, Butler the ancient Labrador flopped out. Sarah rushed forward.

'Oh my goodness, you poor old boy,' she said, looking into his eyes and feeling around his neck. The dog quickly perked up and started wagging his tail. 'I think he's fine, just a bit surprised. Let's let him out of the back door for some fresh air.'

'Who could lock up a sweetie like this?' fumed Daphne. 'There's someone totally evil in this house, that's for sure. Imagine being so cruel to an old dog.'

Sarah patted Daphne on the shoulder, seeing the tears in her eyes. She was sniffing a bit herself at the thought of it. But Butler seemed to be getting over his ordeal by the second, looking from one woman to the other as if to assess which was more likely to provide snacks and/or a nice stroll.

'Come on, boy. Off you go with Daphne. Charles is already walking Hamish. Butler can tag along. And a turn around the grounds will take your mind off things, too.'

'All right. That leaves you with a lot of clearing up, though.'

'Not to worry,' said Sarah. 'Someone had a high old time chucking stuff around, but it won't take me too long to get things shipshape. I'll give the supper some more thought, and see what we've got in terms of tea while I'm at it.'

Daphne disappeared off with the elderly Lab in tow, and Sarah rolled her sleeves up. Whoever was doing this to the folks at Coates House was determined to make life as difficult as possible. Well, it was her job to make sure they didn't succeed.

* * *

Sarah quite enjoyed banging the highly polished brass gong for tea. She had made a few rounds of sandwiches, dug out some chocolate biscuits and brewed tea and coffee. It probably wasn't a patch on the ruined sponge cake, but it would just have to do. All the goodies from the judging tent would be long gone, if she knew Tweedledum and Tweedledee. Supper was still to be decided. One of the PCs had ambled along when Sarah was rushing around getting out the plates, and confirmed that they'd traced Anna's phone and were sending someone to interview her. At least the girl had made it out of the house alive. It had been one of Sarah's many worries.

The last 'bong' had hardly died away when Daphne and Charles turned up at the dining room door with the two dogs in tow. Sarah gave both pooches their regulation share of love and pats, and settled them at the far end of the table. Then Charles and Daphne took their seats, looking hungrily at the neatly laid out treats and twiddling their thumbs.

Helena appeared first. Sarah was surprised; she'd assumed the woman had taken to her quarters for the duration, but she looked all the better for a rest, in a dramatic pea-green linen top with navy silk trousers. Her raven hair looked as though it had been freshly ironed. She had a thin navy cardigan over her shoulders. She shivered as she sat down and pulled it on – not before Sarah had seen a fresh scratch snaking across her forearm.

'That looks nasty,' she said mildly. 'Would you like some antiseptic on it?'

'This? Oh no, it's nothing,' said Helena, apparently unruffled but giving Sarah a hard stare when she thought she wasn't being watched.

Sarah, her mind drawn irresistibly back to the tangle of brambles and nettles around the folly, pushed the sandwiches towards Helena. 'Do help yourself.'

Helena looked askance at the plate. 'I never eat at this time of day. I'll just have a cup of tea. Who prepared those awful doorstops?'

'Well, I did, actually,' Sarah admitted.

'Why on earth? Haven't you got enough to do, snooping around?' said Helena, shoving the sandwiches at Daphne.

'Just thought I'd help out,' said Sarah, with a neutral smile and a warning look at Daphne not to let on about Mrs Bunforth's fate. Did Helena know what had happened at the folly?

'Hmm,' said Helena, letting it go. What the servants got up to was obviously far beneath her notice. 'Where are Letty and Bernard? Not having another domestic, I hope.'

Sarah's ears couldn't help pricking up. 'Haven't they been getting on?'

'I shan't provide you with any more gossip to feed to those plods,' said Helena.

'Well, without those "plods", as you call them, we'll never

find out what happened to your mother and brother-in-law, will we?' Sarah replied.

'I thought the whole point of having you lot around – sorry, Charles, I'm not including you in this, of course – was that you were somehow better than the local constabulary,' Helena said, now looking disappointedly at her empty teacup. 'Do I have to die of thirst?'

'Oh, I'll, er, be mother, shall I?' said Charles, scraping his chair back and taking her cup and saucer over to the sideboard.

Daphne, who'd been tucking in happily, looked up. 'Excellent sandwiches, Sarah,' she said with a wink. 'I expect you want this to be over as soon as possible, Hells. If you like, I could organise a séance for you, and your mother can tell you what happened herself.'

Helena opened her mouth to reply to this generous offer, when, luckily, the door flew open and Letitia stood there, looking as though she was about to faint.

'Are you OK?' Sarah asked, rising from her seat. 'Here, sit down.'

Letitia swayed, then said bravely, 'No, no, I'm fine. Just a bit weak. I've only just heard... about Bunny.'

Sarah immediately cursed whoever had let this information slip. Mariella had been adamant that the incident in the tower should be kept from the family for as long as possible. Unless Letitia knew... because she was the culprit?

'Yes, Mrs Bunforth made these biscuits, they're absolutely delicious,' she said quickly, hoping Helena wouldn't twig.

'Wait a minute,' said Helena, her green eyes gleaming with annoyance. 'I knew there was a reason you'd made those awful sandwiches. What's happened to Bunny?'

'Haven't you heard?' Letitia said faintly, sliding into her chair and putting her head in her hands. 'She's dead too.'

THIRTY-ONE

'Good grief!' said Helena, stretching her eyes wide. 'You can't be serious?'

Sarah wasn't sure whether Helena was putting on an act or not, but finding out how Letitia knew had to take precedence. 'Did someone tell you that?' she asked the younger woman.

Letitia's large, vacant eyes rested on her for a moment. 'No. But I saw the ambulance go off with her in it.' She shrugged. 'Of course she's dead.'

Sarah relaxed a little. Letitia was just guessing. There was still the possibility Mrs Bunforth might recover. She felt personally responsible for her survival, having spent those dreadful minutes alone with her in the folly.

'Well, let's hope that's not the case,' she said. 'Now then, everyone, we need to keep our strength up, so do eat. Have a sandwich,' she said, plonking one on Letitia's plate.

'For goodness' sake,' wailed Letitia. 'This is bread! Do I look like I eat carbs?'

Sarah did her level best not to tut, but Daphne was more forthright.

'Oh honestly, Letty, one won't hurt you. A stiff breeze could blow you away, the size you are at the moment.'

'Well, that's better than...' Letitia began, then thought better of it and nibbled the edge of the sandwich carefully. 'Mm. Actually, this is rather nice,' she said. 'I suppose I do need some energy. Just to support Bernie, you know.'

'Exactly,' said Sarah. 'Helena, a biscuit for you?'

Helena was a tougher nut to crack. She gave Sarah a withering look. 'Do shut up about food. What exactly has happened to poor Bunny? If you outsiders know, then I demand to be told.'

The door opened again, and Bernard appeared, with such large bags under his eyes that they were nearly a full suite of luggage.

'Demanding something, are you, Hells? Some things never change,' Bernard said with a heavy chuckle, taking his place and shaking out his beautifully starched napkin. Sarah suddenly realised there would be no one around to take care of niceties like the household linen any more, now that Mrs Bunforth was out of action and Anna had resigned. She was pretty sure Helena wasn't the only member of the Brett-Coates family who was going to be peeved at the looming drop in standards.

'Sandwich, Bernard?' she said, offering him the platter.

'Mm. Good old Bunny, eh? Amazing, the way she keeps going, what with everything that's been thrown at us,' he said, helping himself heartily. 'Excellent sarnies.'

Sarah couldn't help preening a little, but Helena threw her a dark glance. 'Don't speak too soon. Our pair of amateur sleuths cobbled those together.'

'Very public-spirited of you,' said Bernard, raising his teacup in their general direction. 'All hands to the pump in a crisis. I'm sure Mrs B appreciated a bit of help. That girl of hers is no great shakes,' he said, smiling reassuringly at Letty, who turned her head away.

'You don't understand, Bernard. Or you just won't see. Bunny is out of action. She's the latest victim,' said Helena, seeming to take satisfaction in relaying the awful news.

Bernard, who'd been taking a sip, sprayed tea everywhere and tried vainly to mop at it with his napkin. In her new and unwanted position as chief cook and bottle washer, Sarah hoped it wouldn't stain.

'Victim? What the devil has happened? Why wasn't I informed?'

'Well, I'm sorry, Bernard, but you've got eyes, haven't you? Didn't you notice the police, running about the grounds? Not to mention the dirty great ambulance parked on the lawn.' Helena pulled a plate of biscuits closer and looked at them disapprovingly.

That was interesting, thought Sarah. Despite her earlier pretence, Helena must have had a good idea of what had happened all along.

Bernard got up and peered through the window. The paramedics were long gone, but the churned-up marks on the grass would be there for months. 'Good gracious! Thank goodness Mumsy wasn't here to see the day. She loved that lawn. And, erm, of course Bunny was a treasured member of the family,' he tacked on, and lowered his eyes. His expression was mournful, like a bloodhound who'd been cheated of a nice juicy chop.

'Oh, it's not that bad. Bunny's probably fine. She's just in hospital,' said his sister.

If the situation hadn't been so serious, Sarah would have been amused by Helena's definition of 'fine'. The poor woman certainly hadn't looked too good when she'd been lying on the floor in that claustrophobic turret room, she thought with a shudder.

'Bit of a draught?' Charles said solicitously.

'What? Oh yes. What's the expression? Someone walking over my grave,' said Sarah with an attempt at a smile.

'That's a nasty phrase, particularly in the circumstances,' snapped Helena.

Sarah didn't bother to reply, but turned to Bernard instead. 'It's funny you didn't hear the commotion. Maybe you'd left the grounds?'

'These jobsworth police seem determined to coop us all up here, so I couldn't have gone anywhere even if I'd wanted to,' said Bernard, biting into another sandwich. 'I was upstairs, sleeping. I've not been right since Jonty hit me. And I've had some very disturbed nights lately. Letty will tell you.'

Sarah looked at Letitia, who was in another of her daydreams. 'What?' she said, jerking her attention back to the room. 'Oh, yes. Sure. Whatever Bernie says. Mind you, I'm in the room next door,' she added with a smile.

Not the greatest alibi in the world, thought Sarah, and Bernard didn't look best pleased at having his domestic arrangements laid bare so carelessly, but Charles nodded as though that settled matters for him. Helena, though, was looking thoughtful.

'The police might have some sort of point, Bernard. Anyone at the fair could have attacked Mother. But what about Geoff? He wasn't just in a corner, like you said. He was caged up. And who knew about his phobia, except us? That must have been what they call an "inside job". Thanks to that, we're stuck with this lot,' she said, looking sourly at Daphne and Sarah.

'Unless you fancy cooking all your own meals, you might be grateful we're here,' said Daphne, managing to look pretty cheerful despite Helena's poisonous attitude. 'I've always liked trying my hand at new recipes. It'll be a pleasure to have top-of-the-range equipment for a change. And an excellent sous-chef,' she nodded at Sarah.

Sarah, who wasn't quite so sure she was going to enjoy the experience, was relieved when Mariella knocked and popped her head round the door. 'Just to remind you all, I'm ready to have chats with you, in turn, in the study.'

'Were you going to inform us that our cook has been attacked?' Helena asked Mariella coldly. 'Oh, and where is that scullery maid of hers? Why can't she take over the cooking?' Helena was now glaring at Sarah and Daphne, too.

'Anna has left. She resigned this morning,' said Mariella.

'That little girl with the ears? Why on earth would she do that?' Letty seemed astonished at the news.

'I can't think,' said Mariella drily. 'Anyway, I look forward to seeing you as soon as tea is over.'

'Good grief!' said Bernard. 'Well, that's a bit much. Told the police she was going, did she? She ought to have informed me, by rights. I'm the h—'

'Head of the family. Yes, we know,' drawled Helena. 'Maybe Anna was as impressed by that as the rest of us are,' she said, feigning a yawn.

Bernard looked thunderous, then his expression changed. 'Well, no need to look any further for whoever attacked Bunny. It must have been Anna. And now she's run off.'

'I don't think so,' said Mariella quickly. 'She seems to have left before Mrs Bunforth's, er, accident. Someone's interviewing her now, she's gone to a friend's place in Dartford. Meanwhile, who's first for a little chat?' she added, looking round the table.

'Oh, but we haven't had our second cups yet,' Letitia protested, as outraged as if the detective had suggested they conduct the interviews in the nude with the entire village watching.

'I suppose that's our cue to get to the kitchen and refill the teapot,' Daphne said with a shrug.

She waltzed off, leaving Sarah to collect up all the plates and put them on a large tray. Charles held the door open for her and brought up the rear with the used cutlery. 'I say, it's rather like being in *Downton Abbey*, all this, isn't it?'

Sarah, who'd been a huge fan of the show, couldn't help smiling. 'We've been miscast, though. I think I'd rather be above stairs than waiting on that lot.' Prolonged exposure to Helena was not making her like the woman any better.

'Oh, come on, Bernard's the salt of the earth. Whole family is great fun under normal circumstances,' said Charles.

It was sweet that he was so willing to defend old friends, thought Sarah. But if Charles couldn't see there was a lot amiss with the Brett-Coates clan, he needed an eye test even more urgently than Sarah did herself. And there was something even more seriously awry if being shut up with a murderer was his definition of a good time.

THIRTY-TWO

While Mariella continued her interviews in the study, Sarah found herself on washing-up duty in the kitchen. Worse still, while she was up to her elbows in suds, Daphne was merrily covering the kitchen in flour again. She was attempting to recreate what she insisted would have been prize-winning scones – if it hadn't been for the pesky murderer doing away with the judge before she'd had time to award the gold rosette. These, she insisted, would be perfect for pudding that night. 'I often think it's my light touch that makes all the difference,' Daphne said loudly, banging her bowl down onto the work surface and getting out the rolling pin with a clatter.

'Mm,' said Sarah, scrubbing at the quiche dish. 'Scones might have been better for tea – but I'm sure they'll be lovely later,' she added quickly when Daphne's face fell. 'Have you turned the oven on? It's good to get them cooking the second you've finished cutting them out,' she said.

'Oopsie,' said Daphne, trailing flour from the worktop all the way over to the oven. 'These buttons are weird. Do you know how this thing works?'

Sarah wiped her hands and went across. 'Oh, it's like mine

at home. You just twiddle these two knobs. There, it's pre-heating now. Shall I give you a hand with the rolling out?'

'No, these are going to be all my own work,' said Daphne proudly. 'And besides, you've got enough to do right there in the sink. I've just made a whole lot more washing-up for you.'

'So you have.' Sarah sighed. 'I wonder what we're going to give everyone for their main course at dinner?'

'I had a look earlier, and the freezer is chock-full. We'll just defrost something and do some veg.'

'Good idea. Thanks, Daph, that was very sensible of you to have a rummage. It'll give us a bit more time to work out what on earth is going on in this house. I've thought of a ruse, too, so we can go upstairs and look in the bedrooms.'

'Why would we want to do that?' said Daphne, wrinkling a nose adorned with a light dusting of flour.

'Don't you want to see if there's anything else that's red lying around? If it wasn't pieces of Letitia's dress, then it must be something else... Any thoughts on what?'

'None,' said Daphne, slapping the rolling pin down on the counter.

'I expect it will come to you. Shame Anna's left, I could do with a hand putting the dishes away,' Sarah said, looking sideways at Daphne. 'And what about that missing dirk?'

'Such a strange name for a knife. I'm not totally sure I want to find that,' said Daphne, pressing the cutter into her scone dough.

'What about the motto, though?' said Sarah.

'Oh, don't remind me. So sinister. Honestly, this place is enough to give anyone the collywobbles.'

'Well, at least the ghost's been quiet. She hasn't walked at all, despite us being two family members down,' said Sarah.

'It's no laughing matter, Sarah. And actually it might be useful if we did see it. I could commune with it. My spirit guide,

Pongo, would probably be really useful here,' Daphne said thoughtfully, while she mangled her first scone.

'Um, if you flour the cutter first... Oh, never mind,' said Sarah, as Daphne prised the scone off the floured surface with a knife and dolloped it onto the baking tray. 'I think I've finally finished the washing-up now.'

'If you say so. There's a little bit of flour that could do with sweeping up, though,' said Daphne, brushing great clouds of the stuff off her orange top, to join the snowdrift on the floor. 'I'll just put some egg wash on these and they'll be ready.'

After the kitchen was returned to rights and they'd both enjoyed a cup of strong tea, the scones were removed from the oven. Sarah wished she could say they were beautifully risen, golden on top and looking as fluffy and delectable as anything Mrs Bunforth herself could produce. They weren't – but they were Daphne's best efforts to date.

'Well done, Daph,' said Sarah, trying to keep the full depth of her amazement out of her voice. 'Practice really does pay off, doesn't it? Now then, let's see what we can find upstairs. We can say we're collecting laundry if anyone asks what we're up to.'

'OK, that's so cunning,' whispered Daphne as they made their way into the hall. She tiptoed her way up the stairs, until Sarah pointed out what they were doing was hardly illegal. Then she relaxed and they'd soon made it to the first-floor bedroom corridor. Both their own rooms were here, as was the late Madeleine Brett-Coates's suite.

'Let's go up to the next floor,' said Sarah. 'I've already seen Madeleine's room and I doubt much has changed.'

Off they set, up the thickly carpeted stairs, making almost no sound as they went. As they rounded the final bend, however, they came up against Helena, who was just descending.

'Goodness, you two! You do get underfoot,' she said, as

usual looking immaculate and haughty, but with a slightly furtive air about her.

'Helena, where are you off to?' Sarah asked, trying for a light tone. 'We were just coming to see you.'

'We were?' Daphne said, then coughed. 'Oh yes, we were.'

'Heavens,' said Helena. 'I suppose you want to poke around in everyone's rooms. As if it isn't bad enough being interrogated by the police downstairs.' But she obligingly turned round and led them down the corridor.

'How did the questioning go?' asked Sarah.

'No use trying to sound casual. I know you're burning to find out. And that's one of the many reasons why I'm telling you nothing,' Helena said with a thin-lipped smile, opening a door and waving them in. Once Sarah and Daphne had trooped past her, Helena banged it shut on them and they could hear the sound of the key turning in the lock.

'Drat! I can't believe we've fallen for that trick again,' said Daphne, throwing herself on Helena's unmade bed with a groan.

It was true, someone had played a similar prank on them recently, and it had been incredibly annoying. They'd been shut in a garage then, and only rescued by a sympathetic passer-by. This time, Sarah was reasonably confident they could get out easily. She was sure Helena had left the key in the lock. Kneeling down and squinting through the keyhole confirmed her diagnosis.

'Quick,' she said. 'Pass me that magazine, over on the bedside table.'

Daphne looked at it. 'What, the National Trust mag? This is no time to read about stately homes, Sarah,' she said crossly, but she handed it over. Sarah promptly ripped off the cover, to Daphne's horror. 'Goodness, Helena's going to be as mad as a sack of squirrels about that!'

'She drove us to it,' said Sarah, sliding the glossy cover

under the door. 'I'm sure she's much too self-absorbed to read anyway. Now, is there anything long and pointed lying around anywhere?'

'Oh really, you do ask the oddest questions,' said Daphne, casting about and finally coming up with an eyeliner pencil that had been left on the dressing table along with a host of other beauty supplies. 'For someone who spends so much time scowling, Helena spends an absolute fortune on make-up.'

'Lucky for us that she does,' said Sarah, poking the eyeliner through the keyhole. There was a satisfying jangle, and the key on the other side of the door fell out and landed on the magazine cover. Sarah then very carefully pulled it back towards her, making sure the key didn't get stuck under the door. 'Ta-dah!' she said, once it was in her hand. 'But let's keep the door locked for the moment.'

'Are you crazy?' said Daphne, throwing her head back and looking dangerously close to yelling. 'I want to get out! I need my freedom.'

'Yes, and you'll get it, very soon,' said Sarah, rushing to soothe her. 'But don't you see? This gives us a great opportunity to have a proper look around Helena's room, and she can't do a thing to disturb us, can she?'

'Oh. I suppose she can't,' Daphne said with a deep chuckle. 'Serves her right, the minx. Now, what are we looking for?'

'That's simple, Daph. Anything that can prove Helena is our killer.'

THIRTY-THREE

Twenty minutes later, they had a full inventory of Helena's extensive wardrobe, much of it in wonderful shades of green, and had both admired her extremely covetable jewellery. Daphne was wearing several of her Hermès scarves and Sarah had only just been able to stop her putting on a gorgeous pair of lime silk pumps. Considering Helena was supposed to be the black sheep of the family, and had led a so-called bohemian, alternative lifestyle cavorting out in California with various rock gods, she had a very solid interest in high-end diamonds.

Daphne played with these trinkets, holding up pair after pair of glittering earrings to the dressing table mirror to see how they'd suit her, while Sarah went on searching methodically, until she'd been through everything hanging up. It seemed so intrusive to search through the chest of drawers, where Helena must keep her underwear, but under the circumstances, Sarah felt she had little choice. She tried not to look as she patted her way through the silky piles – but then felt vindicated when her fingers touched something a lot more solid than a pair of knickers. It was a package, wrapped up in a spare pillowcase.

'Look at this,' she said to Daphne, pulling it free of the drawer.

'What on earth is it? I hope it's nothing too... personal,' said Daphne, with a squeamish look on her face.

'I think it's a book,' Sarah said. 'It's the right size and weight.'

'Oh, that's fine then,' said Daphne, flinging the earrings down and sitting on the bed with a flump. 'Quick, open it up. We can't be in here forever. Helena will want to change her diamonds for even bigger ones at some point.'

'OK,' said Sarah, upending the pillowcase. 'Here we go.'

Sure enough, a book tumbled out. The cover was a lurid yellow, with large block lettering shouting out the name of a famous author.

'Funny, I wouldn't have thought Helena was a big fan of SAS vigilante thrillers,' said Daphne with a puzzled frown.

'I don't think she is for one second,' said Sarah, taking the edge of the pillowcase and using it to strip off the book's dust jacket. Underneath was a much more restrained blue cover, with a line drawing of flowers. The title was a simple one: *The Home Handbook of Poisonous Plants*.

'Oh my goodness! You don't think... Can Helena really have—?'

'Well, someone's going to have to ask her that question,' said Sarah, compressing her lips firmly. 'Because look, here's the section on bluebells. And it's been underlined.'

'There's another section marked,' said Daphne eagerly. 'A little further along. The page has been folded over.'

'Gosh, yes. This one's all about mushrooms,' said Sarah, frowning. 'That rings a bell... but we'd better get moving, come on.'

Once Sarah and Daphne had let themselves out of Helena's room, replacing the key carefully in the lock outside, they made their way downstairs. Sarah was clutching the book under her arm, re-wrapped loosely in its pillowcase to preserve any fingerprints. She doubted any would be found, but you never knew. She put out her other arm to stop Daphne.

'Listen, I'll talk to Mariella about what we've just found. Maybe you could find Charles and rope him into helping in the kitchen?'

'Oh, OK then. I definitely don't want to be there when you show Mari that book, she's only going to yell. Good luck.' Daphne made herself scarce as Sarah hesitated on the threshold of the study, which was rapidly becoming the detective's temporary HQ. She didn't want to interrupt if Mariella was still interviewing the family about the events of the day – but she wasn't averse to hearing a bit of the conversation if she was. She leant a little closer, just as the door opened and she almost fell in.

'Sarah. Can I help you?' said Mariella tersely as she ushered Jonathan out of the room. He almost ran up the stairs and Sarah stared at him in surprise. She hadn't been aware that he'd reappeared from wherever he'd been, and now he was off again. She raised her eyebrows at the policewoman, but Mariella just folded her arms.

'Um, yes, Mariella. I have something to show you,' Sarah said, gesturing to the pillowcase.

'Better come in,' said Mariella, looking resigned. 'I don't suppose anyone could make me a cuppa? This house is going to really suffer now Mrs Bunforth is in hospital.'

'I'm sure Daphne will get us some,' Sarah said. 'My phone's in the box in the hall, but you could text her,' she suggested. 'How's poor Mrs Bunforth getting on?' she asked, taking a seat at the wide oak partner's desk that dominated the small, book-lined room.

'It was touch and go for quite a while. But they've pumped her stomach and she's hooked up to every machine imaginable, so it's a question of whether we caught it in time... You'd know much more about all that than I do,' said Mariella a little bleakly.

'She was in good health before all this happened. If it was a poison and it's now out of her system, then she's got the best possible chance of recovery. I agree, the downtime is concerning but she did really well, holding on until the paramedics got there. She's a fighter, and that will help.'

'She would have died without you, that's for sure, Aunty Sarah. Well, thank goodness you and Mum were doing something ridiculously reckless as usual,' Mariella said.

'Going to the folly was just natural curiosity, surely,' said Sarah, deciding not to take offence as the young woman had said it with a smile.

'For what it's worth, there was a crumpled-up piece of paper in her hand, I don't know if you noticed it?'

Sarah's eyes opened wide. 'No, I didn't see that,' she said, kicking herself. She'd been much too focused on Mrs Bunforth's vital signs to worry about anything else.

'Unfortunately it wasn't a written confession from the murderer. It just said "Two p.m., Folly". Typewritten, on bog-standard paper just like that,' Mariella said, pointing to a stack of white A4 on the shelf. 'We've sent the computer off to be evaluated, but I'm betting someone wrote the note on it, printed it off, deleted it and then somehow passed it to Mrs Bunforth. The keyboard had been wiped clean, too.'

'Whoever this is, they're very thorough. But do you have the least idea why Mrs Bunforth was the target?' Sarah's brow was pleated.

'I was hoping you'd have some clever thoughts on that subject,' admitted Mariella. 'At this rate, there won't be any suspects left, they'll all be dead or in the hospital. It's one way to find the culprit, I suppose.'

'Last man standing, you mean?' said Sarah.

'Or woman. We don't discriminate,' Mariella said.

'Talking of women under suspicion... take a peek in that pillowcase,' Sarah said, gesturing to it.

THIRTY-FOUR

Mariella looked at Sarah, shook the book out of the pillowcase onto the desk, and peered carefully under the dummy cover, using a pen. 'Interesting. And this was where?'

'Helena's room.'

'Seriously?' Mariella looked up and stared at Sarah. 'Well, goodness me.'

'Don't get too excited, though, Mariella. I'm really not convinced she's our murderer.'

'Why's that?' Mariella put her head on one side.

'Well, isn't she a bit too self-obsessed and lazy to be printing secret messages and sending wreaths? She mostly prefers sniping from the sidelines, from what I've seen. Mind you, both bluebells and mushrooms would be minimum effort as far as poisoning goes, so I suppose she could have decided to try her hand.'

'Don't like her much, do you?' Mariella raised an eyebrow.

'That's got nothing to do with it,' Sarah said. 'But it's true, she never stops making digs. The whole family is pretty hard going, to be honest.'

'All the more reason for us to sort this out and get away from here,' Mariella sighed. 'The chief constable has been bending my ear again... He's getting on a flight any moment and demanding I sort things out by the time he lands. Honestly, I'm at my wits' end.'

'That sounds completely unreasonable! I hope it's long-haul at least.'

Mariella shook her head. 'Nope. I'm expecting him to ring me up shouting in a couple of hours.'

'If we get this book tested for prints, hopefully that will move us a bit further on,' said Sarah.

'We'll get the new lab on the case. They've got Anna's resignation letter to work on, too. Thank goodness we've found a place that seems quite efficient now, and we're getting back up to speed.'

'OK, well that's good news. Now maybe we should think about why Mrs Bunforth was attacked. She must have seen something, or suspected something,' Sarah mused.

'Yes, but what?'

'Let's see. If Helena poisoned Madeleine, and got rid of Geoff because he guessed something, why would she try and silence Mrs Bunforth? Unless the cook saw Geoff going down into the cellar, followed by Helena?'

'That's a possibility,' said Mariella. 'Any other suggestions?'

'Mrs Bunforth comes into money, following Madeleine's will – would she leave any of it to the Brett-Coates children? She's an odd stick, very protective of the family and her domain.'

'She'll be beside herself when she sees what Mum's done to her kitchen, after only a few hours. I was passing the window while you were making scones. There was flour flying everywhere,' said Mariella.

'That's it!' Sarah was electrified. 'Those big windows in the kitchen, facing out onto the lawn. They would have given Mrs Bunforth a perfect view of anyone out there up to no good.'

'But Mrs Brett-Coates was killed in the tent,' Mariella said patiently.

'Yes, I know,' said Sarah. 'But think of the clues found in the garden, like the red material and the hypodermic syringe. Mrs Bunforth might have been looking out at just the right – or the wrong – moment, and seen the murderer either dropping things carelessly, or laying a false trail. Something that would throw us off the scent, while disguising the identity of the real culprit.'

Sarah and Mariella looked at each other for a moment. It really seemed to fit the facts, and explain why poor Mrs Bunforth was presently in the ICU in Canterbury.

'Have you got anyone on guard outside her hospital room?' Sarah asked suddenly.

Mariella's head shot up. 'She should be fine. It's not like any of the family are going to leave the house.'

Just then, they both heard the dull roar of a car engine turning over, followed by the crunch of gravel. Shooting out of their seats, they ran to the window, where a dark blue Lexus was swishing down the drive at speed.

'Whose car is that?' Sarah asked.

'I think it was the old lady's. So no one should be driving it.'

'But someone is,' Sarah said, as the electric gates at the end swung smoothly open. There was no one to stop them, and the car turned sharp left and disappeared from view.

'For goodness' sake! I told the Canterbury lot to leave a PC stationed on that gate...' Mariella was fuming.

'Just make sure somebody's outside Mrs Bunforth's room,' Sarah urged.

Mariella made the call, and got Deeside's assurance that nothing would shift him from outside the intensive care ward. Sarah looked beadily at Mariella for a moment, then decided she had to act. 'Listen, see if you can round up the family members. A simple head count would help... Meanwhile I'm going to pop along and help your mum out. Otherwise we'll never get supper tonight, and that cup of tea you wanted. See you in a bit.'

With that, she beetled off, not sure whether Mariella believed her or not. She pelted down the corridor to the kitchen, where Daphne seemed to have left vegetable peelings over every possible surface and was now sitting looking sadly at a saucepanful of rather grey liquid.

'I don't know what happened, Sarah. I was trying to get ahead of myself by sautéing some carrots with shallots for tonight. I followed the recipe to the letter – apart from the fact that I couldn't find any carrots or shallots...'

'Never mind that now. We need to get to the hospital as soon as possible.'

'Aren't you well?' Daphne stood up, alarmed.

'Mariella has had to leave Deeside on guard outside Mrs Bunforth's room, and someone has driven off from here as though the hounds of hell are at their heels. We have to make sure that poor woman is OK.'

'Surely we ought to leave this to Deeside? He's a policeman, after all,' said Daphne, wiping a rag ineffectually over some of the many splashes left by her culinary experiment.

'Are you kidding? This is Deeside we're talking about. We'll leave Hamish with Charles, and we'll be back before you know it,' said Sarah optimistically, opening the kitchen door and chivvying Daphne along.

Within five minutes they were in Sarah's car, sweeping out of the gates of Coates House. Sarah could just imagine how furious Mariella would be at seeing them go – but that couldn't be her priority right now. A few minutes more had them drawing up outside the Canterbury hospital and puffing their way down the ICU corridor. Deeside was sitting and peering at his phone. The muted dings suggested he was in the thick of some complicated video game. Without stopping to acknowledge him – and without him challenging them – they bundled into Mrs Bunforth's room. It seemed quiet and serene inside… apart from the bed.

The covers had been thrown this way and that, and the long, thin figure of Mrs Bunforth was sprawling half in, half out, one arm dangling uselessly towards the floor.

THIRTY-FIVE

Sarah and Daphne hoisted Mrs Bunforth back into bed. Sarah took one look at the woman's waxen face and started CPR. In between performing regular compressions on the unresponsive woman's chest, and breathing into her mouth after tipping her chin and closing her nose, she said urgently to Daphne, 'Go outside and yell for help!'

Daphne didn't need asking twice, screaming at Deeside, and calling for a doctor at the top of her lungs. Soon Sarah heard the stampede of feet coming their way – and the shouts of Deeside, trying to shut Daphne up. Just as Sarah's arms were really beginning to tire, the door was flung back and a doctor who looked almost old enough to have the stabilisers taken off her bike burst in and took over.

'Thanks, we'll take it from here. You know the drill, relatives wait outside,' said the young medic, her blonde ponytail swinging as she took over the CPR. A crash cart arrived just as Sarah was leaving and soon she could hear the whine of the defibrillator charging. She knew the statistics – the machine would improve Mrs Bunforth's chances enormously, but this was her second near-death experience today. They would surely be very lucky if she recovered fully at this point.

Having been running on adrenaline ever since she'd spoken to Mariella and realised what was likely to happen, she now felt her veins flooding with rage against Deeside. The idiot had let someone swan in and try to finish the job they'd started earlier. It took all her self-control not to take him by the scruff of his neck and yell at him. He was already being questioned by an officer, though, and it looked like one of the higher-ups from Canterbury. Unfortunately, this would probably rebound on poor Mariella, who had after all made the decision to let him take up this vital post.

'Come on,' she said to Daphne, who was waiting outside like a limp rag. 'Let's see if we can get a cup of tea in the canteen. I really need a sit-down.'

Once they were settled with a strong cuppa and some medicinal bourbons, Daphne let it all pour out. 'I'm fed up with this, Sarah. Who was driving that car? Who's done this?'

Sarah shook her head. 'Whoever it was, they're gone by now. Did you see anyone at the house before we left?'

Daphne shook her head. 'Charles was in the garden with the dogs, that's all I know. The whole family is pretty horrible,' she said. 'Even Bernard, who I used to quite like. I don't know how Charles can stand them. None of them want us there, and now we're going to have to do all the cooking! I'd much rather be at home. Besides, Mephisto will be really missing me.'

Sarah couldn't help sympathising with Daphne, though she was certain the cat would be thoroughly enjoying having the cottage to himself. 'We've been at Vanstone much longer than we thought. And it's frustrating. But I feel it's all going to fall into place soon. Let's just do something simple for supper. No one will be expecting cordon bleu cooking.'

'Are you kidding? Horrible Helena will. I'm fine in my own

kitchen, but it's hard when you don't know where things are kept,' Daphne said plaintively.

'Mm,' said Sarah, who knew that wasn't the problem. She and Daphne just weren't a patch on a professional like Mrs Bunforth. 'Well, let's not worry too much about that. Anyway, talking of getting told off, here's Mariella.'

The young policewoman collapsed, rather than sat, at the table, and Sarah looked at her in alarm. 'I'll get you a tea,' said Daphne. 'And some scones while I'm at it.'

Sarah pushed her plate towards Mariella, and she wordlessly took a biscuit and bit it savagely. 'That bloody idiot Deeside!' she mumbled through a mouthful of crumbs. 'I could strangle him with my bare hands...'

'Please don't,' Sarah said with a smile. 'That would make things much more complicated. But why did he let anyone in?'

'They were wearing a white coat. He assumed it was the doctor. He didn't even get a proper description of the face, sex, you name it. He was so engrossed in his stupid game. Well, he'll spend the rest of his life on traffic duty, if I have my way.'

Sarah now felt a pang of sympathy for the man. 'Quite cunning of whoever it was, you have to admit.'

'Oh yes. There's been no shortage of that, has there? There's zero sign of that dratted car anywhere and the PCs back at the house have just reported that all the family members are accounted for. But whoever it was has had time to dump the Lexus in a layby and walk back by now, so it's meaningless. It was one of them. We just don't know who. I'm so fed up.'

Sarah was worried. Mariella never complained about her ridiculously heavy workload, or the pressures of a job that came with life-or-death situations as a given. 'Listen, something will crack soon. It always does.'

'This time, I'm afraid it might be me,' said Mariella ruefully, managing a smile as Daphne came back with a loaded tray and passed her a tea.

'I've been thinking, while I was stuck in that queue,' said Daphne. 'This whole thing started with scones. I thought we'd got them down pat, but this afternoon showed me otherwise. We've been using our time wrongly, concentrating on things we're not great at. We need to approach this from a different angle.'

Sarah's eyebrows steepled. 'What do you suggest?'

'Jonty,' said Daphne succinctly. 'We've had a go at all the others and got nowhere. Bernard's the human equivalent of a clam, Letty's away with the fairies, and we're no match for Helena.'

'Well, there's been a problem there. Jonty's always doing a runner,' said Sarah.

'He's back now, and I vote we concentrate on him. If both Madeleine and Mrs Bunforth were poisoned, then he surely has to be quite far up on the list of suspects, with his qualifications. There is a literal shedload of foxgloves out there, and even if those weren't used, because they give him the heebie-jeebies or whatever, you can bet he'll know which other toxic plants could do the job. So I say you can carry on with the proper enquiry, Mari, while we grill Jonty. And then we'll let you know when we've cracked this thing,' Daphne said kindly to her daughter.

'Thanks very much,' said Mariella with a tut. 'Nice to know where I come in the pecking order, as far as you're concerned.' She swigged back some tea and clattered the cup back on its saucer.

'Sorry, Mari, I didn't mean that to come out the way that it did,' said Daphne, patting her daughter's hand. 'But you know, you were keen for us to get the inside track.'

'Yes, and look how that worked out. We're no further on, and half the house is either dead or in the hospital.'

'Well, Mrs Bunforth is going to live to fight another day, thank goodness,' said Sarah, trying to pour a little oil on troubled waters.

'As long as she can still remember her own name when she wakes up.' Mariella's face was a picture of gloom.

'She survived the first attack, against all the odds,' Sarah said.

'Let's face it,' Daphne weighed in. 'Anyone that good with a quiche has real staying power.'

Mariella raised a smile at this. 'Right, you two. I'll stay here in case Mrs B comes round. You head back.'

'You're OK with us chatting with Jonathan, then?' Sarah confirmed.

Mariella finished the last of her tea and stood up. 'I'll go up to the ward. See you back at the house. Yes, talk to him. As long as you don't use thumbscrews, it's fine with me. Or actually, do. The faster we find this killer, the better.'

THIRTY-SIX

'What makes you think Jonty's going to open up to you?' Charles asked, as Sarah rubbed Hamish's belly in the drawing room. Daphne was having another go at preparing the supper, insisting she didn't need help.

'I don't know that he will,' Sarah said. 'I'm just hoping he'll realise that hanging onto the family's secrets is doing no good.'

'I must say, I'm keen to get back to my shop. I dread to think how many sales I'm missing, stuck here.'

'Hmm,' said Sarah, as supportively as she could. She did admire his wonderfully optimistic nature. 'Come to that, my garden seedlings will soon need watering. And Daphne's missing Mephisto.'

Charles snorted, but Sarah understood her friend's feelings. 'I'm so glad I could bring Hamish. I wouldn't have wanted to be apart from him all this time.' The little dog panted up at her, knowing he was, quite rightly, the topic of conversation.

'Looks like it's down to us to get this thing moving, then,' Charles acknowledged. 'Where do you propose we stage this intervention with Jonty?'

Sarah was a little taken aback. She was used to making her

enquiries on her own, or with Daphne in tow if strictly necessary. She wasn't sure how things would go if Charles suddenly started throwing questions into the mix. But maybe his presence would put Jonathan at his ease?

'We could sit in the drawing room. I'll get us some tea, and take it there.'

'Righto. See you in a little while.' Charles set off up the wide staircase.

Sarah hesitated on her way to the kitchen. The house was quiet; this could be a good moment to do something she'd been toying with for a while – quickly checking Anna's room upstairs. She wasn't sure the police would have got round to searching it yet, and she had a fairly good idea that there was at least one thing up there that might point her in the right direction.

By the time she got up to the attic, she was panting. At the top of the flight were two doors. She tried the first – locked. Mrs Bunforth's, she supposed. The second swung open when she tried it.

It was a small single, with a fluffy rug covering clean, white-painted floorboards. The slanting ceiling gave the room a gabled effect, and the walls were papered with a pink daisy pattern. Sarah wandered in, disappointed that the place was empty, apart from a couple of photos stuck into the frame of the dressing table mirror, and Anna's trainers under the bed.

Then she pounced. In the wastepaper basket were the ragged remnants of a red silk scarf. As she'd thought, it looked as though this was the source of all those snippets in the garden. The family would be thrilled, if this got them off the hook. Why on earth would Anna be the killer, though? She would have had limited contact with Madeleine Brett-Coates, who no doubt considered her far beneath her notice. She didn't seem either strong or cunning enough to get Geoff into the cellar, and she'd left before Mrs Bunforth was attacked. And why would she have left clues pointing to herself all round the garden?

Sarah scanned the room again, wondering if there was anything she'd missed. Then she took a closer look at the photos wedged in the mirror. One was of a young girl with an older woman. The woman, glaring at the camera, was tall and skinny with long mousy hair hanging down her shoulders, and looked to be in her thirties. The little girl was probably about eleven, wearing thick glasses, with her ears protruding through blonde curls. It had to be Anna.

And the woman? Sarah squinted. And tried to imagine a time, ten or more years ago, when she wasn't in uniform... It was Mrs Bunforth. They were mother and daughter.

It gave Anna a motive, Sarah realised. Though it seemed horrific that anyone would try to kill their mother for £10,000, it was more than possible. She was so shocked by this realisation that she nearly forgot to study the second photo. But when she did, she realised it added another little nugget of knowledge to her store. On the face of it, it was a simple snap of a girl cosying up to her boyfriend. But she'd seen that lanky lad next to Anna very recently. Hadn't she?

Sarah frowned, then realised she'd spent far too much time in Anna's room. She whizzed back down to the kitchen, bracing herself a little before opening the door, but was pleasantly surprised to find Daphne was almost on top of the vegetable clean-up operation and boiling a large kettle.

'Is it OK if I just get a tray together quickly? Charles and I are going to question Jonathan in the drawing room,' Sarah explained, assembling cups and saucers.

'Some people have all the fun,' said Daphne, blowing a lock of hair off her face. She did look a bit pink after her exertions.

'Come and join us, Daph, if you feel like it,' Sarah said. 'I must go, they'll be waiting for me.'

'Harrumph. Might see you in there, I'll just get these

vegetables under control,' Daphne said, bringing a huge knife down on an innocent courgette.

Sarah picked up the tray, and took everything to the drawing room, with Hamish trotting along beside her. Being inside Coates House had become distinctly oppressive, and the hospital visit hadn't exactly provided a relaxing break, but at least here they had a view of the garden. She settled everything on the ottoman and started to pour the tea, hoping Charles would tempt Jonathan along before it all went cold.

She was about to take a sip from her cup when there was a creak right behind her. She wheeled round in consternation.

THIRTY-SEVEN

Bernard strode up, an affable look on his face.

'Oh, it's you, Bernard. I thought you were with Letitia,' Sarah said, putting down her cup and smiling.

'Thought I'd get away for a moment. Looks like you had the same idea,' he said, eyeing the two extra cups.

He sat himself down heavily on one of the sofas before she had a chance to explain matters. Oh well, she thought. Might as well try and get some information out of him, since he'd made himself available.

'What are your thoughts on this whole business?' she asked him, as he took an appreciative sip from the cup she'd earmarked for Charles.

'Mrs Bunforth, you mean? Or... the rest of it?' He shifted in his seat.

'Well, any of it, I suppose,' Sarah said, trying to seem relaxed but hanging on his every word.

'Oh, er, well, now that's quite a— Ah, Charles, old boy! There you are.' Bernard shot to his feet. 'Do sit down. Think I might have taken your seat, haha,' he said, swapping so he was further from Sarah. 'Good, good,' he said, taking up his cup again and draining it in one. 'Well, I should get going...'

But before Bernard could escape, Charles burst into speech. 'Can't seem to find Jonty anywhere,' he said, looking nervously at Sarah. 'Looks like he's done another one of his disappearing acts.'

'Always the way. You'll remember. Whenever he was in trouble, you wouldn't see him for dust,' Bernard chuckled, settling himself back against the sofa cushions.

Sarah thought hard. 'Where did he go, when he used to vanish like this?'

'Oh, to the folly, usually. Er, not that I mean— Oh, well, I'm sure it's different now. Perhaps he's just... having a bath.'

Even Charles's eyebrows rose at that. 'Funny time of day.'

'All right. Well, that's something to check,' said Sarah. 'I was asking you before, Bernard, what you thought was going on. Who has it in for your family, to put it bluntly? It's beginning to look like a vendetta.'

Bernard shifted again, and looked to Charles for help, but Charles was scrutinising his shoes as though memorising every detail. 'Well. You know, if it had just been Geoffrey, I would have thought he'd done away with himself.'

'What, torturing himself to death in the cellar, with his well-known problems with claustrophobia?' Sarah tried to keep the incredulity out of her voice, but a glance from Charles told her she'd failed.

'Apart from that,' said Bernard, rather apologetically.

'I'm not sure what you mean,' said Sarah slowly. 'Are you saying there was a reason for Geoff to kill himself? You know of a motive?'

'Motive, haha, that's a serious word,' said Bernard, looking embarrassed. 'It's just that, well...'

Sarah waited, as patiently as she could – which really wasn't very patiently at all. Thank goodness, Charles intervened before she said something. 'I don't quite catch your drift, Bernard?'

'Oh, all right,' said Bernard, as though they'd put him in the thumbscrews and he was finally agreeing to talk. 'It was Mumsy. She had her suspicions, that's all.'

Charles frowned heavily. 'Not her type, eh?'

'Exactly,' said Bernard gratefully.

Charles smiled at Sarah, as though this made everything crystal clear.

'Are you saying she didn't think Geoffrey was posh enough to be part of the Brett-Coates clan? Or was there something else about him that was substandard in some way?' Sarah couldn't help being a little pointed. It sounded as though Mrs Brett-Coates had been displaying distressingly old-fashioned prejudices.

'Nothing like that,' Bernard said, putting both his hands up as though in surrender. 'It was more that his research on the Brett-Coates line was a bit too enthusiastic, if you get my meaning.' Sarah looked blank, and Bernard obliged. 'All right, if I have to spell it out. He was always snuffling around the place so he could steal from us. Well, you all saw that bagful of stuff he was taking.'

'We saw the holdall but we don't know he stole it,' said Sarah carefully, looking at Bernard.

'Well, who else would it be?' He shrugged. 'Jonty's had a head as big as a prize cabbage since his telly thing took off and Geoff was put out. Swiping the odd thing must have made him feel he was evening up the scales, somehow. He was a bit of a sneaky blighter. You met him, didn't you, Charles?'

'What? Oh, er, yes,' said Charles.

'You haven't said much about him,' Sarah said.

'Well, it would have been at his wedding. You never really get a chance to talk to the er, grooms, do you? And Frankie's drinks parties, I suppose. Always such a crowd, and hard to have a sensible conversation with all the chat going on. Couldn't hear myself think most of the time,' said Charles.

Sarah appreciated that he was always somewhat on edge when mentioning his ex, Francesca, the mayor of Merstairs. In some ways, she was a lot to live up to. Sarah's idea of a cocktail party was pouring a Dubonnet for Daphne. She hoped she'd never have to host the kind of soirées Francesca seemed to throw at the drop of a hat.

'Always puts on a great show, your Frankie,' said Bernard, rather proving Sarah's point. Then he coughed, rather belatedly remembering the changing of the guard. 'That is, yes, awful scrum.'

Everyone sat in silence for a moment, so when Daphne bounded through the door and threw herself onto a chair, it was a welcome interruption.

'I've brought some scones for us,' she said, uncrumpling a napkin and revealing three, looking slightly battered. Hamish wagged his tail appreciatively, enjoying the unexpected shower of crumbs.

'How's everyone bearing up? See Letty, did you?' Bernard said.

'What?' mumbled Daphne. 'Oh yes, I saw her in the garden, through the kitchen window. She seemed fine. Well, no, now I come to think of it. She was looking pretty spaced out. She's wearing one of those fluttery dresses again, it doesn't really help, does it?'

Sarah coughed. 'How was Helena?'

'Oh, still in a filthy mood,' said Daphne blithely. 'She seemed cross Mrs Bunforth isn't back at her post yet. I did explain she might need a couple of days off after someone tried to kill her twice.'

Now it was Bernard's turn to splutter crumbs. The half-scone he'd been chewing went everywhere. 'I thought she'd just had one of her funny turns!'

Sarah stared at him. 'Really? Helena told you about the ambulance. I was there, remember? And now something's happened at the hospital, too.'

'What? Oh, yes, yes. Silly of me,' Bernard said, brushing down the front of his shirt with a pristine white handkerchief, no doubt ironed by Mrs Bunforth in better times. 'I thought it was her usual problem. She's always been prone to passing out. Well, the last few months, anyway.'

'Has she?' said Sarah thoughtfully.

Bernard got to his feet. 'Well, better see how the wife is. Didn't sound too good, from your description, Daphne.'

Daphne shrugged, and they all watched while Bernard got up and shut the door behind him. He was very adroit at avoiding difficult questions, thought Sarah.

'Letty's no worse than usual,' Daphne said. 'Always looks like she'd blow over if you sneezed.'

'But she's here, and so are Bernard and Helena. And Jonty was accounted for earlier, too. He must be in the grounds. At this point, it could be any of them,' Sarah said with a sigh. To distract herself, she looked through the window at the beautiful garden. 'Those hedges remind me of the red bits of fabric. I'm certain they were meant to look like pieces of Letitia's dress – but in fact, they came from Anna's scarf.'

'No, really?' Charles and Daphne stared at her. 'Did Anna do it, then? Or do you think they were just planted in the tent and in the hedges by the killer?' Charles asked.

'Well, either is possible, I suppose,' said Sarah. 'It's interesting because there are elements of these crimes that seem feminine, and others that are very masculine.'

'I don't get what you mean?' Daphne frowned.

'Well, initially it looked as though Madeleine had been strangled with the bunting. That's a brute force crime, very male. Hardly any stranglings are done by women, and of the few that are, the victims are, um, generally much smaller and weaker than the perpetrator.'

'You mean... children? That's horrific.' Daphne looked as though she might cry. Sarah patted her arm before carrying on.

'But that wasn't the case here. Madeleine was poisoned, the bunting was just a cruel bit of staging, making a mockery of the fair, really. And putting the red fabric on her body seems to me to be the sort of crass touch that a bumbling male murderer would think of, sorry Charles. It lacks finesse.'

'There was cunning in tempting Geoff down into the cellar and cooping him up,' Charles said.

'Yes, that could have been a woman's crime. Decoying him somehow, immobilising him and then putting the cage around him when he was down there in the dark. On the other hand, it could just have been brute force too – dragging him there and then physically restraining him.'

'What about the attack on Mrs Bunforth?' Daphne asked.

'That strikes me as more desperate,' Sarah said. 'There didn't seem to be much forethought involved, apart from the piece of paper with the message, which anyone in the house could have printed out in a couple of minutes.'

'Mrs Bunforth's always so busy, I wouldn't have been surprised if she'd just ignored an anonymous summons, given everything that's happened here in the last couple of days,' said Charles.

'I've had a thought about that,' Sarah said. 'You remember her cookery book was open when we went into the kitchen earlier?'

'Was it?' Daphne looked baffled.

'Yes, it was showing a recipe for a velouté of mushroom soup. I thought it was a bit complicated for us... well, the whole book is, to be honest. But it's made me wonder... I think Mrs Bunforth forages for mushrooms. We saw some not far from the folly.'

'So we did!' said Daphne. 'Goodness, I don't think I'd eat a mushroom someone had just gone out and picked themselves. It could be lethal – and most likely would be, in this house. We saw poisonous mushrooms in that book in Helena's room, remember.' She looked horrified at the idea.

'Mrs Bunforth has probably been picking her own for years, though,' Sarah pointed out. 'Jonathan would know more about this, but if you identify them correctly, it's perfectly safe. It's what people did before supermarkets, of course. And if Mrs Bunforth had a habit of foraging near the folly, maybe she saw someone there? So when she got the note, she went because she wanted to talk to that person... and they decided to get rid of her, in a place no one else in the family seems to go near.'

'Well, all this talk of food has reminded me,' said Daphne, changing the subject briskly and collecting up the cups and saucers. 'I suppose we skivvies better get back to the kitchen and get on with the supper.'

Sarah looked at her watch. 'You're right. I'm not sure we'll get as far with the family as Mariella wants us to if we spend all our time cooking, though.'

'Well, I wouldn't be much help with the catering, but I'm happy to keep an ear out. I'll go back and see what everyone's doing,' said Charles. 'Terrible, really, I feel it's so dishonourable.'

'I understand, Charles,' said Sarah sympathetically. 'But on the other hand, you don't want any more of your friends to die, do you?'

'Perish the thought,' said Charles bleakly. 'All right then, let's do this.'

They trooped back to the kitchen with their assortment of crockery, Hamish bouncing along in front. Sarah smiled fondly. Whatever the cloud hanging over the house, the little dog brought a welcome sense of normality. That made her feel a bit better about their prolonged stay with the Brett-Coates family.

They were obviously unwelcome, and with the number of incidents piling up, there was an inescapable sense that any one of them could be next. It was imperative that she sort this whole thing out, and as soon as possible.

The conversation they'd just had was giving her an idea. It would be a test of everyone's nerves if she went ahead with it. But it could be just the jolt that was needed to get some answers to the horrible questions swirling around Coates House.

THIRTY-EIGHT

Back in the kitchen, Sarah strode over to the larder where the big, old-fashioned chest freezer was kept. Inside, it was as neat as a filing cabinet. Mrs Bunforth had methodically packed it with produce from the garden, as well as the odd single portion of soup or stew. Sarah had a pang about her own freezer at home. She'd felt quite organised until she saw this. She flicked through the vegetable section, and then came to a stop.

'Here we go,' she said, plucking out a frosty-looking bag. 'Mushrooms.'

Daphne's jaw dropped. 'Don't tell me we're going to eat those,' she protested. 'We've only just had a conversation about this. You said you wouldn't trust them with a barge pole.'

'I think you're mixing your metaphors a bit there, Daph, and it was you who said you wouldn't be too sure about mushrooms you'd picked yourself – but Mrs Bunforth harvested these.'

'We don't know that, do we? It could be the killer, sneaking them in, after identifying the toxic ones with that book,' said Daphne, backing away.

'I don't think so. Look, this is Mrs B's writing. There's the date at the top, and it even says "Field mushrooms". Mrs Bunforth is so organised, I bet it would say "Death caps" if that's what they were.'

'Can we stop talking about it? This is giving my chakras the willies,' said Daphne with a shudder.

'Well, OK, we won't discuss it if you don't want to, but I'm proposing to make these into a lovely soup and serve them tonight.'

'You can't be serious, Sarah.' Daphne was aghast.

'Oh, but I am. Don't you see, Daph? If there's someone round the table with a guilty conscience, someone who's already poisoned two people in this house, then with any luck we should be able to flush them out with the mushrooms. Whoever it is has a lot of plant expertise, or, as you say, they've done their research with that book. They know just how lethal fungi can be. I think a poisoner will be very reluctant to eat something which is often toxic, and which they seem to have contemplated using themselves. Let's watch everyone's faces really carefully. It's a sure-fire way of making some progress.'

Daphne stared at Sarah, then shook her head slowly. 'All right. I don't like it, but I can see you're determined. My carrot thing didn't really work, anyway, and the courgettes aren't much better. Mushroom soup is one of my favourites too.'

'Great,' Sarah said. 'Do you want to cook it, or would you prefer to have a go at some bread?'

'I've never made bread,' Daphne said thoughtfully. 'But how hard can it be?'

* * *

It could be very hard indeed. The once-pristine kitchen was soon coated in flour again, with small dollops of half-baked dough everywhere, too. Luckily, Sarah unearthed a bread machine in the nick of time, and they set that up to make a quick loaf; otherwise, the soup plus a defrosted lasagne would have made a rather thin supper for a family used to three expertly produced courses whenever they sat down to eat.

Daphne ended up with quite a lot of dough in her hair, so shot upstairs to have a quick shower while Sarah put the finishing touches to a fruit platter they were planning to serve with ice cream for dessert, along with the few scones that were left.

Charles strolled in just as Sarah added some sliced tinned peaches to bulk up the dish. Hopefully everyone would be hungry enough not to make too much of a fuss.

'Anything I can do?' he said affably.

Wiping her hands on her apron, Sarah couldn't help smiling. 'You've timed that perfectly. I've just finished.'

'Ha! Still got it,' said Charles, picking up Sarah's playful mood and waltzing her around the kitchen, which she'd brought back to a flour-free state again.

Daphne burst in, just at that moment. 'You two! We need to feed these people, urgently. They're at each other's throats in there.'

'Well, good,' said Sarah, freeing herself from Charles's embrace a little reluctantly. 'That's what we want. They might let something slip about what's really going on here. Get back into the dining room, Daph, and keep your ears out on stalks. We'll be there in a minute with the soup.'

Daphne beetled off, and Sarah loaded the soup tureen and bowls onto a tray, while Charles carried in some wine and carafes of water. When they got to the dining room and started arranging everything on the sideboard, it was evident they'd interrupted a major row. Daphne was bursting to tell them something, but mercifully held it in, just saying to Sarah, 'Let me come back to the kitchen with you for that thing you've forgotten.'

'Forgotten? I think I... oh, yes, you're right,' Sarah said, catching on rather late. 'The, er, bread and butter. So sorry, everyone. After you, Daph.'

Safely back in the kitchen, Daphne exhaled. 'Well! Talk about brotherly love. Bernie was only telling Helena that she needs to pack her stuff and get out.'

'Goodness me! That's a bit hasty, so soon after the death of her mother. And Geoff too, not that she seems particularly bothered,' said Sarah.

'She might just be suppressing everything,' said Daphne doubtfully.

'Yes,' conceded Sarah. 'They're all under tremendous strain. They must be looking at each other all the time, wondering which of them did these dreadful things.'

'Well, I don't think it can be Letty. She's in cloud cuckoo land half the time,' Daphne said. 'That doesn't leave many options. Who do you think it is, Jonty or Bernard?'

Sarah sighed. 'When you say it like that, it seems so stark. Jonathan doesn't seem to hang around long enough to do anything, but he's certainly got time for planning while he's off wherever. Bernard – you would have thought he was too much the country gentleman. But money does funny things to people.'

'And hatred. We mustn't forget Helena, she's full of the stuff. And calculating, too.'

'I know what you mean,' said Sarah. 'But listen, we need to get back in there and keep an eye on the whole lot of them. Someone turned down the mushroom page of that poisons book for a reason. Hopefully they'll give themselves away when they see my soup. Now, I'll bring the bread and you take this cheese plate.'

'Oh, do we have to go back? I really feel like sneaking out through that door and running all the way home,' said Daphne, looking yearningly out into the stillness of the evening. She was quite right, thought Sarah. The lawn, and the car park beyond it where her trusty Volvo was parked, had never looked so enticing.

'We'll be letting Mariella down if we do a runner. And we wouldn't want to do that, now, would we?' Sarah said bracingly.

Back in the stifling dining room, Helena and Bernard were now studiously ignoring each other. Jonathan had put in one of his sporadic appearances, and was allowing the soup to run off his spoon and back into the bowl again. Letitia, most uncharacteristically, asked for a slice of bread and then gnawed at it like a rodent sharpening its teeth.

'This is as hard as iron,' she observed, opening her eyes wide.

'I thought you didn't touch carbs, anyway. Something wrong with the soup?' said Daphne, switching her gaze from Letitia to Sarah and back again in a less than subtle fashion.

Letitia peered into her bowl and swished around with her spoon. 'Probably not. I just don't like the look of it. When is Mrs Bunforth going to be back?'

'I thought I told you, Letty dear. We're not having a housekeeper any more. We'll manage perfectly well on our own until we sell this dreadful white elephant,' said Bernard, looking around at the beautiful cornices, high ceiling and swagged curtains that made the dining room such an impressive place.

'Still on about that?' Jonathan said with a twisted smile. 'You can't possibly go through with it. You love this place more than anyone.'

'On the contrary, brother dear. I've called an estate agent already. They'll be round in the next few days to measure up.' Bernard took a tiny spoonful of soup and smacked his lips in satisfaction.

'What the hell?' said Jonty, throwing down his napkin. 'Why does no one tell me anything?'

'We can't find you half the time,' said Helena. 'But you knew about our big brother's clever plan to make us homeless. I don't know why you're surprised. He's told me to get out already.'

Jonathan looked thunderstruck. 'I'm begging you, Bernard. Don't do this to your own flesh and blood.'

Bernard gave a dry bark of a laugh. 'Don't be ridiculous. It's about time you both had a dose of cold, hard reality. You've had a free ride for long enough. All the duties of this estate have fallen on my shoulders for years, while you, Hells, were snorting God-knows-what off goodness-knows-who in dens of depravity in the States. And you're no better, Jonty. You were right here on the spot, but you've shown no interest in running things – spending all your time giving that gardener Peabody the eye. Meanwhile Geoff was busy selling off the family silver.'

Jonathan shot to his feet. 'You take that back. Geoff was a saint to put up with me, and living with you lot was driving him mad. He'd never steal from me.'

'He wasn't stealing from you, Jonty. Everything here belongs to *me*. He was taking my birthright, not yours. It's a jolly good thing he's dead if you ask me. Saves me from wringing his neck myself.'

It would have been a speech in poor taste at any time, but considering that Geoff currently lay awaiting burial, it landed particularly badly. Jonathan lunged for Bernard, and started busily choking the life out of him. Charles tried to pry Jonathan's hands off his brother's neck. Then Daphne managed to whack Jonathan across the head with the ceramic water jug.

The blow stopped him in his tracks and he slumped to the ground, liquid sloshing everywhere.

THIRTY-NINE

Sarah darted forward, to check on Jonathan's head wound. 'It's OK,' she said, after feeling the lump carefully. 'Nothing broken. He's just stunned. He'll have quite a headache.'

'Sorry,' said Daphne. 'But I could see Bernard turning blue...'

'No, no, that was quick thinking. You did right,' said Sarah, patting Daphne on the shoulder.

'Yes. The last thing we need is another corpse on our hands,' said Helena, making straight for the drinks tray. 'Anyone want a top-up?'

Bernard, who was sitting slumped in his chair, with Letitia fluttering around him, nodded vigorously. 'Christ, that hurt,' he rasped.

'Hmm. You might be hoarse for a while. And I expect there'll be some interesting bruising tomorrow,' said Sarah.

'Lord alone knows what I'll say to the police about that.' Bernard shook his head. 'Letty, I'm fine, for heaven's sake stop hovering and sit down.'

'Well, pardon me for caring. See what a wonderful wife I am? Even when you're trying to fire the help and make me do all the dogsbody work around here, I still want to make sure you're OK. And that's the thanks I get,' said Letitia, flouncing back to her place and taking a hefty swig of her wine.

'Is it even legal to sack Mrs Bunforth when she's in a coma?' said Daphne thoughtfully.

Sarah had wondered the same thing, and watched Bernard with interest as he squirmed in his seat. 'Sometimes you have to make hard decisions,' was his only reply.

Jonathan, getting himself up slowly under Sarah's watchful eye, rubbed the sore place on his head. 'Well, this is one of the easiest decisions *I've* ever made. I'm leaving this place, and I'm never coming back.'

'Yet another disappearing act?' said Helena with one of her fake yawns. 'Change the record, why don't you?'

'I'm not sure we're allowed off the premises anyway, old boy,' said Charles gently. 'Not till the police have sorted things out.'

Jonathan slumped in his seat. 'Could someone get me some paracetamol, at least?'

Sarah fished in her handbag, producing a packet which she slid over the table to him. He took it silently.

'Well, if everyone's had enough soup and lasagne, I'll go and get the pudding,' said Sarah, getting to her feet. Tensions seemed to have died down a little and she reckoned it was safe to leave the siblings on their own for five minutes.

She and Daphne collected up the plates and bowls, noting that no one had finished the soup, other than loyal Charles. Unfortunately, it was impossible to tell whether that was because they feared the mushrooms – or if it was the sadly more likely possibility, that it wasn't very nice. The bread, too, was largely untouched, but was to stay on the table while the cheese board went round.

Once they were back in the kitchen, which was fast beginning to seem weirdly like a haven, Daphne let out a great sigh of relief. 'Thank goodness we've got away from them for a bit. Honestly, they're all as bad as each other – or rather, each of them is horrible, but in completely different ways.'

'Are they all awful? Or is one of them deliberately winding up the others? Think about it, Daph. I'm getting quite a bad feeling about this,' Sarah said.

'What do you mean?' Daphne gazed at her.

Sarah considered for a second. No point in terrifying her friend. 'It makes you wonder what Madeleine Brett-Coates was like, doesn't it? Did she tolerate all this sniping? Did she even encourage it? Some parents seem to enjoy watching their children having a go at each other.'

'I can't think why,' said Daphne. 'It's miserable. Now, what are we going to give them to cheer them up a bit?'

'There's the fruit salad I made earlier. Can you get the ice cream from the freezer? I'm going to microwave a couple of bars of chocolate to drizzle over as a sauce. People can make their own sundaes. And there are the scones, of course.'

'That sounds brilliant, Sarah! You should do this for a living.'

'I'm not sure anyone else would agree. The soup didn't exactly go down a storm.'

'They don't know what they were missing,' said Daphne stoutly.

'But you didn't finish it either, Daph,' Sarah said.

'Well, you mentioned poison a few too many times while you were making it. That does rather kill the appetite,' Daphne said, sneaking a couple of berries out of the fruit salad. 'OK then, I don't suppose we can avoid them any longer.'

They trooped back into the dining room, and Sarah was relieved to find things seemed mellower now. Perhaps it was the fact that the cheese was the perfect thing to fill up on, if you were a little nervous, either about Sarah and Daphne's cooking or poisoned mushrooms, while the puddings were the type of nursery food all those round the table had grown up with. Even Letitia seemed tempted by the delicious ice cream, much to Sarah's surprise. Helena picked at the Stilton, while looking disapprovingly round at other people's plates.

Bernard was suddenly full of bonhomie again, and seemed to have recovered from Jonathan's death grip on his throat. He left the table briefly, to return with a bottle of port, which was covered with cobwebs. Sarah was sure it must have come from the cellar. She shivered inwardly at the thought of going down there, in the increasingly velvety darkness of night, to ferret around for a bottle where someone had so recently died from stress and claustrophobia. But, to her astonishment, even Jonathan seemed unaffected. He hadn't made good on his latest threat to run off, and he now examined the port with interest.

'Ah, the 1994 Cockburn's. Very nice. I'd say this must be a special occasion, but that would be morbid.'

'Well, we should make the most of these family times, eh, Letty?' Bernard said jovially, pouring the port into small crystal glasses and handing them round with great ceremony. 'Before we all go our separate ways.'

'What?' said Letitia, who was now watching chocolate sauce drip off her spoon onto a pool of melted ice cream, her eyes unfocused.

Bernard waved a hand as though to say, 'Ignore her.' 'Seriously, Jonty. I wish you nothing but the best. You know that.' He raised his glass and sipped the port. The thick liquid caught the light, seeming to glow.

Sarah watched Jonathan curiously. At first, it seemed he wasn't going to return his brother's toast. Then he thought better of it, saluting with his glass even as he winced at the movement. His head was clearly still paining him.

'You can take another two paracetamol in four hours or so,' she said to him in a low voice.

Unfortunately, the reference to the fracas earlier seemed to break the uneasy truce. Helena was the first to set her glass down with a snap. 'Well, much as we want to brush all the unpleasantness of the past day or so under the carpet, there are a few unpalatable facts that just won't go away. Rather like your bread, Daphne,' she said, poking the now concrete-like crust on her plate.

'I say, that's a bit much,' said Charles, always chivalrous.

'Yes, especially as it was Sarah who actually made it,' said Daphne, cheerfully throwing her friend under the bus.

Sarah, giving Daphne a glance, turned to Helena. 'You mean the murders?' she said.

'Yes, I suppose,' said Helena with a shrug. 'And the fact that Jonty and I are being kicked out.'

It was an interesting sense of priorities, Sarah thought. The grisly death of her mother and brother-in-law had been more or less forgotten, while the looming question of what became of her next was very much uppermost in Helena's mind.

'You always were totally self-centred,' said Bernard, summing up Sarah's thoughts pretty accurately. 'We haven't even had the funerals yet and already you've sidelined Mumsy. After all she did for you! The fortune she spent on rehabs, time after time. That last one, in the desert somewhere, why, it cost over a hundred grand. And you're still knocking the booze back.' He gave her a look of disgust.

'For your information, that detox was just for substances, which I have not touched now, ooh, for months. It had nothing to do with alcohol. So it was a complete success and worth every penny.' Helena folded her arms.

'Well, it's not worth a single one of my pennies. You'll have to look elsewhere next time you fall off the wagon, because you won't be getting any help from this quarter.' Bernard looked every bit as angry as Helena.

'Fine. Anyway, you might do well to save up for an intervention a bit closer to home,' Helena sniped, looking sideways at

Letitia. The other woman carried on gazing straight ahead, licking her ice cream spoon. Bernard shifted uncomfortably in his seat. 'That is, if you want to do anything about her little problem,' Helena continued. 'But I'd say it suits you just fine, the fact that she's in a daze half the time.'

'I have no idea what you mean by that, but I resent your tone,' blustered Bernard.

Now Jonathan joined in with a dry laugh. 'God, Mumsy would love this, if she could see it. She adored these evenings, when we were all at each other's throats. Are we doing it for her, now, or is it just habit to attack each other rather than face our real problems?'

'I'd like to know what you think those problems are. To all intents and purposes, we lead a charmed life in this house. We've got enough to eat, a roof over our heads... It's the height of crass behaviour to complain about our lot,' Bernard snarled.

'Except that, as you keep pointing out, you're making us homeless. No roof for us, and no dosh either. I don't know what on earth you expect us to do now. We're constitutionally unable to fend for ourselves, Mumsy made sure of that,' Jonathan said with a smile that pulled his mouth downwards.

'Well, you shouldn't have too much trouble at least, Jonty. You must be making a mint with that TV nonsense. Everyone knows telly folk get paid hand over fist.' Bernard took a hefty swig of his port and refilled his glass to the brim.

Jonathan winced. 'For your information, my show has been cancelled. I was working up to telling Mumsy this weekend. I never got a chance.' He hung his head, and Sarah was alarmed to see tears trickling down his cheeks. She passed him a tissue.

'Oh, spare us the waterworks. What happened? Did the great unwashed public get sick of seeing you tossing those curls in front of some poor sap's flowerbeds?' Bernard was at his most cutting.

Helena, however, clapped her hands. 'You're in the same

boat as me, then! What are we going to do? We need to stick together. I think we should get a lawyer to contest the will,' she said avidly.

Jonathan looked at her in disgust. 'Oh, that's right. Not a word of sympathy for me, as my career goes down the toilet. You're just thrilled I'm in the gutter with you. After all the work I've put into that show! That TV company has got no gratitude. They won't be able to make it work without me.'

'Really? Are they shelving the show?' Helena asked.

'No... they're carrying on with another presenter. But it will be a disaster,' Jonathan said crossly.

'Someone younger and prettier, I expect,' said Bernard. 'What did you expect? Did you think they wanted you because of your special way with a spade? Ha! You must be joking.'

'I have qualifications, Bernard,' Jonathan said through gritted teeth. 'Why do you always have to put me down?' He looked as though he was set fair for a serious meltdown.

'Anyone want more ice cream?' said Letitia, getting to her feet and wafting out of the room.

'Well, if she doesn't take the biscuit? What the hell have you got her hooked on these days?' said Helena furiously to Bernard. 'And does she even know she's taking it?'

'I've no idea what you're talking about,' Bernard sniffed. 'She's highly strung, that's all. You just wind her up. Well, her, and everyone else in this place. Mumsy knew how to handle her, that's the difference.'

'I bet she did. Put her in a straitjacket, did she?' Helena said pointedly. 'We'd better watch out tonight. It's a full moon. She'll be even worse than usual. Looks like there's a storm coming as well.'

Sarah looked towards the windows. Clouds were banked up alarmingly; there was a stiff wind blowing and the cedar trees were swaying crazily. As she watched, the heavens opened and rain began to pelt down.

'Oh, don't be absurd. Letitia wouldn't hurt a fly, you know that,' said Bernard.

At that moment, there was a huge peal of thunder overhead. The dining room door was flung open, and in walked Letitia with a massive carving knife in her hand, its wicked blade flashing as lightning pulsed across the darkening sky.

FORTY

'Letty! Don't do anything hasty, now,' said Bernard, as he got out of his chair and approached his wife carefully. Letitia, the knife trembling in her hand, looked wildly round the room, her huge eyes tracking from face to face.

'Which one of you was it? Who d-did it?' she said in a high-pitched, shaky voice.

'Did what, Letty?' said Helena, managing to sound both bored and angry at the same time. 'Don't you think you should put that knife down? It looks quite heavy.'

Letitia's gaze swung from Helena to the knife in her hand and back again. She looked almost confused that she was carrying the huge weapon. There was a sudden clatter, as she dropped it unceremoniously on top of the cheese plate.

'Oh no,' said Daphne. 'You've squashed that Brie completely. It was really nice, I was hoping for another slice.'

'You can scrape it off the handle,' said Sarah quietly to her. 'But let's wait a minute,' she added, as Daphne put a hand out.

Quick as a flash, Jonathan grabbed the knife, rushed to the window, and chucked it out into the teeming rain. 'There. That's dealt with *that*,' he said.

Letitia looked at him as though he'd taken leave of his senses. 'But what will we cut the cheese with now?'

'Um, there's a cheese knife on the board already, Letty?' said Jonathan, as though humouring a child. He pointed to it; it was mercifully both small and blunt. 'Can I get you a drink?'

Letitia nodded absently and Jonathan set about refilling her glass.

'Do you think you should?' Sarah said. 'I'm not sure she needs it.'

'Letty is not a child, Sarah. If she wants a drink, she should have one. Shouldn't you, darling?' said Bernard, taking the glass from Jonathan and sloshing even more of the port into it. 'Honestly, people can take too much on themselves.'

'Sorry,' said Sarah, feeling chastened. 'It was just that—'

'I'll have some more if you're pouring,' said Charles, with a faint wink at Sarah. He was probably right. There was no point in arguing with Bernard, even though it was clear to her that more alcohol was absolutely the last thing the woman needed, for various reasons.

Sure enough, it wasn't long before Letitia's head started nodding as she slumped in her chair. The electric energy she'd possessed when she burst into the room had ebbed away.

'What was she talking about, anyway?' said Helena suddenly. '"Which of you did it?" That's what she said.'

'I haven't a clue,' said Jonathan, looking surprised.

'Surely it has to be the murders?' Sarah spoke up. 'We're all wondering, aren't we?'

'Pay no attention to Letty. She's just tired,' said Bernard, ignoring Sarah. 'I'd better see you up to bed, hadn't I, poppet?' he added to his wife, with one of those lightning-quick changes to doting husband mode. He hoisted her up and helped her stumble around the table and out of the door, leaning heavily on him. They heard the couple going slowly up the stairs, punctuated with high-pitched giggling from Letitia and low murmuring from Bernard.

Once there was silence, Charles got up and shut the door. 'Well, probably for the best. I'd say she'll have quite the hangover tomorrow,' he said cheerfully.

'That's if she wakes up at all,' said Helena darkly.

Daphne looked at Sarah in horror.

'Why would you say that?' Jonathan pounced.

'Well, we've had the odd unscheduled death around here, haven't we?' Helena replied.

'Bernard must be the most likely victim, if anyone's going to cop it tonight,' said Jonathan, with an almost manic gleam in his eye.

'How do you work that out, dear brother?' Helena said. Despite the amount of drink she'd put away, she still seemed as sober as a judge.

'Well, if he dies, then the will is void, isn't it? Everything reverts back to us.'

'I'd be surprised if that were the case.' Sarah spoke quietly. 'Usually it would just mean that the money would go to Bernard's next of kin if, heaven forbid, anything did happen. Presumably that's Letitia?'

'Ha!' said Helena. 'And good luck getting any change out of that junkie. It's all going straight up her nose, everything Mother worked for.'

'Mumsy will be revolving in her grave, that's for sure,' said Jonathan, glum now.

'And she's not even buried yet,' Helena added.

Sarah couldn't help shivering. It would have been a pretty unsavoury topic of conversation at any time, let alone with two members of the family in their coffins. And yet, was it a chance to get a little further on?

'Some of the clues after your mother's, um, unfortunate death seem to point to Letty. The strips of red fabric – you must both know about those. They didn't come from her dress, but they certainly suggested her. Do you think she left them lying around as a kind of joke, or was someone trying to imply she was involved? Might she have done it, after all, as part of a long-term attempt to get her hands on the money? For instance, if she knew that your mother had rewritten her will?'

'Letty doesn't know what day it is half the time,' said Jonathan dismissively.

'Typical man,' said Helena. 'Always so quick to write a woman off. She was an actress, wasn't she? Before she married our brother.'

'Well, of a sort. She was doing workshops for school-children,' Jonathan clarified.

'Fine. Even if she was terrible, that's still her training. Who's to say she doesn't put on that druggie air? I find it pretty convincing, but then I'm more used to being high than being sober, let's face it. And Bernard is easy to fool, as you should know, Jonty.'

'What do you mean by that?' Jonathan was instantly alert.

'Oh, all this pretending you're heartbroken not to have old Geoff around. When anyone could tell you were sick of his shenanigans and were moving on with Peabody. More's the pity. I quite fancy him myself.'

Jonathan scraped back his chair and towered over Helena. 'Take that back! I loved Geoff. We were happy together...' He burst into tears and pounded the table in front of her, making all the glasses jump and skitter. 'You know we were. Peabody – John, I should say – he was nothing but a distraction. That was all over ages ago.'

'You forget. I have the room next door to yours, thanks to Mother. And the walls are thin. I heard all your screaming rows. I know Geoff was getting through money like water. I don't know what he was spending it on – I just know he was bleeding you dry. And now he's gone. All right, so is your TV job, for now. But you can find something else, and you'll be better off without him.'

'Damn you, Hells. It wasn't like that. It wasn't like that at all.'

Jonathan was now red in the face, and shaking with rage. Helena, as usual, looked as cool as a cucumber, those intelligent, amused eyes raking her brother's disarray and finding him wanting. Jonathan's fists bunched and for a second Sarah was worried he might lash out – but then Bernard burst back into the room.

'Letty's out like a light, poor girl. Overtired. There's been a lot going on. What's happening here? Not you two falling out again? For goodness' sake. They've been like this since childhood, haven't they, Charles? If one says black, the other swears it's white. Well, you need to learn to pick your battles. We have to stick together now.'

Jonathan chose this moment to walk out again, showing exactly what he thought of his brother's idea. Meanwhile Helena spoke up. 'That's rich, coming from you! Not so family-minded when Chivers was handing you the entire estate, were you?' She swigged the rest of her port and slammed down the glass.

'That wasn't Chivers's idea, though, was it? How was I to know what Mumsy had up her sleeve?' Bernard rubbed a hand over his face.

'That's your story, and you're sticking to it. But don't forget, I know you were having little meetings with Mother, right up until the day she died. What were you talking about? You were planning this coup, weren't you?' Helena got up and sloshed the dregs of the port bottle into her glass.

'That was about the fair! It takes a lot of organisation. Not that you'd know, you've never once wanted to get your hands dirty with a real job. Maybe that was behind Mumsy's decision. She was well aware that I know more about running the estate than you and Jonty put together. What do you understand about the real cost of things? That port, for instance, that you're drinking like Ribena. Do you know how much we could get for it at auction?'

'If it's so special, why did you bring it up from the cellar for this lot to guzzle? They wouldn't know fine wine from Sarson's vinegar. No offence, Charles,' Helena said with an on-off smile. He returned it, but rather uncertainly. Daphne snorted, and Sarah tried her best to shrug off this latest insult. 'Anyway, at least you've admitted it at last, Bernard. You're happy with the way things have turned out.'

Bernard looked at his sister's face, animated now after the port. 'I can't help feeling that Mumsy had her head screwed on, as usual. Look at the way you two are losing it over this. It doesn't exactly give the impression that you're competent human beings,' he snapped.

'Competent? I'll give you blasted competence,' Helena said, losing control completely and hurling her wine glass into the fireplace. 'How would you feel if you were about to be thrown out onto the street?'

FORTY-ONE

Sarah and Daphne sheltered instinctively as Helena's glass flew, with Sarah snatching Hamish up to keep him out of harm's way. Butler was safe in his basket at the other end of the room.

'As for you,' Helena shrieked at Sarah. 'Bringing that smelly mutt here, as if your presence isn't obnoxious enough. For goodness' sake, how thick-skinned do you have to be, not to see that you've long outstayed your welcome?'

Sarah couldn't help clutching Hamish all the tighter. Charles stepped between them. 'I say, Hells. Hamish isn't smelly, not like Butler there. Sorry, but it's true, he's getting a bit whiffy in his old age.' He pointed to the comatose Labrador, who'd managed to snooze through the raised voices and breaking glass. 'And where do you expect us to go, after midnight in the middle of a raging storm?'

'I wasn't talking about you, Charles. You can stay,' said Helena, who was now swaying slightly.

'Where Sarah goes, I go,' said Charles steadfastly. Sarah smiled at him.

'You've drunk an awful lot of port, Helena,' Sarah said. 'Perhaps you'd better sit down.'

'Perhaps *you'd* better shut the hell up,' Helena said waspishly, but she subsided into a chair.

'Look, I think we just have to thrash this thing out,' said Bernard. 'Your presence here is seriously disruptive, Helena. You're rude to me, you show no respect for my wife, you go out of your way to offend our guests...'

'Guests! Are you crazy? These people were not invited...' Helena was getting into her stride, when Bernard went up to her, dragged her out of her seat as though she was a rag doll, and escorted her to the door with a horrifying brusqueness.

'They *were* invited. I asked them to stay on. You, on the other hand... Well, it's time you were in bed,' he said, shoving her into the corridor and shutting the door behind her. 'She's impossible when she gets like this. I'm sorry, all,' he said, a hand going up to his brow. 'She's been a nightmare since she was thirteen years old. Mumsy despaired of her. And don't get me started on Jonty. Families, eh?'

'So sorry, old boy. Very difficult time for you all,' said Charles with wonderful understatement.

'Well, I think I'll just get a dustpan and brush and get this glass up; it'll be no good if it gets in poor Butler's paws,' said Sarah. 'Could you hold Hamish?' She tried to pass the little dog over to Daphne, but for once he was not amenable. 'OK, Hamish, OK. I'll take him with me. Can you keep an eye on Butler, just in case he wakes up and treads on any of the bits?'

Daphne nodded and Sarah trooped off to the kitchen. For some reason, the corridor was in darkness. She tried pressing a few of the light switches as she walked along – easier once she'd finally put Hamish down and he'd agreed to trot under his own steam – but nothing seemed to be working. All the lights couldn't have blown at once, surely?

Sarah more or less felt her way to the kitchen, and opened the door with relief. She'd just put a foot over the threshold when there was a mighty clap of thunder, then almost immediately lightning split the sky through the kitchen window – illuminating a dark shape waiting behind the door for her. She clutched her chest in terror.

'For goodness' sake, it's just me,' said Jonathan.

Once Sarah had calmed down and slumped into one of the kitchen chairs, she opened her mouth to speak.

'Before you start,' said Jonathan, 'I had no idea you'd be walking in here or that I'd give you such a turn. I know my way around without switching the lights on, of course. I wasn't skulking in the dark to give you a fright.'

'Of course not,' said Sarah, her heart still beating fast enough to beat the band. 'It's just that... well, the lights aren't working in the corridor.'

'That's odd,' said Jonathan, walking over to a fuse box high up on the wall in the far corner of the room. 'Oh, the switch for the corridor circuit was flipped. It'll be fine again now.'

'It's been quite a night,' said Sarah, a little breathlessly. 'This storm is spectacular.'

'Yes. I always think they hit us differently at Coates House,' said Jonathan. 'Maybe it's because we're on a slightly elevated plain, away from the village, but thunder and lightning seem to rain down on us.'

'And not just the meteorological kind, either. Are things always this tense between you and your brother and sister?'

Jonathan seemed to hesitate, perhaps on the verge of walking out again. Then he decided against it, instead going to a cupboard and fetching a bottle of wine and two glasses. He poured one for Sarah and took the other for himself. Hamish curled up at his feet.

Jonathan tickled the dog for a moment before speaking. 'You'd have to admit, these are special circumstances. I deny any family in the land to keep smiling through what we're going through.'

'Of course,' said Sarah. 'Please forgive me. It was a ridiculous thing to say.'

'It's not that I don't agree with your broader point. We're pretty dysfunctional. I used to hope Mumsy was keeping us here together to make us get on, iron out our differences. It didn't work at all, of course. Then it finally struck me that she enjoyed the rows. After that, I tried to be away as much as possible with the TV show, and then Helena spent years getting treatment in the States anyway.'

'Would you say your mother changing the will was out of character?' Sarah asked carefully.

'What do you mean?' Jonathan sat up a little straighter. 'Are you saying Bernard could have put pressure on her?'

'Would that be a possibility? Obviously he's gained an awful lot, while you two have lost out comprehensively. Yet your mother never warned you this was coming?'

'Don't get me wrong,' Jonathan said, swirling the wine in his glass. 'Occasionally she'd threaten us. "If you don't shape up, then you'll get your comeuppance, all these years of taking me for granted..." Blah blah blah. The sort of thing any parent says to their children.' He was quite offhand.

Sarah, who'd never heard anything like this from her own beloved mother, and wouldn't dream of saying it to her children either, waited for him to go on.

'But I never thought for a moment she meant it,' Jonathan said. 'And I was doing pretty much everything she wanted. Well, I thought so.'

'I'm sure most mothers would be proud of having a famous son,' Sarah said.

'You'd have thought so,' said Jonathan sadly. 'In fact, what she wanted was an heir. It won't have escaped your notice, but none of us has children. And we're all, as Mumsy kept telling us, getting on.'

'Did that matter to her?' Sarah was surprised. It was the first she'd heard of this, though now she thought about it, it did seem a pity there was no younger generation to inherit such a beautiful house.

'Oh yes. She really felt it. She was furious when I married Geoff.'

FORTY-TWO

Sarah sat forward, conscious they might be getting to the nub of the issue. Could this be why Jonathan had been cut out of his mother's will?

'You'll be thinking Mumsy was homophobic,' Jonathan said. 'She wasn't. She just wanted grandchildren.'

'There would be nothing to stop you having them, via adoption or a surrogate,' said Sarah.

'True. If Geoff had been interested. But for all his obsession with history, he wasn't one to think of the future and had no urge to have kids. This place wasn't his anyway. He didn't feel the need to pass it on.'

'But surely he would have compromised, if you were really keen?' Sarah was intrigued.

'Maybe. But I thought we had all the time in the world. Geoff was in his fifties, but I'm ten years younger – bit of an afterthought for Mumsy.' He gulped the rest of his wine, then refilled both their glasses. 'As for Helena, there was never a chance she'd think of anyone but herself. I mean, come on, you've spent enough time with her now.'

There was certainly a steely quality about Helena that

might be hard to square with motherhood. 'But what about Bernard? I suppose Letitia is the right sort of age?' Sarah was fishing now, given her suspicions in that direction.

'What age even is she? Hard to know under all the Botox and cocaine. It must be awful for Helena. She's done her best to stay off the stuff, and there's Letty, going at the coke like a demented hoover.'

Sarah took the tiniest sip of her wine, trying to stay on track. 'The will... Your mother didn't ask Mr Chivers here to go over it. She went to his office instead. Was that normal?'

Sarah's casual tone didn't fool Jonathan for a minute. 'Are you suggesting fraud? But Mumsy signed the new version. She would have noticed any changes she hadn't authorised. No, much though I'd love to blame this whole fiasco on Bernard, I don't think he can have forced her hand. He seemed as astonished as any of us. And he knows I'll be OK in the end. Some other production company will give me work. The question is what to do with Helena. But that's always the issue. She comes over as hard, but inside she's a jelly. That's why she's such a demon for the drugs. They prop her up, or at least she thinks so. Until it all goes pear-shaped again.'

Sarah was impressed by Jonathan's insight, and also his compassion. 'Would you send her to rehab again?' she asked.

'She's not a parcel – we can't just drop her off at the Post Office.' Jonathan hunched over his wine. 'She'd have to want to go – and I'm sure she's probably at the denial stage right now. Don't they say you have to reach rock bottom before you can turn things around? Granted, with her, it's a carousel, with all-time lows flashing past at regular intervals. Besides, Bernard won't be footing the bill. He's made that more than plain, and thanks to Mumsy I can't afford it.'

'Do you think you or Helena might contest the will, as she suggested?' Sarah tried to sound casual again. 'That way Helena could pay for her own treatment.'

'Are you usually this interested in strangers' affairs?' The question was sharp, but Jonathan's expression was amused rather than angry. 'Oh, we're stuck here, aren't we? We might as well talk. The situation must seem intriguing – if you're outside it.'

'I'm afraid it is rather fascinating,' Sarah said. 'I lead a quiet life down by the sea.' This wasn't entirely true – she'd witnessed a lot of hair-raising events recently – but if Jonathan assumed she was a pensioner mesmerised by the activities of this wealthy and rather glamorous family, then so much the better.

'Well, lucky you, I suppose,' he said, in an unconvincing way. It was clear that, despite all the current disadvantages of being a Brett-Coates, he'd still take that over an obscure retirement. 'Still, you'll be back to that soon.'

Sarah gave a smile, trying not to look too thrilled at the prospect. A nice rest in a deckchair on the beach certainly sounded just the ticket right now. 'So... the will?' she reminded him gently.

'What? Oh, contesting it. I don't know. Helena might want to, but how would she pay a lawyer?'

'She does have a lot of expensive jewellery,' said Sarah, remembering all those gorgeous diamond earrings. 'It could raise a pretty penny, I'm sure.'

'Sell her own stuff? Never,' said Jonathan. 'She relies on someone else footing the bill to get shot of her. And don't be fooled by the designer labels – her last boyfriend bought her all that clobber, but it soon went sour. The diamonds may not be all they seem, either. Mumsy gave her a triple-strand pearl necklace years ago, for her twenty-first. In the family for generations. She'd sold it within a week and replaced it with some rubbish from a high street store. Mumsy spotted it straight away and went nuts. I expect Hells still plays the same tricks, but she's probably better now at sourcing her fakes. As for me, I can't face the hassle or expense of legal action. And I'm certainly not going to do it on behalf of my sister.'

'Fair enough,' said Sarah. 'Well, listen. I've probably held you up long enough. I came out here to get a dustpan and brush. I suppose I'd better get on with it.'

'Fine,' said Jonathan. 'I'll stay here and finish this,' he said, lowering his head to drink again. Sarah wasn't quite sure if he meant the glass or the bottle, but she left him to it and took Hamish back to the dining room. Having settled him on Daphne's lap, she set about clearing away the glass as best she could.

'We'd better run the hoover over this in daylight,' she said when she'd straightened up. 'There's bound to be bits we've left. I'd hate anyone to get cut.'

'Especially the doggies,' said Daphne, patting Butler. Luckily, he was at that stage in a dog's life where he was happy to snooze his hours away, unless of course it was time for dinner. He opened one eye to check this was not the case, then subsided back into dreams of younger days.

Charles was looking uneasy, standing by the window watching the rain lashing down. 'Nice weather for ducks, I suppose,' he said, with an attempt at a twinkle. Sarah admired him for trying to lighten the atmosphere, though she feared it was pretty much a lost cause.

Bernard, meanwhile, was slumped in one of the easy chairs, a bottle and glass within reach. In fact, his position mirrored Jonty's, though they were in separate rooms. How sad that this family was so fractured. Madeleine Brett-Coates must have known that her will would put the cat among the pigeons, though there hadn't been much love lost even before Mr Chivers's bombshell.

'It's probably time I went up to bed. It's been quite an eventful day,' Sarah said.

'Yes, and I don't mean to seem unhospitable, but I'd like you packed up and gone first thing tomorrow. Your investigation seems to be going nowhere, in any case,' Bernard said.

'Oh. Of course,' said Sarah. She understood Bernard's point of view but wasn't sure she'd have put it so bluntly.

Daphne gave Butler a last pat, and Charles made as though to leave too, but Bernard waved to him to sit down. 'Not you, old chap. Stay and have a quick one.'

'For the road, as it were?' Charles raised an eyebrow. 'All right then.'

Sarah sighed inwardly and she and Daphne trooped out. 'Do you think they'll be up all night, boozing?' Daphne asked as they climbed the oak staircase with Hamish in tow.

'Charles is more than welcome to Bernard's company,' Sarah whispered, opening the door to her room. 'Well, goodn—' she started, when a bloodcurdling scream rang out from one of the other bedrooms. She and Daphne both jumped a mile, and Hamish started to bark.

FORTY-THREE

Sarah wheeled round. 'Where did that come from?' she asked Daphne urgently, making sure Hamish was safely in her room.

'I think it was up here,' said her friend, climbing the stairs and gesturing for Sarah to join her. 'This one, I think,' she said when they'd reached the landing. She rattled the doorknob ferociously. 'It's locked.'

Sarah knocked on the door. 'Is everything all right in there? Is this Helena's bedroom, or Letty's?' she asked Daphne in a whisper.

'I don't know, they're next to each other, aren't they? I'm not sure, it's so dark up here.'

'I'll try again.' Sarah put her mouth to the door, and said loudly, 'Are you OK? Please say something.' There was no response.

Charles pounded up the stairs, two at a time. 'I heard a scream. What's going on?'

'We're trying to find out,' Sarah said. 'The door is locked.'

Then Helena poked her head round the next door along. 'What's this racket? It's impossible to get a wink of sleep in this place. What are you lot up to?'

She was slurring her words, and her hair was everywhere, but Helena was still strikingly beautiful, her creamy complexion set off by the dark ivy silk of her bias-cut nightgown, which skimmed very good legs.

'Ahem. If everything's OK here, I'll just go to bed...' Charles said, averting his eyes.

'Charles, no. Helena is fine, which must mean it's Letty who screamed. We need to get her door open,' said Sarah.

'I suppose I'll just have to break it in,' said Charles glumly, after rattling the handle with about as much effectiveness as Daphne.

'Wait a sec,' said Sarah. 'Let's try calling her again. She might only have had a bad dream or something,' she said.

Helena stepped forward and rapped sharply on the door. 'Letty! What's going on in there? Are you all right?'

There was silence, and everyone looked at each other. 'Oh, Christ,' said Helena. 'Let's hope she hasn't done anything stupid.'

'Why would you think that?' Sarah was alarmed.

'Well, because she *is* stupid,' said Helena bluntly. 'Before you smash the door, I'll get the spare key. She's done this before.' She returned in a few moments, and unlocked the door. It swung open, and everyone hesitated on the threshold.

'We can't all go in, we'll frighten her out of her senses,' said Daphne.

'Not that she has any, but all right.' Helena shrugged. 'I'll be back in my bed if anyone wants me,' she said with a glance at Charles.

'Right,' said Sarah. 'Charles, you stand guard. I'll go in. Daphne, you ring Mariella.'

'I'll nip downstairs for my phone and be right back up,' Daphne said.

Sarah stepped forward into the darkness of Letitia's bedroom.

FORTY-FOUR

The room smelt of Letitia's floral scent. Sarah could hardly see a thing. She just about made it to the window and pulled the curtains open, revealing the howling night. Now she could make out the rumpled bed – it was empty. She flung open the floor-to-ceiling wardrobes next, but revealed only serried ranks of frilly dresses. Letitia must be in the ensuite bathroom. Sarah snapped on the light, but there was nothing but a tangle of wet towels on the floor and bottles of Letitia's favourite perfume and body lotion on the shelves. Sarah stepped closer. It was Penhaligon's Bluebell.

That couldn't be a coincidence, could it? This case kept dancing around bluebells like a spring breeze, and all the while Letitia was merrily spritzing herself with their essence. Sarah sniffed the bottle, and the sweet scent transported her back to the myriad flowers near the folly. For goodness' sake. Could nothing be simple in this house? And where was the blasted woman anyway?

She was bracing herself to do a proper search of the bedside tables when there was a loud crash from downstairs. Tearing outside, she bumped into Daphne and Charles, both looking rather disconcerted in the half-light.

'Where did that bang come from, do you know?'

'I think it was the kitchen,' said Charles. 'I'm going to get a poker from the drawing room. Never know what you might find in a place like this,' he said.

'OK then, let's all go,' said Sarah. Daphne nodded and brought up the rear as they trooped downstairs to the drawing room and then went in procession to the kitchen, with Charles in the lead brandishing the poker.

'What are we waiting for?' Sarah whispered while Charles hesitated on the threshold.

'Um, nothing,' he said, gripping the poker more tightly. 'Just wondering where Mariella's got to. Daphne rang her, what, at least five minutes ago?'

Daphne nodded. 'Poor Mari. It's no fun having to get out of bed in the middle of the night.'

'Well, we can all sympathise there,' said Sarah. 'Not that we've even managed to get to bed yet. Now, shall we just see what's going on in this kitchen, then?'

'You don't want to wait for reinforcements?' Daphne dithered.

There was a scrabble in the hall and Hamish trotted up to them, very intrigued by this new game. 'I thought I'd shut my door to keep you in,' said Sarah. 'But great, now that you're here, you can protect us, can't you, boy?'

With that, she reached around Charles and grabbed the doorknob. The door fell open with a creak, and they stepped inside, Hamish pattering after them. There, on the floor, was Jonathan Brett-Coates, moaning faintly.

Sarah rushed forward and examined him. He was lying curled up, and seemed to be clutching his forehead. 'May I have a look?' she asked, moving his hand gently out of the way. There was a big contusion just above his eyebrow on the right-hand side. 'Has someone hit you again?' It wasn't long since Daphne had clonked him on the head with that jug, though luckily in a different spot.

Jonathan swallowed a couple of times and spoke, while remaining on the floor. 'No. No, nothing like that. I'm afraid it's a bit ridiculous... too much to drink. I must have been nodding off, and just toppled from the chair. Hit that stone hot water bottle Mrs B uses as a doorstop. So stupid. Could you help me up?'

Charles stepped forward and got his hands under Jonathan's armpits, struggling to lift him. Daphne got the chair and put it back in position. Staggering slightly, Charles managed to manoeuvre Jonathan into it.

With a sigh, Charles then took a seat too, and so did the women. They all looked expectantly at Jonathan, who was searching in vain for his wine glass. It was in smithereens on the floor. Sarah saw the shards and picked Hamish up before he pricked a paw.

'This floor needs doing again! Honestly, we must have cleaned it a dozen times since we've been here,' Daphne huffed.

'If you take Hamish, I'll give it a quick going-over,' said Sarah, handing her the little dog. She decided to use the dustpan and brush, rather than get out the hoover. As the house seemed to have subsided into quietness, the last thing she wanted to do was wake Bernard up. When she'd finished, she flopped down in her chair. 'Now. I suppose we should talk about what's really going on here.'

'Oh heavens, must we?' Charles ran a tired hand over his forehead. 'Could it wait until morning, do you think?'

'Well perhaps – if Jonathan will explain what happened just now.'

'What do you mean? I've told you everything. I was drinking, probably too much as usual, and it's late – I simply dropped off.' Jonathan crossed his arms.

'In an upright kitchen chair like that one?' Sarah gave him a beady look. 'I don't think so. Even if you hadn't slept for a week, you'd be hard pressed to snooze in that chair.'

'Well, if you think you're so clever, perhaps you'd like to tell me what happened, then?' Jonathan said, infuriated.

'If you insist,' said Sarah serenely. 'I think you were down here on your own, yes, and drinking more than is strictly advisable, too. But then you saw something. Out of that window. Your chair is perfectly positioned to get a view of the garden.'

'That's absurd. What could I possibly have seen out there? Apart from anything else, it's pitch dark, if you hadn't noticed. With the light on, all you can see is the reflection of the kitchen. Look, you can see it's the truth.' Jonathan pointed, and sat back.

'Ah, yes. But we've been having quite a storm, haven't we?' Sarah was insistent.

'No one's going to deny that. It's been raining all night long. That just makes visibility worse, if anything,' said Jonathan, more relaxed now.

'What about the lightning, though?' said Daphne suddenly.

'Lightning?' Jonathan looked blank – deliberately so, in Sarah's view.

'Exactly, Daphne,' said Sarah. 'That would illuminate the garden beautifully. Granted, only once in a while, and for a few seconds at a time – but when it struck, you would be able to see the whole of the lawn, right down to the car park, clear as day. I was in here earlier, so I know it's true. Isn't it, Jonathan?'

Sarah stared at the man, and after a few seconds, he dropped his eyes. 'All right, then. Suppose you're right. Suppose I saw something I couldn't... shouldn't...'

'Exactly,' said Sarah. 'You saw something so shocking that you fell right off your chair. Now what was it?' She moved towards the window, and Daphne and Charles followed. All three stared out, but it was hard to see anything except the raindrops cascading down the glass.

'It was... it was...'

And, just as Jonathan was about to speak, there was another flash of lightning, and they all saw what had transfixed him.

'Oh my God!' shouted Sarah. 'We've got to get out there right now.'

FORTY-FIVE

Sarah could feel raindrops washing down her face, while water seeped into her socks, making every step that little bit colder and more unpleasant. But she couldn't stop; none of them could. They had to reach the figure they had all seen lying motionless on the lawn.

But, by the time they rounded the kitchen outbuildings and got to the spot where the lightning had struck, all that was left on the grass was a sodden coat. Sarah wheeled round, peering as best she could at the hedges surrounding the lawn, and the car park beyond, but she couldn't see a soul. Whoever had been there was gone.

'Who on earth was that? Did you see?' Charles asked.

'No... I could have sworn... but it can't have been,' said Sarah, picking up the coat. It was cold and wet to the touch. Something heavy fell out of it and stuck fast into the ground. They all looked at it.

'Is that... It's not that weird family knife, is it?' said Daphne, horrified.

'It is. Don't touch it, Daph,' said Sarah quickly, before her friend could grab it. 'Though it's so wet out here, there probably won't be any prints. I'll use the coat to pick it up. Come on, let's get back inside. There's nothing more we can do here,' she said.

She spoke slowly, while all the clues that had been nagging at her for the past day suddenly came together. It was as though a thunderflash had struck, illuminating the darkest mystery she'd yet come across.

'Could you ring Mariella again?' she said to Daphne as they made their way back into the kitchen, dripping on the floor. Sarah draped the wet coat on a chair and wrapped the dirk in a clean tea towel. 'We're going to need her. And if she doesn't respond, just dial 999. We need all the reinforcements we can get.'

'What shall we do until she gets here?' Daphne asked. 'I can't possibly go to bed, after all this. I feel wide awake again.'

'I don't think any of us will sleep until we get this properly sorted out,' said Sarah, suddenly businesslike. 'I think it's time we had a good hard look at what's really been going on at Coates House. We need to assemble everyone.'

'How do you propose to do that, my dear? You can't gather the clan if they're all asleep, can you?' said Charles.

With the light of battle in her eye, Sarah marched straight into the hall with the wrapped dirk, took up the beater and whacked the dinner gong until the very walls of the ancient house shook with the noise.

'I say! That'll wake the dead, Sarah,' said Charles, standing with Daphne, both of them with their hands clamped over their ears.

'It's done the trick, though,' she said, pointing upwards.

Sure enough, a rather white-faced Letty was descending the stairs slowly in her frothy dressing gown. As they watched, Helena pushed past her rudely and shouted down at the little group at the foot of the flight of stairs. 'Which one of you idiots did that? Some of us are trying to get a wink of sleep, you know!'

'Helena, Letitia, perhaps you could follow Daphne into the

drawing room,' said Sarah, ignoring the outburst. 'We're just waiting for Bernard and Jonathan now.'

While she was speaking, a tired-looking Bernard wandered down, in a red woollen dressing gown. Meanwhile, Jonathan came down the kitchen corridor, a half-full wine glass in his hand. 'What's all this nonsense?'

'I'll explain once we're all settled in the drawing room,' Sarah said pleasantly.

The two men moved somewhat reluctantly at her chivvying, but soon they were all collected together in the comfortable room, taking up the sofas and fireside armchairs.

'I'll put the dirk up here on the mantelpiece, out of harm's way,' Sarah was saying, when the doorbell pealed. Mariella came in, while the two constables who'd come with her headed for the garden.

'I think we'd all appreciate a bit of clarity on why we're here at, um, twelve thirty a.m.,' said Mariella, squinting at her watch..

'Daphne rang you initially because we heard a scream upstairs, then we saw something out on the lawn – something that definitely shouldn't have been there,' Sarah said. 'Those situations resolved themselves. I think it was Letitia who screamed, maybe because she saw... someone outside. But it left me thinking about all the other strange little clues that have been popping up, ever since Madeleine Brett-Coates died. It's as though our attention has been directed to one person after another, all the time.'

'You mean somebody's been trying to put the blame for the deaths onto people who are innocent?' said Daphne.

'Exactly that,' said Sarah.

'Oh, for goodness' sake,' said Helena, not bothering to hide her fury. 'Who the hell do you think you are? You're just an old woman who fancies herself as an armchair detective. You don't know any more than we do.'

'It's absolutely true,' said Sarah, not abashed at all by Helena's withering tone. 'I don't have any special knowledge or skills. But I have spent a lot of time examining people over the course of my long career, and diagnosing what's amiss. That's what I've been trying to do here. You might not like what I'm going to say, but at this point, do you really have much to lose by listening?'

'Well yes,' said Helena. 'Hours of beauty sleep. But still, you've got us all here now. You might as well get on with it.' She crossed her legs, wrapped her silk gown more tightly, and stared crossly at the fire.

Charles got the hint and poked at the embers, then put some more logs on as Bernard spoke up.

'Look, I feel it's incumbent on me to say a few words about this,' he started.

'Oh, for heaven's sake,' said Jonathan, slamming down his wine glass and spilling half the liquid in it. 'Spare us.'

'Maybe I should just talk everyone through my findings instead,' said Sarah with a shrug. 'It really shouldn't take too long. How about that?'

Bernard looked furious, but remained silent. In the absence of any eruptions or protests from the rest of the family, and after a nod from Mariella, she got to her feet.

'The way I see it is this. Madeleine Brett-Coates was an overbearing mother. She had you all on a tight leash. Bernard, she entrusted you with more responsibility than your brother and sister, but she still scarcely gave you a chance to run a bath without supervision.'

'Here, I say,' said Bernard, growing red in the face. 'Charles, can't you get her under control?'

Charles, still tending the fire, merely directed a small smile at Sarah, who carried on.

'Jonathan, she reproached you for not having children. Maybe she did that once too often? Or did she suspect your TV company had dropped you? Whichever, she made life uncomfortable for you and Geoff. It sounds to me as though she barely tolerated your husband, which must have been very difficult. No wonder you started to feel murderous towards her.'

'Now hang on a minute,' shouted Jonathan, leaping to his feet. 'If you're trying to accuse me of something, why don't you come out and say it?'

'All right then. It does look as though you're the most likely person to have done away with your mother,' said Sarah. 'You knew about plants, so you would know the properties of foxgloves, and could easily have been faking your phobia about them. Equally, you would have known that the bluebell stems and bulbs were just as lethal, and you could have put them in Madeleine's food.'

Jonathan, still standing and gazing wildly round at his siblings, burst out, 'Guys, she can't be serious! She's deranged. You've said it yourself often enough, Hells. This is ridiculous.'

FORTY-SIX

'Why don't you sit down, Jonty? I don't think Sarah has finished yet,' said Charles with all his usual courtesy.

'When it came to your husband, Geoff,' Sarah said, 'the entire household knew about his hatred of confined spaces, but it would probably be easier for you than anyone else to persuade him into the cellar. And as for Mrs Bunforth, we all know you had a great relationship with her. It wouldn't have taken you a second to run off that sheet of A4 inviting her to the folly. Then it would just be a question of dosing her up to get her out of action—'

'The lab's come back on that. It was digitalin, so the foxgloves were used after all, just not on Mrs Brett-Coates,' Mariella said.

'Right,' said Sarah. 'Well, again, you could have been faking that phobia, Jonathan. You could have ordered the wreath and dictated the note; you could have driven to the hospital and tried to kill Mrs Bunforth there too. And you could have gone out into the garden before anyone else, and dropped the dirk there, so no one would find it in your room.'

'Have you quite finished?' Jonathan looked dejected. 'So,

that's it, then? You've decided it was me. I killed my mother and my husband – and all for what, exactly? I don't inherit a penny from Mumsy.'

'But you do from Geoff. And if he really was selling off the family silver, then you'd have that money to look forward to. By killing your mother, you'd also silence that nagging voice always telling you that you hadn't lived up to your heritage,' said Sarah quietly.

Jonathan put his head in his hands and started to weep. 'Look, I can't prove I didn't do these awful things. But I'm telling you, it wasn't me.'

Sarah looked at him for a moment, then went over to him and patted him on the back. 'That's all right, Jonathan. I know it wasn't you.'

'You do?' Jonathan raised his tearstained face. 'Then why put me through that?'

'I wanted to see how your brother and sister would react. Whether they would come to your aid. And now we know. They didn't,' said Sarah.

'Just a minute,' said Helena, sitting up straighter. 'How do you know it wasn't Jonty? Not that I particularly think it was you,' she added belatedly, as Jonathan turned to stare at her.

'Well, I do believe he has a genuine phobia about foxgloves, which would take him out of many of the elements of the case. But more simply because, at the time someone went to the hospital to try and kill Mrs Bunforth for the second time, Jonathan was downstairs here, in the cellar. Weeping at the spot where his husband was killed. Tweedledum saw him. Sorry, I mean PC Dumbarton,' said Sarah.

'That's true,' said Mariella. 'He's confirmed it.'

'Is there no privacy in this house?' Jonathan sobbed. Daphne patted his hand kindly, and Hamish went over to put a paw on his knee.

'Hang on. That only alibis him for one of the incidents,' said Bernard dismissively.

'True,' said Sarah. 'But we have to consider his motive and behaviour, too. Killing his mother only silenced a negative voice. It didn't bring him any other advantage. The death of his husband has caused him terrible distress, as we can all see. And it's hard to believe a murderer would voluntarily spend time with the parents of his victim, as Jonathan did when he went to comfort Geoff's family.'

'Oh, I don't know,' said Helena. 'Let's face it, Jonty'd do anything for a bit of attention.'

'What about you, Hells? You're more than capable of bumping Mumsy off yourself,' said Jonathan crossly.

'Maybe.' Helena smiled mirthlessly. 'But I'd never go anywhere near Geoff, would I? So how would I get him in the basement?'

Sarah coughed. 'Well, you could have told him you had something you wanted to sell – jewellery, for instance. He'd be quite a useful contact, for someone who was, say, wanting to pawn items or to have them copied.'

Helena glared at her. Then she laughed, unabashed at this secret coming out. 'For your information, I'd tried that, and Geoff was hopeless. He got pennies for some of my best sparklers.'

'You mean your diamonds aren't real? That's so disappointing,' said Daphne.

Helena ignored her. 'And why would I try anything with Bunny? She's useful to me. She gets the stains out of my cashmere sweaters and sorts out my shoes. My Jimmy Choo suede slingbacks aren't going to brush themselves, you know.'

'I can imagine. Don't worry, Helena. I've had to rule you out,' said Sarah. 'For reasons I'll explain later. I'd like to turn to Bernard, now.'

'Oh, for goodness' sake,' said Bernard, addressing Mariella.

'How much licence are you going to give this crackpot? I think *she* should be arrested, never mind anyone else.'

'I'll bear your views in mind,' said Mariella. 'But for now, I'd like to listen to what Sarah has to say.'

'Well, Bernard, as you've mentioned once or twice, you're the head of the family now,' Sarah said. 'You're the only one of the siblings to have benefited directly from the death of Madeleine Brett-Coates – though you insist you didn't know your mother had changed her will. You weren't a fan of Geoff, as you keep making plain. You could easily have slung a few bits of silver in a bag, to accuse him of theft. You didn't, however, gain from that death either – unless Geoff saw something untoward, and the murder was to silence him. Then did Mrs Bunforth in turn witness you luring Geoff to his death? It all seems very convoluted. And there is a person here who has a better motive than you do, Bernard.'

'Who? Tell us, can't you, you stupid—' Bernard bit his lip, as Sarah turned to face him.

'Why, it's your wife, of course,' she said softly.

Everyone swivelled in their seats, to gawp at Letitia. She was entirely unaware of their scrutiny, concentrating on a hangnail that she was nibbling with her small white teeth.

'There! Got it,' she said in triumph, then stretching out her hand to admire the effect. She looked up, her eyes seeming to focus at last, and did a double-take when she saw everyone craning her way. 'What are you all staring at? Do I have lipstick on my teeth?'

'No,' said Helena in that silky, detached voice. 'But it seems you do have blood on your hands.'

FORTY-SEVEN

Letitia seemed to realise the seriousness of the situation at last, and got to her feet. 'I didn't touch Madeleine! And you're all crazy if you think I did,' she said, looking wildly from face to face.

'Funny, now you *do* seem to know what you're being accused of, after all,' said Helena thoughtfully.

'Oh shut up, you stupid snob. You've got no reason to look down your nose at me. And as for you, Bernie, why are you sitting there and letting her be so mean?' Letitia said plaintively, looking at her husband.

Sarah couldn't help wondering the same thing. He was hardly a supportive partner. She spoke up. 'The thing is, Letitia, you do benefit hugely from Madeleine's death. Not only did it rid you of a very difficult mother-in-law, but via your husband you come into a fortune. You drift around, apparently aimlessly, but you could easily have drugged Madeleine's food with the bluebells you love so much, you could have spun Geoff some story to get him into the basement and drugged him with the foxgloves, and you could have sent the wreath and the note. Then there was red fabric on Madeleine's jacket, and snippets of it in the garden, suggesting that you'd been on the scene of the first death, and were perhaps involved in hiding syringes in the garden.'

'Why would I do all that?' Letitia looked thoroughly perplexed.

'I agree,' said Helena. 'And why would she hide her drug use? We all know she's high as a kite half the time.'

'We do know that the fabric didn't come from Letitia's dress, though,' Mariella put in.

'Ahem. And what about dragging Bunny to the folly?' said Charles. 'Letty's a slip of a girl.'

Letitia smiled mistily at Charles and Sarah spoke up again. 'That's where it all falls down,' she said. 'With the best will in the world, I can't see Letitia hefting a full-grown woman all that way through the woods, let alone up two rickety flights of stairs.'

'Well, exactly,' Letitia said. 'I could have told you. I'm innocent.'

'I rather think you are,' Sarah admitted. Letitia sat down abruptly, and went back to scrutinising her nails – but with a smile on her face. 'And the same goes for Helena, for the same reason.'

'Well,' said Bernard, looking around the room, and coming back to Mariella. 'Fat lot of use our silver sleuth has been. We've had to sit through a bunch of appalling slurs, and all for what? She says none of us could have done it. Time for the real detective in the room to haul her away, surely, so you can get on with your job.'

'Ah, but I didn't say none of you could have done it, did I?' said Sarah. 'I only said that Letitia had a better motive than you did. That doesn't mean that you didn't do it.'

There was dead silence for a moment, as everyone took in the implications of what Sarah had said.

Then Bernard burst into speech. 'What? This is utterly

preposterous,' he spluttered. 'Of course I didn't do it! Charles, old boy, I've asked you to get this woman under control.'

Charles looked at Bernard and, for the first time, a note of disapproval came into his voice. 'I really think we'd better listen, don't you?'

'My mistake was thinking that the change in your mother's will was as much of a shock to you as it was to the rest of us,' said Sarah. 'You knew full well what she had done. And that's why you killed her on the day of the fair, when you knew there would be loads of people around to provide a distraction, and hopefully be accused instead of you. You weren't to know the crack Neighbourhood Watch team would rule out everyone except the family.'

'How on earth could I have known that Mumsy had altered her will?' Bernard blustered. 'I don't have second sight, do I?'

'No,' said Sarah. 'But you did have a spy in the camp. That was a term that was levelled at us, ironically, though it was you who'd roped in a useful ally where it counted.'

'Well, who on earth would that be?' Bernard put his hands on his hips, as if challenging her to do her worst.

Sarah looked levelly at him, and then apologetically at Letitia. 'It was Anna. She had a boyfriend who worked for Mr Chivers. Jenkins, the rather colourless young man who accompanied him when he read the will. And that's why Chivers recognised Anna when he came here that day. It should have struck me at the time, but he called her by her name, when she took his coat. He'd said himself he hadn't been to the house for years, and Anna only started working here the year before last. So how did he know her? And then, up in her room, there was a photo of her with a young man – Jenkins.'

'Oh yes,' said Jonathan slowly. 'I saw her in the village once with someone. Tall, gangly kid. But why would Anna tell Bernard what her boyfriend said about the changes to the will?'

'Do you want to explain, or shall I?' Sarah said, looking at

Bernard. He gave her a look of disgust, and turned his face away. 'All right then. I'll fill in the blanks, as it were. Bernard knew his mother had a meeting with Chivers, and he'd found out where Anna's boyfriend worked. Maybe he promised Anna some of the money. Possibly he promised her marriage, if his present wife should overdose, say. I don't know what he told her. But he leant on the girl to get information about his mother's new will out of Jenkins.

'Once you knew you were going to inherit everything, Bernard, I imagine you got bored with waiting,' Sarah continued. 'You didn't enjoy living with your siblings, and there was always the risk that your mother might spend another fortune on a detox for Helena, or lavish support on Jonathan while he looked for work, if you'd found out about that. Using plant poisons on your mother and Mrs Bunforth was an easy way to point your finger at your expert brother, but the book on toxic plants showed even Helena could have dosed your mother with the bluebell bulbs and drugged Mrs Bunforth too. The wreath of foxgloves helped to suggest that Jonathan was unhinged – maybe dangerously so. But it could also have been the sort of spiteful thing Helena would think of. I think you quite enjoyed it, directing me one way and then another.

'Then something spooked Anna earlier, and she made a bolt for it,' Sarah added. 'Maybe she's feeling remorse – after all, she betrayed her boyfriend, who in turn let his employer down terribly. Worse still, she's been abetting a murderer. Or maybe she just thought she might be next for the chop.'

'Lucky for her she ran when she did,' said Mariella. 'She knows enough about you to put you away for many years, Mr Brett-Coates.'

'What do you mean? I never said a word to that bi—' Bernard realised what he'd said, and clammed up.

'Well, that's torn it, Bernard,' said Jonathan, looking disgustedly at his brother. 'So it's true. You were in cahoots with the help, you with all your ridiculous notions about lineage. You killed Mumsy and... and, my God, you killed Geoff!' He got out of his seat, and was about to lunge, when Mariella grappled him.

'Are you going to sit down, or do I need to get the PC outside to cuff you?' Mariella asked.

Jonathan subsided, glaring at his brother. Meanwhile, Letitia blinked a couple of times. 'I'm sorry, I must have missed something. What did you say you've been up to, Bernie?'

'For heaven's sake,' said Helena. 'He's been having a fling with Anna, you idiot.'

'Oh, of course,' said Letitia dreamily. 'But I knew that.'

There was a thunderstruck silence. Helena broke it. 'Well, you've finally surprised me in a good way, Letty. Didn't you mind?'

'About what? Anna? No, of course not. You carry on, Bernie, that's what I say,' said Letitia with a lopsided smile.

'Well, I don't think he'll be able to, not where he's going,' said Charles heavily.

'Perhaps it's time we made a move down to the station,' said Mariella, getting to her feet.

'Good grief, yes. Get him away from us. The sooner this is over and done, the better,' Helena said with a shudder.

'You realise it never will be finished, don't you?' said Jonathan. 'This will be known as the "Murder House" for evermore, and we'll be the poor saps who didn't realise their brother was a killer.'

'Well, look on the bright side. You can present lots of awful true crime documentaries about it,' sniffed Helena.

Jonathan seemed to cheer up distinctly at the prospect, while his brother was yanked to his feet by Mariella and Charles. But as they started to move off, Bernard stepped forward, twisted out of their grip and made a bolt for the mantelpiece, taking down the dirk.

'Ha! Thought you were going to bundle me off the premises? Not a chance,' Bernard said, brandishing the dagger and eyeing everyone in turn. 'Now you two, shove out of the way and let me pass,' he said, making a stabbing motion towards Charles.

Charles bravely stood his ground for as long as he could, then reluctantly – and not a moment too soon, in Sarah's view – stepped back. Mariella did the same, and Bernard ran for the door. But, as he charged forward, his foot caught on the side of the ottoman between the sofas.

He crashed to the floor in an untidy heap. Then he lay still.

The others stared at him in astonishment and confusion. The silence lengthened. Charles was the first to speak up.

'Bernard, um, old thing, I'll give you a hand up – as long as you put the knife down,' he said, advancing slowly towards him.

'Be careful, Charles,' Sarah couldn't help saying. 'Don't get too close!'

'Oh, you wouldn't stab me, would you, Bernard?' Charles said in jovial tones, while moving carefully forward.

When Bernard didn't move a muscle, Mariella darted over to him. 'There's something wrong. Help me get him up.'

Charles hefted Bernard up by the shoulder, and started to shift him. Just then, Letitia screamed out. Charles's pale blue shirt was now streaked with red, as were his hands.

Bernard's blood was everywhere.

FORTY-EIGHT

When they'd turned the man over, they could see all too well what the problem was. The Brett-Coates dagger, which Bernard had been obsessed with, was now sticking out of his chest. Sarah examined him briefly, but she'd been pretty sure it was game over from the moment he'd fallen so heavily and then lain so still.

'I'm very sorry, Letitia, Jonathan, Helena. I'm afraid Bernard is dead. He must have landed right on top of the blade. It looks like it's gone clean through his heart.' She looked towards Mariella, who stepped quickly out of the room, phone in hand.

Letitia gasped, and seemed to black out, flopping back in her chair. Suppressing a sigh, Sarah moved away from the body and tended to the young woman. 'Daphne, could you get me some water?'

Daphne stood up, dithered for a second, then came over with the glass she'd been drinking from, and unceremoniously threw it over the unconscious woman, who came round shaking like a wet dog.

'Well, that's one way of doing it,' said Sarah, looking at her friend.

'What? She's awake, isn't she?' Daphne was not repentant. 'When are we going to be allowed to go?' she added in a very loud stage whisper. 'Being in this room with... Bernard – well, it's enough to give my heebie-jeebies the collywobbles.'

Sarah couldn't help but agree. The sight of the poor man, stretched out on the floor, his head lolling and his chest stained all around the dagger's blade, was quite chilling. She noted the bottoms of his pyjama legs were still wet, from when he'd been outside planting the dirk – another little bit of proof if Mariella needed it. In death, he looked absurd and diminished. But should she really feel pity? After all, she reminded herself, this was a double murderer, who'd tried to kill again and had seemed to have no remorse whatsoever for his crimes. He'd escaped a lifetime behind bars – this was truly the easy way out for him.

'Unfortunately, this is a crime scene, and we're all a part of it,' said Sarah, taking a large woollen throw from the back of one of the sofas. 'But I do agree, it might be more fitting if we covered Bernard up – if that's OK with you, Mariella?'

Mariella looked up from her phone, where she was busily trying to coordinate the response to a sudden death. She nodded once and Sarah arranged the blanket over the corpse, then went to sit down again.

'It's probably too early to be asking this, but have you thought about what you're going to do, any of you?' Sarah asked, looking at Letitia and the siblings.

Jonathan stared at her bleakly. 'You can't expect us to have a plan, Bernard's only just... it's... It's going to take us ages to process this.'

There was a wail from the corner of the sofa where, to everyone's astonishment, Helena had burst into tears. 'I actually can't believe he's g-gone,' she sniffed.

'Oh, do shut up, Hells,' said Jonathan. 'You spent Bernie's last days carping and moaning at him, so don't pretend you're sad now. Anyway, he killed Mumsy and Geoff. Good riddance, I say.'

Helena sighed. 'I suppose he'd want us to believe that stupid family motto foretold it. Well, I'm planning to stay put here anyway. Letty's going to need help running the place.'

Jonathan snorted. 'Are you really telling me you're going to live here and give her a hand? I've never heard you say one nice thing about her.'

'She has good taste in shoes,' Helena shrugged.

'Thanks,' said Letitia with a dazzling smile.

'You will need help, Letty, though, won't you? In your condition?' Sarah said carefully.

'Oh,' said Letitia, her smile dropping. 'How did you guess? I've only just realised myself. I-I didn't even get a chance to tell Bernard.'

'Tell him what?' said Jonathan blankly, rubbing a hand over his face.

'Letty's expecting a baby,' Sarah said.

FORTY-NINE

There was a brief, rather heavy silence, then Butler lumbered to his feet, waddled round to where Bernard lay, and let out a bloodcurdling howl. Coming from such a benign old creature, it was a terrible shock, and at once brought home Bernard's death in a way nothing else had.

Daphne jumped up to comfort the old dog, and Hamish pattered over to help. The Labrador's distress seemed to underline the fact that there was now one fewer of the Brett-Coates clan left in the world.

'Congratulations... and I'm very sorry for your loss,' Mariella said to Letitia, Helena and Jonathan. 'Well, losses. The medical services are, um, on their way. As you can imagine, I'm going to be needing some quiet time alone with each of you later this morning to take statements, but before I do that, I'd like a word with Sarah, Charles and my mother elsewhere. There will be a constable outside this room.'

The trio trooped out after Mariella and sat themselves down in the dining room. The policewoman got out her notebook and pen, and sighed. 'Look, I know how hard this has been on you all.

Not least the last few minutes.' She looked at Daphne, who still appeared shell-shocked. 'You are witnesses, though, so it's important we get your stories down while they're fresh in your minds.'

'Must we?' said Daphne. 'I'm exhausted. And I really want to go home.'

Sarah patted her arm. 'I know how you feel, Daph. Let's just wrap this up. Then we'll go.'

'Exactly,' said Mariella. 'So, Sarah, when did you first suspect Bernard?'

'I should have realised it was him from the start,' Sarah said ruefully. 'When I first met him, right by the tent, he must have thanked his lucky stars, finding me creeping out of the place where he'd just murdered his mother. I was a ready-made suspect who'd take the heat off him, or so he thought.'

'He misjudged you,' Charles said.

'Well, hardly. I have a horrible feeling that's why he more or less insisted we all stay on, after Geoff's death. He must have thought we were going to muck everything up. Maybe the way we rushed around after clues made it easier for him to go about his horrible, sneaky business, too. Though I must admit, everything was pointing to him by the end. It was only the fact that he always seemed so responsible, with all that "head of the family" stuff, that confused me.'

'It was so evil, the way he tried to keep putting the blame on his brother and sister. Even his wife,' Daphne said.

'Yes. Bernard was trying to frame them, one after the other. Look at what he did to Geoff, too. The man might have been a bit light-fingered, but I don't believe he was stealing that whole bagful of silver. He was clearly trying to leave, when he almost forced us off the road. It's tragic that he changed his mind and went back, maybe to try and persuade Jonathan to come with him, only for Bernard to kill him in that dreadful, sadistic way. Geoff must either have seen Bernard do something suspicious, or guessed what he was up to, and signed his own death warrant.' Sarah shuddered.

'No wonder it felt like there was almost too much information all the time,' said Charles.

'Exactly,' Sarah said. 'But yet there was nothing much indicating it could be Bernard – and that in itself was telling. I was trying not to let on to Bernard that I'd begun to suspect him. The figure out on the lawn earlier was Bernard, of course, with the dirk. Either he was considering running, or he was planning who to kill next – I suspect it might have been Peabody, because that would have pointed back towards Jonathan as the killer.'

'Peabody! He's about the only person I never suspected,' said Daphne.

'He was a possibility. He must know about plants, after all, and could have left the silk trail or the syringe – but in the end only Bernard ticked all the boxes,' said Sarah.

'You know, it seems wrong to suspect a lady,' said Charles. 'But there were times when I almost thought Letty could have done it.'

Sarah smiled at Charles's innate gallantry. 'Bernard wasn't above dragging his own wife into the picture. She certainly looked deranged when she came in with that knife when the lightning struck. I'm sure he was dosing her up with something, to make her look as unreliable as possible – which is appalling, given her pregnancy.'

'Did he know about that? Daphne asked.

'We'll never be sure,' said Sarah. 'But would he have cared? He was completely ruthless. He said that Mrs Bunforth had had fainting attacks recently – I think that was him, testing out his poisons on a convenient guinea pig. He could have easily killed her by accident while doing that, and then he tried twice in earnest. All he wanted was to get his hands on the money and Coates House. I don't believe he wanted to sell the place; he just wanted to throw everyone off the scent with that idea. Maybe he was lining Anna up to be the place's next mistress.'

'It's all rather sad for Letty's baby. It will have no father, and quite a ditzy mother, to say the least,' Daphne reflected.

'Yes. Letty sometimes seems like a wilful child herself. It's been distressing, seeing her carry on drinking. Hopefully it will be early enough not to have too much of an impact,' said Sarah thoughtfully.

'On the other hand, the baby will grow up in this marvellous place, rolling in money,' said Daphne, with her usual irrepressible smile. But it faltered as she said, 'Goodness me, Letty will need to watch out for the curse, though.'

'The curse?' Sarah frowned.

'Yes, Sarah, you're really not concentrating. That's what did for Bernard. "*Dreich the day the dirk does go, To them that steal it false steps and woe.*"'

'Well, I suppose he did take the dirk out of the dining room into the garden,' shrugged Sarah.

'Exactly! And what could be more of a false move for him than falling over and getting that horrid old blade right through his heart?' said Daphne. 'It was always in his stars.'

'Hmm,' said Sarah, not entirely convinced but knowing Daphne would hang onto the idea like Hamish with a bone. 'Well, yes, but remember the second part. "*Until an heir untouched by horror, Drives the devil from this door.*" Maybe that's Letitia's baby. And I wouldn't be surprised if its aunt and uncle stay on in the end to help Letitia out,' said Sarah. 'After all, they've got nowhere else to go. And without Bernard cleverly winding everyone up the whole time, who's to say they won't get on a lot better?'

FIFTY

In one way, Madeleine's dearest wish was finally coming true – there would be a little Brett-Coates to take over the house and ensure her line went on. But what a legacy it was. Sarah could only hope that the best of Letitia's genes would outweigh the darkness that was tragically so apparent in her husband's bloodline.

Sarah loaded the last of their motley belongings into the Volvo. Daphne settled into the back seat with Hamish in his harness, letting Charles and his long legs take the front. The little dog had said a fond farewell to Butler, but the old Labrador had opted to remain inside, still confused about where his master had got to and determined not to abandon his post in case he finally showed up.

Mariella, supervising the removal of the last traces of the SOCOs from the drawing room, came out to say a quick good-bye. 'I've had a word with the chief constable. He's not that happy about the final outcome – I think he played golf with Bernard, and to say he's shocked doesn't even cover it. But at least he hasn't had to come back into the office straight after his holiday. He couldn't argue with the evidence, when I presented it to him. On this case, I'd call that a win. Now that it's over, it's very clear what Bernard did, and how he accomplished it. Oh, and we've found Madeleine's Lexus – it was parked in a lane five minutes from here. Better still, Bernard's fingerprints are all over the steering wheel. He must have been in so much of a hurry that he forgot about gloves, so that's the final confirmation we needed.'

Daphne hung out of the car window to give Mariella a hug. 'Well done, darling! That's fantastic news. Your first success in Canterbury. We must celebrate later.'

'Lovely idea,' Sarah said enthusiastically. 'We could all meet for a drink. Or, I tell you what, there's the café in Vanstone itself, isn't there? We could stop off for tea and scones right now. How about that, Daphne?'

'Are you kidding?' said Daphne, her face a picture. 'Scones got us into this mess in the first place. I never want to eat another as long as I live. And as for Vanstone, I've had more than enough of it. Take me home to Merstairs immediately!'

A LETTER FROM ALICE

Welcome back to Merstairs!

Thank you so much for reading *A Country Manor Murder*, my fifth book featuring retired GP Sarah Vane, her Scottie dog Hamish, and her friends Daphne and Charles. I love the breezy Kent coast and it's a joy to set Sarah's adventures in such a beautiful spot. If you'd like to find out what Sarah and the gang are up to next, please sign up at the email link below. Your email address will never be shared and you can unsubscribe at any time.

www.bookouture.com/alice-castle

If you enjoyed this book, I would be so grateful if you could post a review on Amazon or Goodreads, so that other people can discover Merstairs too.

I'm also on social media, so do join me there. Happy reading, and I hope to see you soon for Sarah Vane's next outing.

Alice Castle

alicecastleauthor.com

facebook.com/Alicecastleauthor

x.com/AliceMCastle

ACKNOWLEDGEMENTS

Thank you so much to my fantastic agent, Justin Nash of KNLA, my lovely editor Natalie Edwards, and all the team at Bookouture, for making Merstairs real.

PUBLISHING TEAM

Turning a manuscript into a book requires the efforts of many people. The publishing team at Bookouture would like to acknowledge everyone who contributed to this publication.

Commercial
Lauren Morrissette
Hannah Richmond
Imogen Allport

Cover design
Tash Webber

Data and analysis
Mark Alder
Mohamed Bussuri

Editorial
Natalie Edwards
Imogen Allport

Copyeditor
Rhian McKay

Proofreader
Lynne Walker

Marketing

Alex CrowMelanie Price

Cíara Rosney

Martyna Młynarska

Operations and distribution

Marina Valles

Joe Morris

Production

Hannah Snetsinger

Mandy Kullar

Nadia Michael

Charlotte Hegley

Publicity

Kim Nash

Noelle Holten

Jess Readett

Sarah Hardy

Rights and contracts

Peta Nightingale

Richard King

Saidah Graham

RAISING READERS

Books Build Bright Futures

Dear Reader,

We'd love your attention for one more page to tell you about the crisis in children's reading, and what we can all do.

Studies have shown that reading for fun is the **single biggest predictor of a child's future life chances** – more than family circumstance, parents' educational background or income. It improves academic results, mental health, wealth, communication skills, ambition and happiness.

The number of children reading for fun is in rapid decline. Young people have a lot of competition for their time, and a worryingly high number do not have a single book at home.

Hachette works extensively with schools, libraries and literacy charities, but here are some ways we can all raise more readers:

- Reading to children for just 10 minutes a day makes a difference
- Don't give up if children aren't regular readers – there will be books for them!

- Visit bookshops and libraries to get recommendations
- Encourage them to listen to audiobooks
- Support school libraries
- Give books as gifts

There's a lot more information about how to encourage children to read on our websites: **www.RaisingReaders.co.uk** and **www.JoinRaisingReaders.com**.

Thank you for reading.

Printed in Dunstable, United Kingdom

82839114R00160